The critics on Tami Hoag

'Lock all the doors and windows and turn on all the lights . . . a spine-chilling thriller' *New Woman*

'Tami Hoag writes the kind of can't-put-it-down suspense that keeps you on the edge to the final sentence' John Saul

'This is a book best read in a well-lit room, with the certain knowledge that all locks are securely bolted and all closets uninhabited. We are all afraid of something, and Tami Hoag has a good handle on what it is' *Mostly Murder*

'This is a taut, intelligent thriller, which is genuinely scary, with a strong sense of place' *Sunday Times*

'[Hoag] skilfully handles a complicated plot, and makes us care about her central characters. The whodunit is compelling' *Kirkus Reviews*

'Accomplished and scary' *Cosmopolitan*

'Well-crafted . . . a tautly written account of life in a small Minnesota town . . . the investigatory techniques are all presented intelligently and provide a strong framework for this gripping suspense tale. Highly recommended' *Library Journal*

D1390525

Since the publication of her first book in 1988, Tami Hoag has penned 23 novels, including five consecutive *New York Times* bestsellers, and has won numerous awards for her writing. Prior to settling on a career as an author, she worked at a wide range of jobs, from photographer's assistant to training show horses to selling designer toilet seats. She claims writing is the ideal profession because: 'You get to go to work in your pyjamas, tell lies all day, and get paid for it. There aren't many other jobs where a person can do that kind of thing without danger of prosecution.' Tami Hoag lives on a horse farm in Virginia with her husband and an ever-growing family of animals.

Also by Tami Hoag

Cry Wolf
Still Waters
Lucky's Lady
Sarah's Sin
Dark Paradise
Night Sins
Guilty as Sin
A Thin Dark Line
Ashes to Ashes

MAGIC

Tami Hoag

ORION

An Orion paperback
First published in Great Britain in 1995 by Orion Books Ltd,
Orion House, 5 Upper St Martin's Lane, London WC2H 9EA

Fourth impression 1999

Printed and bound in Great Britain by
Clays Ltd, St Ives plc

MAGIC

PROLOGUE

University of Notre Dame, South Bend, Indiana
spring 1977

"Okay, everybody, this is it—the final portrait of the Fearsome Foursome. Make sure your caps are on straight, ladies. I'm setting the timer now." Bryan Hennessy hunched over the 35-millimeter camera, fussing with buttons, pausing once to push his glasses up on his straight nose.

Decked out in caps and gowns, three women stood on the damp grass near the blue expanse of St. Mary's Lake. The clean, cool air was sweet with the scents of spring flowers, new leaves, and freshly cut grass. Bird song mingled with Alice Cooper's "School's Out" blasting from a boom box in a distant dorm.

Peering through the viewfinder, Bryan focused

1

on his three best friends: Faith Kincaid, Alaina
Montgomery, and Jayne Jordan.

It didn't seem the least bit odd to him that his
three best friends were women. He happened to
like women. These three were like sisters to him,
surrogates for the siblings he had left behind in
Chicago. He valued their company, their views,
their support. He cherished their friendship. He
missed them like hell and they hadn't even parted
company yet. Just the idea of it made his heart
ache.

He adjusted the camera lens, blurring the images before him then bringing them back into
focus, willing his memory to hold their likenesses
with the same sharp clarity.

Faith Kincaid, her dark eyes bright with innocence and unshed tears, adjusted the shoulders of
her gown and checked her cap, poking back long
spirals of burnished gold hair. With a little sigh
she settled herself and her sunny smile in place,
doing her best to look brave and optimistic.

Bryan had always thought of her as their Ma-
donna figure—sweet, serene, kind, and forgiving.
It frightened him a little to think of Faith going
out into the real world. She was too trusting. Who
was going to look out for her? Who was going to
steer her clear of men who would take advantage
of her innate innocence?

That was the last worry he had about Alaina,
who stood to Faith's right. Tall, cool, and poised,
Alaina didn't trust anybody. Bryan doubted there
were many men who wouldn't back off from her
"ice princess" look. But were there any who would

be brave enough to look past those barriers of hers to find the lonely woman on the other side?

She seemed tense now, and Bryan realized she was dreading what was to come—the ceremony that would aggrandize their parting, the phony celebration afterward with her social butterfly mother and the latest in a string of stepfathers. Alaina might have been cynical and as practical as the short style of her dark chestnut hair, but Bryan knew that beneath the brusque exterior lay a tender heart that had adopted the other three members of their group as the only real family she had ever known. He could already feel the sharp ache of loneliness echoing inside her.

At the other end of the line stood petite Jayne Jordan, her pixie's face dominated by wide black eyes and a cloud of wild auburn hair. Jayne was the observer, taking in every detail of the scene around her and committing it to memory. She was their resident flake, a student of all things mystical. She was his soul mate in a lot of ways. Jayne understood about magic and mystery. But who would understand Jayne?

These were Bryan's three best friends in the world. They had banded together their freshman year. Four people with nothing in common but a class in medieval sociology. Over the four years that followed, they had seen one another through finals and failures, triumphs and tragedies, and doomed romances. They were friends in the truest, deepest sense of the word.

Depression threatened to smother him like a wet woolen blanket. Bryan did his best to ignore

it. He set the camera's timer and hustled around
to stand behind his friends, his cap askew. Had
he been able to be in two places at once, standing
in line and behind the camera, he could have
objectively viewed himself. He was tall and athletic
with a strong, honest face, and tawny hair that
tended to be a bit shaggy because he tended to
forget little details like barber appointments. The
girls always had to remind him about things like
that—haircuts and dates and eating meals. What
was he going to do without them?

"Okay. Everybody smile," he ordered, his voice a
little huskier than usual. "It's going to go off any
second now. Any second."

They all grinned engagingly and held their collective breath.

The camera suddenly tilted downward on its
tripod, pointing its lens at one of the white geese
that wandered freely around St. Mary's Lake. The
shutter clicked and the motor advanced the film.
The goose honked an outraged protest and waddled away.

"I hope that's not an omen," Jayne said, frowning as she nibbled at her thumbnail.

"It's a loose screw," Bryan announced, digging a
dime out of his pants pocket to repair the tripod
with.

"In Jayne or the camera?" Alaina queried, her
cool blue eyes sparkling with teasing mischief.

Jayne made a face at her. "Very funny, Alaina."

"I think it's a sign that Bryan needs a new
tripod," said Faith.

"That's not what Jessica Porter says," Alaina remarked slyly.

Bryan felt a blush creep up to the roots of his hair as the girls giggled. While he had never been romantically involved with any of them, he had an active social life, something the girls teased him about unmercifully.

Not that he was a masochist, but he was going to miss that. The girls helped him keep things in perspective. He tended to fall in love at the drop of a hat. Romances came and went in his life, flaring brightly and burning out like shooting stars, but Jayne and Faith and Alaina were always there to sympathize or console . . . or make a lewd remark.

"If you want a sign, look behind you," he said as he fussed unnecessarily with the aperture setting on the camera.

The girls turned together and immediately caught sight of the rainbow that arched gracefully across the morning sky above the golden dome of the administration building.

"Oh, how beautiful," Faith said with a sigh.

"Symbolic," Jayne whispered.

"It's the diffusion of light through raindrops," Alaina said flatly, crossing her arms in front of her.

Bryan looked up from fiddling with the camera to frown at her, his strong jaw jutting forward aggressively. "Rainbows have lots of magic in them," he said, dead serious. "Ask any leprechaun. It'd do you some good to believe in magic, Alaina."

Alaina's lush mouth turned down at the corners. "Take the picture, Hennessy."

Bryan ignored her, his wise, warm blue eyes taking on a dreamy quality as he gazed up at the soft stripes of color that painted the sky. "We'll be chasing our own rainbows after today. I wonder where they'll lead us."

They each recited the stock answers they'd been giving faculty, friends, and family for months. Jayne was leaving to seek fame and fortune in Hollywood as a writer and director. Faith was heading to a managerial position in a business office in Cincinnati. Alaina was staying on at Notre Dame to attend law school. Bryan had been accepted into the graduate program of parapsychology at Purdue.

"That's where our brains are taking us," he said, pulling his cap off to comb a hand back through his hair as he always did when he went into one of his "deep thinking modes." "I wonder where our hearts will take us."

He knew three of the answers to that question. He was the confidant the girls entrusted with their secrets. He was the only person on earth who knew Alaina's deepest wish was for emotional security. He knew Faith longed for a simple life with a husband and children. Jayne's quest was for understanding and acceptance.

"That's the question we should all be asking ourselves," Jayne said, wagging a slender finger at her friends. "Are we in pursuit of our true bliss, or are we merely following a course charted by the expectations of others?"

"Do we have to get philosophical?" Alaina groaned, rubbing two fingers to each throbbing temple. "I haven't had my mandatory ten cups of coffee yet this morning."

"Life is philosophy, honey," Jayne explained patiently, her voice a slow Kentucky drawl that hadn't altered one iota during the four years she'd spent in northern Indiana. The expression on her delicately sculpted features was almost comically earnest. That's a cosmic reality."

Alaina blinked. Finally she said, "We don't have to worry about you. You'll fit right in in California."

Jayne smiled. "Why, thank you."

Faith chuckled. "Give up, Alaina. You can't win."

Alaina winced and held her hands up as if to ward off the words. "Don't say that. I *abhor* losing."

"Anastasia," Bryan declared loudly. He gave a decisive nod that set the tassel on his cap dancing. The word would have seemed straight out of left field to anyone who didn't know Bryan Hennessy and the workings of his unconventional mind, but he knew his compatriots would understand immediately.

Anastasia was the small town on California's rugged northern coast where the four of them had spent spring break. While watching the surf crash against the rocky shore, they had made fantasy plans to move there and pursue idealistic existences. Jayne's dream had been to have her own farm. An inn with a view of the ocean had been Faith's wish. They had somehow gotten Alaina to admit to a secret desire to paint. Bryan had wanted to play the role of local mad scientist.

"That's right," Faith said with a misty smile. "We'd all move to Anastasia."

"And live happily ever after." Alaina's tone lacked the sarcasm she had no doubt intended. She sounded wistful instead.

"Even if we never end up there, it's a nice dream," Jayne said softly.

A nice dream. Something to hang on to, like their memories of Notre Dame and one another. Warm, golden images they could hold in a secret place in their hearts to be taken out from time to time when they were feeling lonely or blue.

Bryan set the timer on the camera once again, then jogged around to stand behind Faith. "Who knows?" he murmured, almost to himself. "Life is full of crossroads. You can never tell where a path might lead."

And the camera buzzed and clicked, capturing the Fearsome Foursome—wishful smiles canting their mouths, dreams of the future and tears of parting shining in their eyes as a rainbow arched in the sky behind them—on film for all time.

ONE

Anastasia, California,
the present

"Great big head. Eyes of red. Don't know how long he's been dead. Has anybody seen my ghoul?" Bryan sang softly in his pleasant tenor voice as he worked. He paused as he adjusted the angle of the still camera and smiled broadly into the wide-angle lens, as if posing for a self-portrait. Then he pushed his old-fashioned gold-rimmed spectacles up on his nose, moved on to the next piece of equipment, and continued on with his song.

Ghosts. His life was filled with them. He searched for them and lived with them. Sometimes he wished he were one, he thought darkly, his enforced good mood slipping. The whole point of going back to work was to get away from depres-

sion. He was finding that returning to his former
upbeat, optimistic self was as tough a job as any
manual labor he'd ever done. Squaring his shoulders with determination, he double-checked his
photographic equipment, the video camera on its
mount above the carved oak door, the light stands
set in their strategic positions around the wide
foyer. He checked the still camera last.

Finally satisfied that everything was in place and
in working order, he flipped off the hall light,
turned, and trudged up the first short flight of
stairs, his usually lithe step somewhat weary. He
had been raised an athlete in a family of athletes.
His brother J.J. was a former professional quar-
terback, his sister Marie was a world-class figure
skater. Bryan himself was no slouch on a tennis
court, but these days he felt every day of his thirty-
six years, and then some.

With his back pressed to the mildewing wallpaper he slid down to sit on the dusty hardwood floor
of the landing. He settled back into the shadows,
not caring that the floor was cold or that a draft
wafted down the stairwell. Those kinds of discom-
forts were not unusual in his line of work. He'd
crouched in the damp, cramped holds of ships,
waiting. He'd spent night after night in castles
built long before the invention of central heat,
waiting. A run-down Victorian mansion like this
one was actually fairly cozy by comparison. Besides, it had been a long time since he'd paid any
attention to physical discomfort. It was probably a
victory of sorts that he had even noticed the draft.
The girls would be proud of him.

It was funny how they had ended up there after all. The Fearsome Foursome had disbanded to chase four different rainbows, and still they had ended up in Anastasia, the place they had dreamed of and fantasized about years ago. Faith had her inn and her family. Jayne had her farm and a husband who may not have understood her precisely, but who accepted her nevertheless. And Alaina had finally found a place where she belonged, a family to love and who loved her in return.

Bryan had come to Anastasia to seek solace and sympathy, and his old friends had given it to him in ample measure . . . for a while. They had consoled him and given him a place to heal his broken heart. Then each had begun to hint in her own way that the time had come for him to start living again.

Faith had been gentle about it. That was her way, gentle, diplomatic, sympathetic, skills that had been polished to perfection by six years of motherhood. Alaina had been blunt. Jayne had been empathetic and philosophical.

It had been the girls' collective idea that he investigate Addie Lindquist's house for paranormal activity. Bryan had to smile. He had always been the one to look out for and look after them, but here they were, banding together to see to his emotional well-being. You couldn't custom-order better friends.

He knew they were right. A man couldn't go on mourning forever. Yet, there was a small measure of resentment inside him. There was a certain perverse comfort in grief. In clinging to his grief he was clinging to Serena. If he let the grief go, if he involved himself in work again and made new friends and stopped devoting all his time and energy to missing her, he would be letting her go. Her memory and the memory of the pain of losing her would dim, and a part of him didn't want that. He had loved her so deeply, even holding on to painful memories was better than nothing at all.

So, he had reached a compromise with himself. He would go back to work, ease back into the routine, but deeper involvement with people would have to wait. For the time being he just didn't have anything left to give.

Settling back more firmly into the corner, Bryan heaved a sigh. Soft gray moonlight spilled into the foyer from the narrow windows that flanked the door. All was still in the hall below. All was still inside him. He didn't sense anything in the air around him except mold. So far, Drake House wasn't exactly proving to be a hotbed of psychical activity. Of course, as out of touch as he'd been with his own gift, there might have been spiritualistic manifestations all around him, and he wouldn't have noticed.

Addie Lindquist claimed there was a ghost in this house. Addie claimed she spoke with this ghost on a regular basis. Perhaps *claimed* wasn't quite the right word. *Declared* was more like it. Addie was sixty-six, opinionated, and imperious. Of course she spoke with Wimsey, she had announced to Bryan, her blue eyes flashing with impatience. She couldn't understand why other people thought it unusual that she spoke with Wimsey. She didn't understand that she was the only one who had ever actually seen Wimsey.

Whether or not the ghost existed was the matter in question. There were people in Anastasia who vaguely remembered stories of strange goings-on at Drake House told by previous owners, but no one had firsthand experienced. Addie was the only one with that, and Addie's mind was going round the bend on greased tracks, as Jayne's husband put it.

In fact, Addie's doctor had been trying for weeks to contact Rachel Lindquist, Addie's daughter, to let her know about her mother's condition. Whether or not the woman would respond was anyone's guess. No one in Anastasia had even known of her existence.

Bryan hated to think of what would happen to Addie. Not that he was getting involved in her situation, he told himself stoutly. It was just sad, that was all. It didn't sound as if Rachel Lindquist cared what happened to her mother. Addie would probably be packed off and forgotten, dead in all the ways that mattered most, the shell of her body left to the care of strangers.

"I could win a prize for being morose," he mumbled, disgusted with himself and his morbid frame of mind.

It wasn't like him, really. He had always been an optimist, a great believer in magic and rainbows. Besides, he was supposed to be thinking about the case, about the possibility that Addie's Wimsey was in fact a psychic disturbance of some sort. He knew nothing would happen to Addie as long as he was staying in Drake House, and he had no immediate plans to leave.

Producing a playing card from inside his shirt-sleeve, he walked it between the fingers of his left hand with careless dexterity, wondering only vaguely at the sudden strong sense of anticipation that surged through him. It was a pleasant feeling, both soothing and exciting, like a promise of something good. The warmth washed through him, chasing out the chilling ache. Tension seeped from the muscles in his broad shoulders, and his eyes drifted shut as he let himself enjoy the sensation without questioning where it came from or what it meant. His glasses slipped down his nose as his head bobbed forward, and the playing card dropped from his fingers.

TWO

The scream could have pierced steel.

Bryan jolted awake, his body exploding out of its cramped position on the landing. His actions were purely instinctive. He had no idea who or what had issued the sound. All that registered was the buzzing of his alarm telling him that sensors indicated a presence in the downstairs hall. He was halfway down the stairs when the flash of his still camera went off, blinding him. Unable to see and unable to stop himself, he stepped out into thin air.

"Aargh!"

His cry of surprise was abruptly cut off with a grunt as he bounced the rest of the way down the steps, rolling like a human tumbleweed. Another otherworldly scream split the air as he hit the marble-tiled floor in a heap and sprawled out, groaning.

The sound had a definite ghostlike quality, he thought excitedly as he struggled to sit up. He was going to have bruises from here to Hyannis, but they would be well worth it if he had captured something on film or tape. He could already see his articles in the scientific journals. Funding for studies and documentaries would come out of the woodwork. Maybe he'd even get invited to the *Tonight Show*. At the very least he'd get a segment on *Unsolved Mysteries*.

Wincing, he hauled himself to his feet and fumbled for the light switch beside the front door. His breath hardened in his throat as the foyer was flooded with amber light from the old chandelier. He'd caught something all right, and she was beautiful.

Bryan straightened his glasses and stared, his heart beating a curious rhythm. The woman before him was quite real, vision though she seemed. The professional in him acknowledged an appropriate amount of disappointment at that, but the basic male in him could find no regret. It would have been physically impossible for a red-blooded man to have been anything but awestruck by the young woman gazing up at him.

She had the face of an angel—gently prominent cheekbones with slight hollows beneath, a chin that looked as if it were made to be cupped by the hand of a handsome lover; a slim, tip-tilted nose; and full pink lips that looked so soft and kissable, they almost made him groan aloud. Her skin was like rose-tinted cream, so tempting, he nearly reached out to touch her cheek. Instead, he pulled his hand back and splayed his fingers across his chest, as if he were having a heart attack.

The overhead light caught in the woman's halo of pale golden hair, adding to her ethereal quality. She wore it up in a loose chignon, but soft tendrils escaped all around her head, framing her feminine features. She stared at him, her periwinkle blue eyes wide and brimming with terror.

Her obvious fear struck him like a slap in the face. He cleared his throat nervously, peeled his hand off his chest, and offered it to her, attempting a genial smile.

"Bryan Hennessy."

Rachel flinched at the sound of his voice. The silence had held her spellbound, now she was jolted out of the trance. She stared first at the big hand hovering before her, then her gaze traveled up a considerable distance to take in the rest of the man.

He was fairly tall with shoulders so wide, they seemed to block out the stairwell behind him. His hair was disheveled. The strands falling across his broad forehead were a color somewhere between blond and brown. With panic overruling her other senses, the only thing she noticed about his face was the strong jaw and the five o'clock shadow that darkened it. His clothes—worn jeans with bits of paper sticking out of one front pocket, and a chambray shirt that was tucked in on only one side—were rumpled.

All things considered, she thought, he looked

dangerous, maybe even unbalanced. He certainly didn't look like anyone her mother would invite into her home. The woman she remembered wouldn't have sat next to this guy on a bus. How, then, had he come to be the one to greet her at the door? The possible answers were not reassuring.

She choked down what fear she could and called on years of vocal training to project a confident tone when she spoke. "What have you done with my mother?"

"I don't know," Bryan said, bemused. He was too thrown off by her remarkable beauty and by his reaction to it to think straight. He pulled his hand back and combed his fingers through his hair. "Who is she?"

Rachel swallowed hard. She started to back away from him, wondering what her chances were of making it to her car and from there to the police station. Not good, she figured. He appeared to be in wonderful physical condition. That was probably essential when one was running from the law. As she took a step back, the man took a step forward. She held up a hand to ward him off.

"If you touch me, I'll scream," she promised.

"You've already done that," Bryan pointed out ruefully. "Quite well, I might add. My ears are still ringing. Now I know the full meaning of the word *shrill.*"

"I know karate," Rachel blurted out. She braced her feet, squared her shoulders, and raised her hand as if she were preparing to take on Bruce Lee. It was ludicrous, of course. Bryan Hennessy dwarfed her. He wasn't the stocky, no-neck, mus-

cle-bound type, but he was big and athletic-look-
ing; and she was all of five feet seven, a hundred
and twenty pounds. She decided she would have
to make up the difference with her temper.

Bryan's brows bobbed up and his face lit with
genuine interest. "Karate? Really?"

Now was not the time to be overly honest, Rachel
reflected as she frantically cast her gaze about for
a handy sharp-edged instrument with which she
might defend herself.

She thought of her mother and a terrible pang
reverberated through her. All the years they'd
wasted! And for what? Now she was finally returning, hoping she and Addie could patch up their
relationship. What if she were too late? Dr. Moore
had told her it wasn't safe for Addie to live alone
any longer, that her mother's impairment made
her forget things like turning off the stove and
who to allow inside her home. Had her mother let
this man into the house thinking he was a friend?
It was entirely possible.

On the drive to California from Nebraska, Rachel
had thought about what time she would have left
with her mother—the mother she knew and
loved—not some vacuous stranger existing in her
mother's body. And she had vowed to make the
most of it. Time for them may have been snatched
away. The thought filled her with a sense of almost
overwhelming loss.

"Rachel," he said abruptly.

Her eyes widened at the sound of her name. The
stranger's voice was husky and warm, but the fact
that he knew her name sent chills down her back.

Bryan nodded decisively. "You're Rachel Lindquist. You're Addie's daughter. I should have recognized you right off. You look a lot like your mother."

He stared at her hard, his straight brows drawing down low and tight over his eyes. A slight frown of disapproval turned the corners of his mouth. It wasn't triggered by Rachel Lindquist's appearance or her identity, but by his own reaction to both. This was the daughter who had not bothered to visit her mother in five years, the girl Addie herself had labeled ungrateful. This was the young woman who had run off with a folk singer, the young woman he had thought of as selfish and uncaring. And he was damned attracted to her.

It came as a very unpleasant surprise, that warm, curling sensation deep in his gut. It was something he hadn't felt in a long, long time, but he was too strongly, basically masculine not to recognize it for what it was—desire. The primitive male in him was responding to a pretty female, and he heartily resented it, resented *her* for stirring that dormant need inside him.

"So, you decided to come back after all," he said coldly, trying to distance himself from her emotionally as well as physically.

Rachel willed herself to stand still while Bryan Hennessy's gaze bore through her. He moved back and a little to her left, and the light from the old chandelier fell more fully across his face. He looked as if he'd just awakened from a sound sleep. Behind his glasses his eyes were bleary and bloodshot, but there was nothing truly dangerous in their stare. He looked annoyed more than anything. More than anything except male. He looked very male—big and brooding and sexy with his tousled hair and beard-shadowed cheeks.

The silence between them swelled with unspoken messages, messages Rachel didn't want to hear or understand. Just the same, she felt a strange fluttering deep inside her, and she pressed a hand to her stomach as if she could push the sensation away. It was probably just hunger. Most of a day had passed since she'd eaten.

Tearing her gaze away from Bryan Hennessy, she gave herself a mental shake. She was experiencing hunger, all right, but it wasn't the kind that she could appease with a sandwich. If she had learned anything over the course of the past five years, it was to be honest with herself. The kind of hunger coursing through her had little to do with prime rib and everything to do with primal attraction.

The realization shocked her. She had lived to the ripe old age of twenty-five and had never experienced such a strong physical reaction to a man, not even to Terence, whom she had once loved. She hadn't expected ever to feel it. It simply wasn't in her nature. She certainly hadn't expected to feel it for a complete stranger, especially one who was suddenly regarding her with subtle disdain. She didn't like it, didn't want it, and she most definitely didn't need it. The reason she had come to Anastasia loomed over her like a dark cloud. There would be no time in her life now for anything but Addie.

"Where is my mother?" she asked firmly, effectively breaking the strange spell between them.

"Upstairs. Asleep, if she's lucky," Bryan said, shouldering his way past her, "though I'd be surprised if there's a dog in this county you didn't wake up with that shrieking."

"Shrieking!" Rachel said indignantly. She pressed her lips into a thin line and planted her hands on her slim hips as she watched him fiddling with the array of equipment clustered in the foyer. Anger surged through her as other feelings subsided. "Of course I was shrieking. I step into my mother's house and am virtually attacked by mechanical contraptions.

"What is all this junk?" she asked impatiently, gesturing sharply at the stuff. "What's it doing here? What are *you* doing here? Who do you think you are anyway?"

"Most of the time I think I'm Bryan Hennessy," Bryan said dryly. He righted a light meter that had tipped over and tapped it gently with a finger, relieved to see it was still functioning. "I got hit in the head with a shot put once, and for about three hours afterward I thought I was Prince Charles, but that was fifteen years ago. I've pretty much gotten over it, except for a strange yen to play polo every now and again. And I was once mistaken for Pat Reilly, the actor." He shot her a Cheshire-cat smile that made Rachel's heart flip. "Personally, I don't think we look all that much alike, but the lady tearing my shirt off didn't agree."

Warmth bloomed under the surface of Rachel's skin as her imagination conjured up an unusually

vivid picture of this man with his shirt half off.
Her image of his chest was smooth and solid with
well-defined muscles, a sprinkling of tawny curls,
and a tiny brown mole just above his left nipple.
She could almost feel the heat of his skin against
her palms, and her nostrils flared as she caught
the faintest hint of his male scent. It was an
altogether weird experience, one that had her
fighting to get a good deep breath into her lungs.

Oblivious to Rachel's predicament, Bryan had
turned back to his machinery. He checked each
item thoroughly. At the moment he couldn't afford
to have a piece needing repair. His finances weren't
in the healthiest of states. In fact, he was more or
less broke.

"This 'junk,' " he said, "is highly sensitive electronic surveillance equipment essential to my
work. I'm a psychic investigator specializing in
locating and defining paranormal phenomenon."

It came as a complete surprise to Rachel that a
man who looked as rumpled and ratty as Bryan
did was capable of speaking in more than mono-
syllables. She tucked her chin back and frowned
as she tried to translate his explanation into gar-
den-variety English. "Is there a generic term for
what you do?"

He flashed her a smile that revealed even white
teeth worthy of a toothpaste commercial. This
time his eyes twinkled with amusement, the corners crinkling attractively behind his spectacles.
"I'm a ghostbuster."

Rachel blinked at him, certain she had heard
him wrong. "You're a what?"

"You know, a ghostbuster. When people hear things that go bump in the night, I'm the guy they hire to find out what those things are. Is it Aunt Edna coming back to get them for all those jokes they made about her pot roast, or is it just bad plumbing?" His broad shoulders lifted in a shrug. "Is that disgusting ooze in the basement crud from hell, or do they just need a new septic tank?"

"People actually pay you money to do that?" Rachel questioned in disbelief. The idea went completely against her innate sense of practicality. "You actually take money from people to do that?"

"A crime against humanity, isn't it?" Bryan said sardonically. He was used to dealing with skeptics. When one made his living investigating things a great many people refused to acknowledge, one learned to handle criticism in a hurry. But he made no effort to argue his case to Rachel Lindquist.

Let her think what she liked, he told himself. He was going to be much better off simply leaving her alone. Between his involuntary attraction to her and his anger over the way she'd treated her mother, there was no telling what would happen if he let himself get involved. Not that he wanted to get involved, he amended hastily. Noninvolvement was his credo these days. He was just minding his own business, looking for ghosts.

"You play on the superstitions and fears of lonely old women," Rachel said, her anger building. He was a con man. Thank God she had arrived when she had. There was no telling how much this handsome charlatan might have bilked Addie for.

"You set up a lot of electronic gizmos, spout a bunch of scientific-sounding mumbo jumbo, and take money for it. I think that's deplorable."

Bryan's shoulders stiffened, and his hands stilled on the light stand he had righted. He gave her a hard look, the expression in his warm blue eyes severe. "Yes, well, we all have our own ideas as to what amounts to deplorable behavior, don't we, Ms. Lindquist?"

"Just what do you mean by that?"

"Oh, just nothing," Bryan muttered, tearing his gaze away from her.

Dammit, how could he feel so drawn to her knowing what he did about her? Even as he stood there fuming with righteous anger, a part of him never once stopped assessing the gentle beauty, the exquisite femininity Rachel Lindquist possessed. This indiscriminating lust dawning inside him was a disconcerting new character flaw, to say the very least. With a considerable effort of will he attempted to block it from his consciousness.

Rachel could feel his disapproval of her like an icy rain, and it rankled. The man was little better than an out and out thief, and he was looking down his nose at her! What could he possibly know about her? Nothing. Unless . . . Addie had told him something. That idea irked her even more, that her mother would share family secrets with this stranger.

"I don't know what my mother may have told you, Mr. Hennessy, but she is not a well woman. She has Alzheimer's disease."

"I'm aware of that, Ms. Lindquist," Bryan said

pointedly. "I've been dealing with Addie on a daily basis. I dare say, I know a hell of a lot more about her condition than you do."

The blow was on target. Rachel flinched at his words and at the burning guilt that immediately flooded through her. Still, she pulled herself together and lifted her chin. "Dr. Moore wasn't able to contact me until just last week."

"Oh. Pardon me for thinking you might give your mother a call every once in a while," Bryan said dryly. "You know, once a year or so."

Tears stung the backs of Rachel's eyes. She had called Addie over the years. She had tried to bridge the chasm that had divided them. Addie had hung up on her every single time. Every letter she'd sent had gone unanswered. Every overture of peace had been met with bitter, stony silence. But none of that was Bryan Hennessy's business, and, despite all she had been through, Rachel had too much pride to enlighten him.

She pulled her shoulders back and gave him her haughtiest look. "You will pack your things and leave this house, Mr. Hennessy."

"No, I won't," Bryan said evenly.

"I won't have you taking advantage of my mother."

Won't have me taking advantage of her inheritance is more like it, Bryan thought. He gave her a black look that only darkened as he leaned over her and caught a whiff of her perfume, an elusive scent so delicate, he almost thought he'd imagined it, and yet it lured him closer.

Tempting fate, he bent his head so he was almost nose to nose with her—well within kissing distance. Her full, soft lips beckoned like a siren's call. It was as if their bodies were communicating on a level of their own, impervious to opinions on character. His heart thumped hard, then slowed against his breastbone, and his lungs fought every shallow breath he tried to take. It was unlike anything he had ever experienced.

"Addie and I have a deal," he said softly, straining to concentrate on the subject at hand. "More to the point, we have a contract. And most important to me, I gave her my word I'd find out what's going on around here. That may not mean much to you, but I stand by my promises."

Rachel barely heard his words. They were absorbed into her brain on one level while her conscious awareness dwelled on the man. She felt overwhelmed, enveloped by his masculinity, and she felt her body responding to it. A satiny warmth unfolded through her, down her arms and legs and into her breasts, making them feel heavy and full. Her gaze fastened on his mouth. In a way she couldn't begin to explain or understand, she could almost taste his lips, could almost feel them on her own. The sensations were so vivid, they frightened her, and she took a step back from him in obvious retreat.

Bryan turned away and speared both hands back through his hair as he dragged in a deep, cleansing breath. Dammit, he swore inwardly, more shaken than angry at the moment. He'd never felt anything quite like the power that had held him in its grasp as he'd stared down at Rachel

Lindquist's petal-pink lips. He shook his head to clear it.

It must have had something to do with a combination of exhaustion and celibacy. Once he might have called it magic, but he couldn't call it that now. Magic was what he had shared with Serena. All his magic had died with her. What he was feeling now—well, it was something he wanted no part of, certainly. He was there to do a job, that was all. That was all he could handle right now. That was all he wanted to handle.

"Hennessy?" an imperious voice sounded from the top of the stairs. "What in God's name is going on down there?"

"I wish I knew," Bryan mumbled to himself, shaking off the last of the sensation that had stunned him so. He planted his hands at his waist and looked up as Addie Lindquist descended the grand staircase.

Addie moved like a queen. She kept her thin shoulders square and her back straight. Age had shrunken her some, but she did not see that as an excuse for bad posture. Her hand skimmed the mahogany banister lightly. She held her head high. Her frazzled braid of silvery blond hair was draped over her shoulder. She looked like she should have been wearing a velvet cloak instead of a flannel nightgown.

"Who's down there with you?" she demanded, squinting. "Is it Wimsey? The rascal. I haven't seen him all day. I can't imagine where he's taken himself off to."

"No, it isn't Wimsey, Addie," Bryan said, heartily

wishing it were the elusive ghost of Drake House. He stepped to the left so Addie would have an unobstructed view of her visitor.

"Well, who is it, then? You'd better not be cavorting with the kitchen help again."

"She sort of thinks I'm her butler," Bryan whispered, tilting his head down so Rachel could hear him.

But Rachel wasn't listening. She was seeing her mother for the first time in five years. When had Addie gotten so old? The beautiful, vital woman Rachel remembered had faded like a photograph left in the sun. Her hair was paler. The vibrant glow that had always radiated from Addie had dimmed. She seemed smaller, and, while she still had a beautiful complexion—something she had always taken great pride in—her face was deeply lined. In the time they had been apart Addie had slipped from middle age to old age. Suddenly the five years that had passed seemed even more of a waste.

As Addie stared down at her, Rachel suddenly felt as she had at sixteen when she'd been caught coming home after curfew. A hundred fears and anxieties tumbled inside her. How would Addie react to her coming here? It was Dr. Moore who had contacted her, not Addie. Addie wouldn't even accept her phone calls. How would her mother receive her now that she was there in the flesh?

If you leave with that cheap musician, don't think you can ever come back here, Rachel Lindquist. If you leave here now, if you defy me, I will cease to have a daughter.

The ultimatum rang in her ears as if her mother had delivered it only yesterday.

Addie's gaze settled on the pretty young woman standing beside Hennessy in the hall below her. At first there was no spark of recognition in her mind whatsoever, but, as she moved down one step and then another, she felt her mind shift gears. A quiver of fright ran through her as she realized this was someone she should know but couldn't place. The feeling lasted only a second or two, but its intensity sapped the strength from her, and she had to pause on the landing before descending the last few steps. Then the fog of confusion cleared abruptly and recognition startled her so, she nearly gasped.

"Rachel," she said, her pale eyes round with wonder. She didn't smile or rush forward, but held still. If she moved toward this vision, there was every chance it would vanish. If she was still, she could soak it up greedily and pray that her memory would hold it.

Rachel. Lord, when had she become a woman? She was beautiful. She was dressed like a cheap Gypsy in faded jeans and a purple sweater that hung to the middle of her slender thighs, but it made no difference; she was beautiful.

Her daughter, the child she had thought lost, was there before her, a woman. Emotions ran riot inside her, joy and regret and anger swirling and tumbling around in her brain and overwhelming her. She could only stand on the landing of the grand staircase and stare and say her daughter's name. "Rachel."

Rachel shivered, rooted to the spot. She wanted to rush forward and embrace her mother, but that was not the way of the Lindquists. They had never been the type for hugs and kisses and "vulgar" public displays of emotion. Instead, she tried to swallow down her fears and simply said, "Mother."

It was a simple word full of complex feelings. There was so much between them, such a complicated history, so many memories, so much pain. Rachel pressed a hand to her pounding heart. Since she had received Dr. Moore's call, she had thought of little besides her mother and how they would handle the situation. But now she realized that never once in all that time had she allowed herself to recognize the hope she'd harbored for this moment.

Bryan watched the exchange between mother and daughter with interest. What kind of family was this? His mother would have had him in a bear hug the instant he'd come through the door. Addie and Rachel stared at each other as if there were an invisible wall between them.

Perhaps there was.

The look in Addie's eyes was guarded, almost defensive. Rachel appeared to be more frightened than joyful. Had she caught that second of blankness in her mother's gaze when Addie had almost certainly failed to recognize her? Bryan tried to tell himself it served her right. She was the one who had left and not come back for five years. She deserved to be frightened. But he couldn't stop the rush of sympathy that welled inside him. The expression in Rachel's eyes was a little girl's, hopeful and repentant. If she had looked at him that way, he knew he would have forgiven her anything.

"Rachel," Addie said again, stepping down from the landing. She held herself perfectly erect.

This was the daughter she had devoted her life to. This was the daughter who had chosen to throw away all their dreams to chase after a two-bit drifter who had an adequate voice and a beat-up guitar. This was the daughter who had left her. Her deteriorating mind had no trouble recalling these facts while it ignored the attempts at peace-making. All the old hurt and bitterness boiled inside her anew, obscuring the joy and the guilt. Her mind wasn't capable of dealing with many emotions at once, and so it seized upon the strongest. Stubborn pride tilted her chin up as she stared into the face that so resembled the ghost of her own past. "What are you doing here?"

Rachel felt disappointment crush her. She didn't try to stop the tears from springing into her eyes, but she did manage to keep the sorrow out of her voice. "I came to help you. Dr. Moore called me and told me about your illness." *Why didn't you? Why couldn't you put that damned pride aside long enough to tell me you needed me?*

"Broderick Moore is a Nazi and a fool. There's nothing wrong with me. I don't need your help," Addie said coldly. She turned toward Bryan. "I have Hennessy to help me."

Bryan took an involuntary step backward. He already felt like a voyeur, watching the interchange between mother and daughter; now he felt like an interloper as well. Rachel glared at him, her violet-blue eyes luminous with tears, and he held his hands up in a gesture of surrender. He shot a look at Addie. "Addie, you know I'm here only to look for Wimsey."

"Well, I don't know why you can't find him," she grumbled as her mind tuned out. "He's all over the place." She turned and started to shuffle down the hall, her green rubber garden boots scuffing against the marble floor. "I'm going to feed Lester. I'm sure you forgot to do it. No doubt practicing your smooth lines in front of a mirror again. Big Irish rascal."

Bryan rubbed a hand along his jaw, realizing dimly that he had forgotten to shave. He didn't know quite what to say to Rachel, who stood in the foyer looking like a piece of crystal on the verge of bursting into a million shards. It suddenly didn't matter what kind of daughter she'd been, it was obvious Addie's cold reception had hurt her, and almost certainly the decline of her mother's mental state had shocked her. He couldn't feel anything now but sympathy for her and the desire to take her in his arms and hold her.

"Dangerous thinking, Hennessy," he mumbled to himself. "Don't get involved. Make a note of that—don't get involved." He patted his shirt pocket, looking for his pencil, but it was gone again. "And don't forget to shave tomorrow."

"What was that?" Rachel asked. If she could not function in any other way, she could at least be polite, she thought ruefully. Wasn't that one of the Lindquist rules of deportment? A hysterical little laugh threatened but never emerged from her throat.

Bryan blushed a bit. "Nothing."

Rachel hugged herself, trying to ward off a chill that came from within. "I suppose I shouldn't have expected anything better than that," she murmured to no one in particular. Her gaze followed her mother down the hall into the nether reaches of the big house. "She never wanted me here before. Why should she want me here now?"

"You tried?" Bryan blurted out. Shame crawled around in his stomach. It hadn't occurred to him that Addie's side of the story might have been biased.

Rachel gave him a cool look, her pride returning to rally around her. "There are lots of things you don't know, Mr. Hennessy."

Bryan pushed his glasses up on his nose and nodded. "Oh, yes. I readily admit there are lots of things I don't know." He tossed her his most inane grin in an effort to lighten her mood and said, " 'A man doesn't know what he knows until he knows what he doesn't know.' Thomas Carlyle. I've adopted that as my motto."

"I see," Rachel murmured, though she clearly didn't.

Bryan was unconcerned. The point was, Rachel's eyes had lost their tragic quality. She was no longer staring after Addie with an expression of shattered hope. She would have to deal with those feelings later, he knew, but at least the intensity of the impact had been defused.

He stuffed his hands into the front pockets of

his jeans and gazed up at the chandelier, his blue eyes drowsy with thought. "Of course, John Wooden once said, 'It's what you learn after you think you know it all that counts the most.' For instance, did you know that an alligator's length in feet is the distance between his eyes in inches?"

Rachel opened her mouth to comment, then closed it and simply stared at him. How had he gotten on this topic? Who in his right mind would try to measure the distance between an alligator's eyes? The man was a lunatic. A rumpled, handsome lunatic.

She shook her head, deciding she had to be a little off the beam herself to be going on this way about how sexy this strange man was. Finally she decided to ask a question that seemed more pertinent. "Who's Lester?"

Bryan sobered and sighed. "There is no Lester. Um . . . your mother thinks she owns a parakeet." He shrugged apologetically. "If she does, I haven't been able to find it."

"Oh."

"I keep meaning to buy her one, but I forget things. I'm sure I've written myself a note about it," he said, pulling a fistful of paper scraps from his pants pocket. He sorted through them, frowning.

"That's all right," Rachel said.

Addie thought she owned a parakeet. This man, who was a virtual stranger, intended to buy her one to placate her. How sweet. What a sweet, sexy, rumpled con man he was. Her heart warmed, then she caught herself and shuddered, cursing her wildly swinging emotions. She felt as if she were trying to keep her balance on the deck of a ship pitching violently in a stormy sea.

Stuffing his notes back in his pocket, Bryan watched her from under his lashes. She looked so lost. In a way it made him think of Addie at the instant her mind snapped from normal to non-functioning. But then Addie would retreat into her fantasies. Rachel didn't have that option.

Without thinking, he took a step toward her. Odd, but he felt almost as if he'd been pushed toward her. When he caught himself he had already begun to reach out to her. Stopping in his tracks, he slapped his hands together and tried to look decisive. "You must have a suitcase or something out in your car. I'll go get it."

He turned and let himself out, taking big gulps of the cool night air as he crossed the porch and jogged down the steps.

"Holy Mike, that was a close call, you moron," he grumbled to himself. His sneakers crunched on the gravel drive as he headed for a beat-up little Chevette that was parked beside Addie's old Volvo wagon.

The farther he got from the house, the steadier he felt. The sea air was refreshing. Moisture from the fog that had rolled in at sunset dampened his skin. He leaned against the roof of the little car and let the sound of crashing waves wash the tension from him.

Drake House stood on a cliff overlooking the bay on the very northern edge of Anastasia. Because of the lay of the land and the size of the estate, its nearest neighbor was a quarter mile away. The house on its lonely precipice was a giant sentinel, a gaudy reminder of a bygone age.

It might have looked like a happy, magical place once with its turrets and gingerbread and gables. Now, run-down and in dire need of a coat of paint, it looked like something out of a horror movie. The land that stretched out before it had at one time been a beautifully manicured lawn. There had been gardens and even a maze. He'd seen pictures of it in *Anastasia's Architecture: A Pictorial Essay.* The gardens had long since gone to weed and the maze had become a tall, tangled mass of wild brambles.

The few people who came to visit Drake House called during daylight hours, bowing to superstitions they would never voice. Most of them came to browse through the antiques Addie had collected to sell. The kids of the town sometimes came to the end of the driveway at night. Bryan had seen them—groups of four or five kids who weren't brave enough to come any closer. They stood down at the gate, shoving each other through the portal but never farther. They were thoroughly convinced the place was haunted. They were also scared to death of Addie.

Addie. Bryan glanced up at the house and caught a glimpse of her silhouette as she passed a window. He knew she was going to all the bird cages she had collected, filling the little dishes with seed. In the morning he would clean the trays out before she got up, or she would be upset thinking there was something wrong with Lester.

It never seemed to bother her that Lester wasn't in any of the cages. Unless, of course, she was seeing birds that weren't actually there. Ghost birds.

He found his pencil and a crumpled bit of paper and made a note of that, then shook his head as he tucked the scrap of paper into his hip pocket and forgot about it. Addie could be fairly lucid. At times she was sharp as a tack. Then in the blink of an eye she would be talking to people who weren't there, feeding birds she didn't own.

It was a sad situation, but it wasn't any of his business, he reminded himself. He'd dealt with his own sad situation; he didn't need to get wrapped up in another.

Rachel watched her mother go from bird cage to bird cage, panic tightening her throat. Addie couldn't be this bad already. The possibility that she was terrified Rachel. The further her mother retreated from reality, the less chance there would be for them to reconcile.

In her own mind, because she had only just learned of the problem, Rachel felt as if her mother had just developed this illness. She wanted to forget that Addie's decline had doubtless begun several years earlier, and her mother had either ignored or hidden it for a long while.

Addie had moved to Anastasia upon her retirement from teaching music in Berkeley, not long after Rachel had gone on the road with Terence. According to Dr. Moore, the people of Anastasia had labeled her erratic behavior "eccentric," and, by the good doctor's own admission, the town had more than its share of oddballs, so Addie hadn't really stuck out. It was only after she had backed her Volvo clear across Main Street and into the front of the movie theater that anyone had thought to alert Dr. Moore.

"Mother, it's very late," Rachel said wearily. She leaned against the door frame of the parlor, letting it support her weight for a moment. Now was not the time to try to deal with any of this mess—the illness, the emotional baggage, Bryan Hennessy. "You should be in bed."

Addie set her birdseed down and turned toward her daughter, arching a brow. Resentment burned through her. She resented Rachel for leaving her, for abandoning their dreams, for trying to tell her what to do now. She resented the fact that it had taken a call from that idiot Moore to bring her daughter home. The pressure of her feelings built inside her like steam, which she vented on Rachel.

"I won't have you telling me what to do, missy," she snapped, eyes flashing. "I'm not some incontinent old woman who needs to be taken care of like a child."

Rachel reined in her own ready temper, forced a sigh, and hung her head. She was so tired. She'd driven clear from North Platte, stopping to sleep only once for just a few brief hours. Before the marathon drive had been the marathon fight and subsequent end of her relationship with Terence. And before that had been the devastating news of her mother's illness. All of it weighed down on her now like the weight of the world on her shoulders.

At the moment she would have given anything for someone to lean on, just for a minute or two.

The image of Bryan Hennessy drifted through her mind. For an instant she could have sworn she felt a man's arms around her. How absurd, she thought, shaking free of the strange sensation.

"What room should I take?" she asked. "I'm going to bed."

"Not in my house."

Rachel's head snapped up as her heart skipped a beat. "What?"

"I don't want you here," Addie said bluntly. "Go away."

Rachel stared at her mother. She couldn't have moved if her life had depended on it. Maybe she couldn't have expected to be welcomed with open arms, but she hadn't expected a total rejection either.

Addie raised her fists suddenly and jigged around like an old-time prizefighter, her braid bouncing, a truculent light in her eyes. "Go away! Get out of my house!"

"Mother, don't!" Rachel ordered, wincing as Addie popped her one on the arm.

"You're a traitor! I don't want you here!"

"Mother, stop it!" Rachel shouted, dodging away from another blow.

She couldn't believe this was actually happening. She had been bracing herself for a fight, but not one like this. As she backed into the hall and toward the front door, she kept thinking that any second she would wake up and discover it had all been a dream, a strange black dream. But how far back would the nightmare go, she wondered dimly. A week? A year? Five years?

"Get out! Get out!" Addie chanted. She couldn't seem to stop herself from saying the words over and over, but she couldn't bear to look at Rachel's face as she said them, so she turned her back to her daughter and went on shouting. It was as if the floodgates on her emotions had been suddenly thrown wide. Anger and hurt spewed out unchecked.

Rachel pressed her hands over her ears and squeezed her eyes shut. Abruptly it all become too much. She turned and bolted for the front door, knocking over half of Bryan Hennessy's equipment as she went. She flung the heavy door open and ran out onto the porch, where she stopped and leaned against a post, feeling dizzy and sick.

"What happened?" Bryan asked, setting her two suitcases down on the ground at the bottom of the steps.

"She threw me out," Rachel whispered, stunned. "She doesn't want me here. She meant it. She told me to leave and never come back, and she meant it."

She sounded so small and lost. Bryan's heart twisted in his chest.

Rachel hugged the wooden column as if it were the only solid thing in a world suddenly turned to illusion. "I have to help her," she murmured to Bryan beseechingly. "She's my mother. I have to help her. She's my responsibility now. But she doesn't want me here."

"Look," Bryan said, climbing the steps to the

porch, "it's late. Addie gets really irrational when she hasn't had a good night's sleep." He wanted to tell her that everything would seem better in the morning, but the bald truth was Addie could be irrational at *any* time. There was no guarantee of her behaving any differently tomorrow.

Rachel faced him, leaning her back against the post. She wrapped her arms across her middle, fighting to hold herself together. In a matter of days her whole world had torn loose from its moorings. All the dreams she had believed in had died. The rainbow she had followed away from home hadn't ended in a pot of gold. And the home she had returned to was full of strangers. The nightmare wasn't going to end when she opened her eyes in the morning. The bad dream had just begun.

"My mother is losing her mind." She uttered the words as if she had only just realized what they meant and what the ramifications for her own life would be.

She looked up at Bryan through a shimmering window of tears. It suddenly didn't matter that he was a stranger or that she had questioned his motives. He was someone's son. He had a family somewhere, a home he would return to one day. Maybe he would understand a little of what she was feeling, and she needed so badly to share it with someone, just for a minute or two.

As the first fat tears teetered over the barrier of her thick lashes, she said, "What am I going to do?"

Bryan instantly forgot his vow of noninvolvement. What man could stand there and watch this lovely creature crumple like a wilting rose? He could offer her his strength if nothing else. He took her gently into his arms, as if her body were as fragile as her spirit, and pressed her cheek to his chest. Sobs tore through her, terrible, wrenching sobs. She didn't seem strong enough to cry so hard, he thought. He could feel her sobs echoing through his chest, and he had to fight down the knot in his throat.

She was hurting—not physically, but with the kind of pain that comes from confusion and broken dreams and mourning a lost future. He could understand that all too well. He could understand her need to be held. He couldn't understand his own overwhelming need to hold her, but even as his brain tried to decipher it, his arms tightened around her and his lips brushed against her temple.

"Shhh . . . you're too tired to think straight. Let's get you settled in. We'll talk about it in the morning," he murmured, not even aware that he had included himself in her dilemma.

Even though he whispered something about going inside, he made no move to leave the porch. He simply rocked her gently back and forth as the mist swirled around them and the sea crashed in the distance. He knew a strange contentment in holding her, but he didn't question it. For the first time in a long time something was soothing the ache in his heart. He didn't dare wonder why.

THREE

They entered the house through a back door, passed through a corner of the large dark kitchen, and went into an old-fashioned pantry, where Bryan opened what appeared to be a tall cabinet set into the wall. Rachel followed him, mute, as they went up a dusty, unembellished servants' staircase, a place hung with cobwebs and bare light bulbs dangling from thick black cords in the ceiling.

"I'm sorry about breaking down that way," she said, embarrassed now that the tears had dried. "I don't ordinarily do that kind of thing."

"That's okay. You don't ordinarily get chased out the house by your mother either," Bryan said. "Careful on this step. Stay to the right. Dry rot, you know. You have to watch for stuff like that in these old houses."

44

Rachel glanced down at the crack in the wooden tread as she bypassed the step altogether, wondering how much of the rest of the house was rotting away. She had hoped to get by without investing much in repairs before they sold the place. What money of hers she had managed to keep out of Terence's slippery hands wasn't going to go far. Her mother had been running an antiques business for several years, and then there was the money from her father's police pension fund, but their expenses were going to run high. She had to consider Addie's medical bills, the deposit on an apartment in San Francisco, and their day-to-day living expenses. She had no idea how Addie had taken care of her money recently. If Bryan Hennessy was an example, she had been squandering it with a lavish hand.

A ghostbuster. Rachel shook her head.

They exited through a door that blended into the paneled wall of the second-story hallway.

"Here we are," Bryan said softly. He put on a pleasant smile and slid the hidden door shut with the toe of his battered sneaker. "Just like in the movies, huh?"

Rachel took in little of her surroundings. Her normal curiosity had been diluted by the circumstances of her visit. Maybe in a day or two she would find it interesting that the house had a secret stairway and real mahogany paneling, that the floor in the foyer below was made of imported Italian marble. Right now none of that penetrated her senses. Nor did the musty smell of old carpets and draperies. For the moment it was all she could do to put one foot in front of the other and follow Bryan Hennessy down the hall.

"Don't read too much into your mother's reaction tonight," he said quietly, slowing his long strides and turning to regard her with a serious expression. He carried a suitcase in each hand and his faded blue shirt was stained dark from her tears in spots across his chest. "You took her by surprise. She doesn't handle surprises very well."

Rachel thought of Terence and Addie's reaction to him, and she smiled sadly as she reached up to tuck a strand of hair behind her ear. "No, she never did."

"She'll probably be perfectly composed tomorrow."

A weak smile was the best Rachel could manage. She hoped her mother was perfectly composed in the morning, but that wouldn't help her tonight. She felt shaken to the very foundation of her soul. If she lived to be a hundred, she would never forget the wild fury in her mother's eyes as she'd shouted at her to get out of the house. Remembering the scene now sent a shaft of pain through her so sharp, it nearly stole her breath from her lungs. She had known it would be difficult coming back, but she'd never imagined anything like the bizarre scene she'd been a part of. It didn't even help to know it was the illness that made Addie behave irrationally. There was just too much true emotion beneath the madness to easily push the outburst aside.

"You can take my room for tonight," Bryan said, shouldering open a door and standing back in invitation for her to precede him into the room. "It's the only spare bed with sheets on it."

"I can't throw you out of your bed," Rachel protested, going to stand over the heat register, hoping it would chase away some of the chill that was permeating her bones.

"A little while ago you were ready to throw me out of the house," Bryan said with a charming smile, trying to tease an answering smile out of Rachel. He kept his gaze on her as he bent to set her suitcases down beside the dresser.

Rachel closed her eyes and sighed. She managed a wry twist of her lips, but that was all. There was no way she could handle this man on any level—teasing, arguing, anything. Aside from being tired enough to drop, her feelings toward him were completely tangled. He was a stranger, a man who was taking her dotty mother's money to hunt for ghosts. He was an antagonist who seemed to disapprove of her. He was inane one minute and serious the next. He was an attractive man, arousing needs in her that had been left unattended for too long. He was a compassionate human being, offering her comfort and support. That would have been a confusing mix for a person to handle on the best of days, and this was most certainly not the best of days.

"Get some rest," Bryan whispered.

He didn't remember crossing the room. He didn't remember making the decision to touch Rachel Lindquist, but his finger was crooked beneath her chin and he was tilting her face up as if he had every intention of kissing her. It took a considera-

ble effort not to do just that. Her lips were slightly
parted. Her thick lashes were lowered, laying like a
pair of delicate lace fans against her pale cheeks.

Desire ached all through his body, throbbing a
little harder behind the suddenly close confines of
his jeans. He cursed his rogue hormones. What
was the matter with him—acting like some randy
stallion when this poor girl was so physically and
emotionally exhausted she seemed near collapse?
What was he doing feeling attracted to her anyway? For all he knew she had come there to pack
Addie up and hustle her off to a rest home. The
only significant facts he knew about her were that
she had run off five years ago and hadn't come
back.

But she had tried to call . . . and she had cried
on his shoulder . . . and she looked so small and
sad. . . .

He shook his head for the umpteenth time that
night, amazed by his sudden, strange feelings.
True, he had always had a soft spot in his heart
for a damsel in distress, but he wasn't interested
in getting involved with one just now. No. His life
was falling back into order; that was all he wanted
to concentrate on now. He wasn't interested in
taking on the problems of a complicated mother-
daughter relationship or the raft of troubles that
would accompany Addie's illness. He didn't want
to concentrate on Rachel Lindquist and all the
pain and broken dreams he'd seen in her eyes.

She opened her eyes and stared up at him, and
yet another blast of heat seared through him.

"Get some rest," he murmured again, backing away before he lost all sense.

"Where will you sleep?"

"Don't worry about me," he said, forcing one of his silly, sunny smiles as he moved toward the door. He had the distinct impression he wasn't going to sleep at all. "I'm a magical being; I can sleep anywhere. Tables, chairs, stairs. I once spent the night in the trunk of a Mercedes-Benz, but that's a long story and I'm really not at liberty to divulge the details. Suffice it to say they put all the luxury features in other parts of the car."

Rachel stared at him, amazed. She wanted to laugh. After all the horrid things that had happened in the past few days, she wanted to laugh at Bryan Hennessy because he was silly and funny in a way unlike anyone she had ever known. It amazed her that she still had a sense of humor. She felt a little warmer inside because of it.

"You're a very unusual person, Mr. Hennessy," she said with a wry smile.

He beamed. "Why, thank you."

Rachel chuckled. "It wasn't exactly a compliment."

"It was to me. We Hennessys pride ourselves on being unique."

"You're certainly that," she said, trying unsuccessfully to stifle a yawn.

"The bathroom is down the hall on the right," Bryan said over his shoulder as he started out the door. "Watch out for the faucet in the sink, it sprays like a geyser every once in a while for no apparent reason. I think it may be possessed.

Poltergeists often take up residence in the plumbing, you know. No doubt the result of faulty toilet training when they were toddlers. That's my theory anyway."

"Mr. Hennessy," Rachel blurted out, a part of her loath to have him leave.

"Bryan," he corrected her, turning back and bracing a forearm against the doorjamb. He felt old enough as it was these days; he didn't need this lovely little thing calling him mister. He had to have ten years on Rachel Lindquist—at least. At the moment she didn't look a day over fifteen, and still he wanted to kiss her. That thought left him feeling like a lecher.

"Bryan," she said hesitantly, clasping her small white hands in front of her. "Thank you for giving me your room and . . . for . . . everything."

She couldn't quite bring herself to say "holding me." She wasn't comfortable with the idea of having turned to a stranger that way, pouring her pain out to him. She couldn't remember the last time she'd cried in front of someone. Not even when her mother had told her she could never come home had she let the tears fall with a witness present. She hadn't cried in front of her mother, nor had she cried when she had gone outside and gotten in the car with Terence. Her fierce pride hadn't allowed it.

But tonight she hadn't been able to keep the tears in check. They had fallen in torrents onto Bryan Hennessy's solid chest. And he had held her as if it had been the most natural thing in the world.

Bryan stared at her for a moment from his position in the doorway. She stood beside the bed, looking vulnerable in her baggy purple sweater, her baby-fine hair framing her face in wisps. Her skin looked as soft and rich as cream. Her eyes were like pools of twilight. Longing ribboned through him. Without a word he left the room, closing the door behind him.

Immediately Rachel felt lonely. Lonely for a lunatic. How silly, she scolded herself. She was lonely for a con man just because he had a nice smile and a weird sense of humor. That was hardly like her normal, practical self.

To take her mind off her feelings, she busied herself getting ready for bed. She was so tired, it took all of her flagging concentration to accomplish that simple task. She pulled her nightgown out of one battered suitcase and changed into it quickly. It wasn't a nightgown precisely, but an extra large T-shirt with a bust of Bach silk-screened on the front above the words "I go for baroque." Foregoing her nightly ritual of washing her face and brushing her teeth, she removed the pins from her hair and let it fall in waves past her shoulders. She pulled back the covers of the bed and slipped between them, groaning in relief as her weary body settled into the mattress.

As exhausted as she was, she couldn't sleep. She lay in the bed, staring at the ceiling for a long while, trying not to think of anything at all. But she wasn't able to blank her mind. Thoughts kept creeping in from the edge of her consciousness—

thoughts of Addie, of Terence, of the past, of the future, of Bryan Hennessy.

The pillow she lay her head on carried his scent. The sheets that enveloped her body had covered his. The mattress beneath her had dipped beneath the weight of his lean, athletic body. Those thoughts seemed almost unbearably erotic to her. She moved restlessly, sexual awareness arousing all her nerve endings so that the gentle rasp of the sheets against her skin had all the impact of a caress. Her suddenly fertile imagination conjured up an image of him lying beside her, his big hands stroking her soothingly, his lips feathering kisses along her jaw. Her nipples tightened, and a dull ache coiled low in her belly.

Joining all the other emotions jumbled inside her was a vague sense of guilt and shame. She had no business thinking such thoughts about a man she hardly knew. It wasn't like her to indulge in sexual fantasies anyway. She had never been a particularly sexual person. She discounted her feelings as a reaction to stress. She was feeling overwhelmed. It was only natural to want to turn to someone, to be held, to forget.

And there was so much she would have liked to forget—the dreams she had abandoned, the ones that had drifted away, the opportunities she had squandered.

Finally giving up on the idea of falling into a peaceful sleep, Rachel turned on the ancient lamp that sat on a lace doily on the stand beside the bed. She propped her pillow against the massive carved headboard and leaned back against it.

The light cast its glow on only half the room, leaving the farther corners shrouded in shadows. There was an enormous, sinister-looking armoire standing opposite the bed with one door open and athletic socks hanging out of the top drawer as if they were trying to slither out and escape. To the right of the bed an assortment of junk lined the wall—old steamer trunks, wooden chairs, and a bird cage large enough to hold a vulture. To the left of the bed was a dressing table with a cracked mirror. There were books piled on it, and charts and notes were strewn across the top of it as if it was being used as a desk.

On the nightstand beside the bed was additional evidence that Bryan Hennessy occupied the room. There was a watch that was either running down or was set for the wrong time zone. Rachel picked it up and examined it more closely, telling herself she had a right to know who this man was her mother had invited to stay in her home. It was a nice watch, gold with a brown leather band that was curved by long use to the shape of its owner's wrist. It had an old-fashioned face—no glowing digital readout, but script numerals and delicate hands. The back was engraved WITH LOVE, MOM AND DAD. 1977.

Carefully replacing it on the table, Rachel glanced at the snapshot held in a plain gold frame. A younger Bryan Hennessy stood in a cap and gown behind three smiling young women—a blonde, a brunette, and a redhead. At least he wasn't prejudiced, Rachel thought with a strange spurt of something akin to jealousy.

Pushing the unwelcome feeling aside, she looked at the crumpled scraps of paper that had been tossed across the dusty surface of the nightstand. They were notes with odd messages like "Jayne says to eat breakfast tomorrow," "Go to library—background, Drake House," "Dinner with Faith and Shane, seven sharp. Get a haircut!" "Addie capable of hidden psychokinesis? That could explain object movement in grid nine."

Was it possible Bryan Hennessy was truly a scientist of some sort? It seemed unlikely a con man would be so thorough as to leave notes like that last one on his nightstand on the off chance someone with a fully functioning mind might stumble across them. On the other hand, a ghost hunter seemed too farfetched for words.

Rachel couldn't find it in her to believe in ghosts. Reality was proving tough enough to deal with; she didn't have time to wonder about the supernatural as well. She knew she had to focus on the here and now. She had to concentrate on the grim practical aspects of her future and her mother's future. In view of what had happened in the past few years, she knew it was pointless to waste time on dreams and wishes. There was no such thing as magic or happily-ever-after. There were no such things as ghosts.

As if to mock her, the image of Terence Bretton filled her head. Handsome, smiling Terence, as he had been when she'd met him at a coffee house located just off the campus of Berkeley. She'd been a sophomore, diligently studying classical music on a scholarship, dutifully pursuing the career in opera her mother had been grooming her for for her entire life. Terence had been a breath of fresh air to a girl who had lived a sheltered, structured life of voice lessons and practice and study. Terence, with his disarming, lopsided grin and twinkling green eyes. Terence, full of big dreams but lacking the ambition to make them come true.

Only she hadn't know that at the time, Rachel reflected with a wistful smile. She had fallen for Terence's charm and his dreams and his honest, untrained voice. He had offered her love and freedom, and she had embraced both.

Her initial attraction to him had been calculated. Terence, a folk singer who led a Gypsy's life, was everything Rachel knew her mother would detest. She had loved her mother, but rebellion was a natural part of growing up. Rachel's had come later than most, she knew. She had abruptly become fed up with the control Addie had wielded over her life. She had suddenly burned out on the hours of training, the discipline, the lack of a normal social life, the constant reminders of how hard Addie worked to secure her future. She had gone to the Coffee Mill out of defiance and had determinedly fallen for the handsome young man playing the guitar on the small stage there.

It didn't seem like five years ago. It seemed like a lifetime ago. Another lifetime down a trail of broken dreams.

Terence had never made it big, and the burden of his mediocrity had fallen on Rachel's shoulders. Terence didn't like to deal with the realities of booking gigs and balancing books. Sensible and practical, Rachel had taken on the responsibilities. Their relationship had gradually cooled from lovers to friends.

Her love for Terence Bretton had slipped away until a part of her had almost come to hate him. According to Terence, it was always someone else's fault he didn't hit the big time. According to him, there was always another golden opportunity around the corner just waiting for him.

The news about Addie had been the final straw. Terence's reaction had been no less than Rachel should have expected. Still, she had held on to the last of her hope that he would somehow redeem himself, would somehow make up for all the disappointments he had handed her over the years. All she had wanted was his friendship and his support. It hadn't seemed so much to ask. What a fool she'd been.

"Put her in a home."

"She's my mother."

"She disowned you."

"She raised me by herself after Dad died. She took care of me. I should do the same for her."

"If her mind is going, she'll never know the difference, Rachel. Put her away someplace. We've got our lives to live. We've got plans. We can't stop now. I'm going to make it big, Rachel. I need you there beside me."

"So does my mother."

Now Rachel sighed and hugged the spare pillow to her chest as sadness overcame her. Terence wasn't going to make it big. He didn't have plans, he had dreams, and he spent his time expecting them magically to come true with little or no effort on his part. Rachel had learned the hard way that there was no such thing as magic.

In the end her choice had been clear. In fact, there had been no choice to make. She had known the instant after Dr. Moore had told her the news that she would go to Addie.

Now she was there and Addie didn't want her.

They would get over that hurdle somehow. Beneath the hurt and the uncertainty, Rachel had bedrock determination, no doubt inherited from her indomitable mother. She would reconcile with Addie somehow. She would deal with the reality of Addie's condition somehow. As they had after Verne Lindquist had been killed, the two of them would get along . . . somehow. It wasn't going to be fun. It wasn't going to be easy. But they would manage it. Somehow.

And what about Bryan Hennessy?

A sharp pang ran through her, and she hugged her pillow a little harder. Bryan Hennessy was a stranger. He had nothing to do with their situation. He couldn't. She had all she could handle with Addie. A relationship with a man was out of the question. Why she was even thinking about it was beyond her. She didn't know Bryan Hennessy from a goose. He might have been a con man or a killer or another Terence Bretton. Judging from all his nonsensical piffle, he was probably worse than Terence. At least Terence aspired to something. To what could a ghost hunter aspire?

She was just overreacting to him because she was exhausted and he had been gallant enough to offer her his shoulder to cry on and his bed to sleep in. He wouldn't want to get involved with her, at any rate. What fool would volunteer to take on the problems she was facing?

You have to help her.

Bryan scowled. He shifted positions in the blood-red leather wing chair. The study was located in grid nine of his chart of the first floor of Drake House. Addie had told him she'd seen things move in this room—move with the assistance of Wimsey. According to her, Wimsey had twice rearranged the furniture because "he likes it the way he likes it." She had moved it all around once, just out of stubbornness, but Wimsey had put it back.

Bryan had chosen this room to spend the night in because he knew damn well he wasn't going to sleep, and he was hoping against hope for a distraction—the appearance of Wimsey, a book falling off the shelf by itself, a sudden cold breeze, anything. Anything that would help get his mind off Rachel Lindquist sleeping in the same bed he had slept in, wrapping the sheets around her slender body, burrowing her angel's face into his pillow.

He groaned as his blood stirred hot in his veins. He could just imagine what she looked like sleeping: soft and tempting with her wild honey-gold hair mussed around her head. She was probably wearing a T-shirt, and the soft fabric would mold around her breasts the way his hands wanted to mold around them. The thought had him more than half turned on.

He swore under his breath. What kind of depraved creep was he turning into? There was poor Rachel, exhausted, frightened, hurt, trying to manage a few hours rest and escape from her troubles, and here he was lusting after her!

She's very pretty.

"Yes, she's pretty," he grumbled. "She's very pretty. And she's got a lot of problems, and I don't want to get involved."

For the first time he wondered about the folk singer Rachel had run off with five years before. Where was he? What kind of jerk was he that he would send Rachel to deal with this crisis on her own? Clarence something. "A common tramp" Addie had called him. Somehow, Bryan doubted Rachel would run off with a common tramp. Despite her casual style of dress, she radiated class. It was there in the way she held herself, in the way she moved, in the way she spoke.

There was obviously a lot more to the story than an "ungrateful" daughter taking up with a "cheap folk singer." Bryan was a little disappointed in himself for so readily believing the worst. Especially since it had come from Addie, who was disoriented much of the time. Maybe Rachel Lindquist was rotten to the core, but it wasn't his place to make that judgment without having all the facts. On the other hand, his life would be a whole lot simpler if he believed the worst and stayed away from her.

Even as he thought it, he had the sinking realization that it wasn't going to happen. It wasn't in him to judge people harshly. It wasn't in him to stand by and watch a lady struggle with a load that was too heavy for her to carry, either.

He had always taken care of the women in his life. His sisters first, and then Faith and Alaina and Jayne. Then Serena. Now Serena was gone, and the three lovelier members of the Fearsome Foursome were being taken care of by their mates. Enter Rachel Lindquist with her big violet eyes and incredible pink mouth and stubborn pride tilting her little chin up.

Fighting an inner battle, Bryan flung himself out of the chair and paced the width of the room, head down, his hands combing back through his tawny hair again and again.

You have to help her. She needs help.

"No, not me. I can't help anybody. I can't even help myself. She can get help from the doctor. She can join a support group. Just leave me out of it."

He paced some more, feeling the pressure in a strangely tangible way, as if it were pressing in on him from all around. It was not unlike diving deep into the black depths of the ocean, a silky nothingness pushing in on him from all sides, threatening to crush his chest. To escape it, he threw open the French doors and strode out onto the stone terrace.

As it had earlier, the cool air calmed him. He dropped onto a bench and leaned over, his elbows on his thighs, his hands rubbing the back of his neck.

He had known Serena was dying when he had married her. He had loved her, and the thought of letting her face death alone had been incomprehensible. Her decline and ultimate death had been the worst thing he could ever imagine going through. He had endured it for her, but he had vowed to himself never to go through anything like it again.

Rachel isn't facing death.

"No, but she's facing pain, and I've had enough pain to last me a lifetime."

What about her? You could ease her pain. You could lighten her burden.

"How?" he asked his inner voice as he pulled his glasses off and rubbed the bridge of his nose with a thumb and forefinger.

Magic.

Bryan laughed at that. He wasn't sure he knew what magic was anymore. Was he supposed to believe he could pull a rabbit out of his hat, and Rachel and Addie's troubles would disappear? It wouldn't happen.

But it might help.

After settling his glasses back into place, he reached into the breast pocket of his shirt and withdrew a short black wand, not more than five inches long and as big around as a cigarette. With a flick of his wrist, it became a silken red rose with a thin stem that abruptly drooped over his hand. A smile lifted the corner of his mouth.

"If I can't dazzle her with my magic, maybe I can be a source of comic relief," he said dryly, tucking the wilted rose back into his shirt pocket.

He hadn't been able to perform the simplest of tricks for months now. Though he kept trying, deep down he was afraid he had lost his magic forever.

He pushed himself up from the bench and wandered back into the house. His broad shoulders sagging under the twin burdens of exhaustion and stress, he picked up the glass of whiskey he had left on the leather blotter of the walnut desk. He had hoped the excellent liquor he'd found in a bottle in a desk drawer would help him sleep. The glass was nearly empty. Bryan frowned. He could have sworn he'd left a good inch in it when he'd gone outside. He didn't notice the stain near his feet on the old woolen carpet or the scent of liquor seeping up from the fabric. He noticed only that his whiskey was gone, and he didn't feel like pouring another.

Shrugging, he dismissed the question and tossed back most of what was left of the drink. Remembering things had never been his strong suit.

The study was quiet. This room was supposed to be a hotbed of paranormal activity, but not one thing out of the ordinary had happened in the few days he'd been there. Worse than that, Bryan felt nothing unusual, sensed nothing whatsoever.

As he gazed around the dark room, he wondered morosely if he was losing his touch professionally as well as with his magic. He had always had phenomenal success seeking out psychic disturbances. He had always been able to tune in to the scene and feel things others couldn't. His special sensitivity had led him to his career. Had it deserted him?

Too tired to think about it, he wandered from the room and down the hall to search for something comfortable to stretch out on.

FOUR

Rachel awoke early from a fitful sleep. Soft gray light seeped into the room through the window. She struggled with the covers that were tangled around her, and pushed herself up in the bed so she could lean back against the headboard. She was exhausted. The mere idea of getting out of bed made her groan, and when she thought of what she would have to face, she almost crawled back under the covers. Not that it would have done her any good. She hadn't gotten a moment's rest during the night. Dreams had haunted her, one right after another, interweaving and intermingling until they couldn't be separated. Even now emotions assailed her, panic chief among them.

The main theme of the dream marathon had been Addie. How were they ever going to get through what was ahead of them if her mother

wouldn't accept her help? It was one thing for
Rachel to say she was going to take care of Addie.
Accomplishing that task was going to be another
thing altogether. Addie had never been the kind of
woman who stood to the side, wringing her hands
and letting other people run her life. She had
always been so strong, so independent, such a
dictator, running their lives like an admiral on a
tight ship.

Rachel was a woman now and hardly the subser-
vient, obedient little thing she had been in her
youth. Because of Terence's lack of responsibility,
she had been forced to the role of leader. She had
handled the job with the same grit and determination her mother had always shown. She knew
from experience how to take charge of a situation.

But she didn't know how to take care of Addie. It
seemed completely unnatural to assume her mother's role as head of the family and relegate Addie to
second place. And she knew with a sense of dread
that was like a lump of ice in her stomach that
Addie wasn't going to go down without a fight.

The first logical step was the appointment Rachel had scheduled with Dr. Moore. Perhaps he
would be able to make Addie see reason. Hopefully
Bryan had been right in saying Addie would be
more composed in the morning, better able to
understand and to cope with the changes that
were inevitable.

A tiny flame of hope flared to life inside her, and
it burned a little hotter as she continued to think
about Bryan.

A strangely clear image of him waking up filled

her imagination. His tawny hair would be tousled,
his blue eyes bleary and heavy-lidded. He would
rub his hand along the stubble on his strong jaw.
She could almost smell his warm male scent, could
almost feel his warm weight in the bed beside her.
That warmth crept into her and swirled lazily
through her body.

Rachel forced her eyes open wide and all but
leapt from the bed.

"What are you doing, thinking that way, Rachel
Lindquist?" she demanded, staring at her reflection in the cracked mirror. With her cheeks
flushed and her hair a wild tangle around her
head, she looked like a strumpet. A scowl turned
down her pretty mouth. "What's the matter with
you? Bryan Hennessy is not now, nor will he ever
be a part of your life. You are going to see to that
first thing this morning."

Whether he was a legitimate scientist or not
didn't enter into it. She couldn't afford to pay him
for his questionable services. She had things like
doctor bills and rent to consider.

It still made her angry to think he would take
money from Addie. Her mother was obviously not
in full command of her faculties. This ghost business of hers was most probably some result of the
Alzheimer's. Rachel had read that some victims of
the dementing illness experience hallucinations.
This ghost, this "whimsy," was probably just
that—whimsy. The mother she remembered
would no more believe in ghosts than she would
believe in Santa Claus.

Rachel padded across the cold floor to the window for her first glimpse of the view from Drake House. Stepping over a large pair of battered loafers and around a bird cage, she peeled back one of the sheets from the glass. Fog obscured the view. She could hear the distant crash of the ocean, but she couldn't see the lawn, let alone the cliff edge or the blue water beyond.

"How symbolic of my life at the moment," she said dryly.

She turned away from the window and set herself to the task of preparing to face the day. With an eye toward pleasing her mother, she dressed in a conservative white blouse and a hunter-green jumper, painstakingly restored order to her hair, then turned to make the bed. That was when she found the rose.

A single yellow rose, slightly mangled, was peeking out from beneath the spare pillow she had hugged and punched and tussled with throughout the night. She picked it up by the end of the stem, staring at it in shock and disbelief as a petal dropped off and drifted to the bed.

Warmth surged through her before she could check it. A rose. How lovely. How thoughtful. How sweet. Then a blush bloomed on her cheeks and indignation rose up inside her. Bryan Hennessy had snuck into her room! He'd come into her room while she had been asleep.

Of all the low, strange things to do. How long had he stood beside the bed, looking at her? A minute? Five minutes? The very idea was mortifying! She might have been talking in her sleep or snoring or drooling, while this man she barely knew watched her!

Leaving the housekeeping for later, Rachel turned on her heel and stormed purposefully from the room to go in search of her midnight caller.

Bryan woke slowly, knowing instinctively that he would be better off unconscious. All the clues were there as his mind reached cautiously up out of the depths of sleep: an ache here, the beginnings of a pain there. Still, his eyes came halfway open, and he rubbed his hand along his jaw, rasping a two-day growth of whiskers against his palm. He really did have to remember to shave later.

The light in the billiard room was dim. It was early, he guessed, early enough for him to get to the bird cages before Addie did. Groaning, he pushed himself upright on the felt-covered slate of the old billiard table and swung his long legs over the edge. His body protested in more places than he cared to count.

"Maybe I'm getting too old for this kind of thing," he reflected as he retrieved his spectacles from the cue-stick rack and put them on. He looked at himself then in the ornate mirror that hung on the wall, taking up a space equal to that of the billiard table. Even through a couple of decades worth of dust he looked bad. He looked like a vagrant. His shirt was rumpled beyond redemption, the tails hanging out of his equally wrinkled pants. His wilted magic rose drooped over the edge of his shirt pocket.

A shower, a shave, and clean clothes were the

order of the morning, he thought as he slicked his disheveled hair back with his hands. But first, the bird cages.

He went into the parlor and unearthed the coffee can filled with bird seed Addie kept stashed behind a burgundy velvet fainting couch. Also behind the couch were a dozen unopened bags of bird seed and a foot-high stack of mail. Addie was notorious for stashing things away, like a squirrel hoarding nuts for the winter. And, like a squirrel, she often forgot where she had buried her booty. She never forgot her bird seed, however. She only forgot that she didn't have a bird.

Bryan wondered what her frame of mind would be this morning. He hoped for Rachel's sake Addie would be in one of her more normal periods. The two of them had a lot to talk over, a lot to settle between them, and not much time to do it. That was the one sure thing about Addie's illness: it would progress. There would be no remission, no reprieve. What needed settling between mother and daughter needed settling as soon as possible.

"Not that I'm getting involved," Bryan mumbled as he opened a wire cage and scraped the seed out of the little dish and into the coffee can. "I'm just here minding my own business, doing my little job."

To distract himself from the inner voice that was trying to tell him differently, he began to sing softly to himself. "I got a ghoul in Kalamazoo—"

"Mr. Hennessy." Rachel paused in the doorway of the parlor, ready to launch into her tirade, but the sight of Bryan brought her up short. He was crouched over a little bamboo bird cage—just one of dozens of bird cages in the room—digging bird seed out of the tiny dish with one large finger.

"Addie gets upset if Lester doesn't eat," Bryan explained, his expression serious.

Rachel's heart turned over in her breast. Not many men of her acquaintance would have catered to an old lady the way this one did. But then, he was getting paid for it, she reminded herself, steeling her resolve.

She marched across the room and thrust the bedraggled flower in his face. "Would you care to explain the meaning of this?"

Bryan rose slowly to his full height, wincing absently at his stiff muscles. His gaze moved from the flower to Rachel and back again. He took a deep breath, pondering. His eyebrows rose and fell, and he pushed his glasses up on his nose.

"It's a rose," he said finally.

"I know it's a rose," Rachel said irritably. "Would you care to explain why I found it on my pillow this morning?"

She was staring up at him with fire in her violet eyes, as if finding a rose on her pillow were some horrible affront to her sensibilities. Bryan couldn't stop the soft, thick warmth that filled his chest. She was lovely. There was no denying that. She had to have just combed her honey-colored hair back and arranged it at the nape of her neck, but already wisps had pulled loose to curl around her face. She was no doubt trying her darnedest to look indignant, but her features were too soft and angelic for her to quite pull it off.

"Mr. Hennessy," she repeated, her tone clipped. It was the tone of an irate schoolteacher. "I'm waiting for an explanation."

Bryan sighed a bit, dragging his gaze off the lush, kissable curve of her lower lip. He gave her a bright smile. "Is this a riddle? I do like a good riddle."

"It's an infringement on my privacy, and I don't like it at all," Rachel said, thumping the bedraggled flower against his chest. "I know I was sleeping in what is technically your room, but that doesn't give you the right to just walk in—"

"I wasn't in your room."

"Then how did this get on my pillow?" she asked, shaking the flower for emphasis. Yellow petals floated to the floor.

Bryan's broad shoulders rose. Behind his spectacles his blue eyes sparkled. He smiled his most engaging smile. "Magic?"

Rachel frowned in disapproval. "I don't believe in magic, Mr. Hennessy."

"My name is Bryan," he corrected her soberly as he lifted the flower from her small fingers. "Everyone should believe in magic, Rachel," he said. He held her gaze with his as he performed a little sleight of hand, making the rose disappear and a playing card appear in its place.

His eyes went wide. The trick had worked! He had his magic back!

Trying to swallow some of his excitement, he handed the queen of hearts to Rachel.

She looked at it and went on frowning, unimpressed. "Card tricks?"

"It's the best I could do on short notice," he said cheerfully. "I'm not the kind of fellow who keeps silk scarves tucked up his sleeve, you know. You must know, or you wouldn't have thought I was the one in your room last night."

"It had to be you," Rachel insisted. "Who else could it have been?"

"Addie, I suppose." He rubbed his chin in thought, and his eyes brightened suddenly. "Or Wimsey. Did you see anything, hear anything? Did you notice any change in the air temperature?"

"I don't believe in ghosts, either," Rachel said. "No sensible person does. Which is another reason I've come to see you. I'm going to have to ask you to leave, Mr. Hennessy."

"Oh, dear." Bryan sighed. "I thought we'd settled this. My deal was with Addie."

"My mother isn't . . . up to . . . making decisions like that," Rachel said, avoiding the word *competency* and its legal ramifications. "Really, I think it's quite cruel of you to play on her illness this way. I should probably report you—"

"Whoa there, angel," Bryan said, a thread of steel in his soft voice and the glint of it in his eyes. His jaw hardened as he stared down at her, all traces of the innocuous magician gone. "Let's get something straight here right away. I'm not taking advantage of Addie. I'm not taking a red cent from her, and I heartily resent that you think I would."

"But you said you have a contract—"

"That's right. Addie has agreed to let me stay here and search for the ghost."

"There is no ghost," Rachel said in exasperation.

"Don't you understand? Addie isn't well. This ghost is just what she calls it—whimsy."

Bryan stared at her, solemn and sad. "Just because you don't believe in something doesn't mean it isn't true, Rachel. Trees fall in the woods all the time, and they make plenty of noise even though you're not there to hear it."

Rachel refused to listen. Her mind was made up. "My mother is a lonely old woman who has invented this whimsy to keep her company. There's no reason for you to stay, Mr. Hennessy."

"I'm going to start walking with a cane if you don't stop that mister business," Bryan grumbled, combing his hair back with his fingers. He took a deep, cleansing breath and started in again. "I am aware of Addie's illness. Has it occurred to you what it must be like to know your mind is slipping away a little bit at a time and realize there's nothing you can do about it? Have you considered what it must be like to have everyone in town think you're some kind of lunatic and not believe a word you say?

"You may not believe in ghosts, Rachel, that's your prerogative, but Addie believes in Wimsey, and I believe there's every chance that he's a genuine, bona fide entity. If I can prove that, I can give Addie a little bit of her dignity back. Don't you think that's worth having a nuisance like me around for a little while?"

Rachel couldn't find any words for a rebuttal. She felt ashamed of herself for the things she had accused Bryan of. Worse, she felt a strange flutter of panic in her throat. If he had been a con man, she could have gotten rid of him. If he had been a crook, she could have sent him on his way and held on to her righteous anger. But he wasn't a con man or a crook. He was a temptation. Her heart rate shifted gears at the realization.

She had wanted him gone not only to protect her mother, but to protect herself. There was something about Bryan Hennessy that attracted her beyond reason, and she couldn't allow that. She was there because of Addie. Addie would need her undivided attention. She couldn't waste her energy on an attraction to a man who made up silly songs and pulled playing cards out of thin air.

"What do you say, Rachel?" Bryan queried softly. He suddenly felt compelled—almost *propelled*—to step closer to her. It was too early in the day to question the wisdom of getting too near, so he gave in to the urge. He inched a little closer so she had to tilt her head back to look up at him. It would have been so simple to raise his hands and frame her face. The desire to do that and to lean down and kiss her swam through him.

His held breath burned in his lungs as he waited for her answer. Would she let him stay? Why did it matter so much? This trembling hope inside him had to do with something other than Wimsey, but he refused to think of what it could be. He told himself he needed this job right now because he needed something to focus on. It wasn't that he was interested in getting involved with Rachel. Despite the argument his inner voice had put up the night before, he wasn't convinced he could help her.

But as he looked down at her, at the uncertainty and the questions that filled her eyes, the need to have her say yes grew inside him to mountainous proportions. And the attraction both of them would rather have denied strengthened and tightened its hold.

"What do you say, Rachel?" he asked, his voice a whisper. "Will you give me a chance?"

Rachel swallowed hard. Her heart was pounding, her knees were wobbling. There was something more in his question than permission to work in the house. She read it instinctively as she stared up into his earnest blue gaze. She felt it in her heart, and fear cut through the haze of this strange desire. How could she cope with a man who believed in magic?

In some distant part of the house a door banged and voices sounded.

She couldn't, Rachel whispered to herself. The last thing she needed was a man who believes in magic.

Bryan flinched slightly. He had heard the words spoken only in her soul, and they went straight to his heart.

Before he had a chance to wonder about it, the voices that had sounded faraway were suddenly sounding again—just outside the parlor. Then the doorway was filled with the substantial form of Deputy Skreawupp. The deputy hooked his thumbs behind the buckle of his belt, his arms framing his pot belly. He scowled, his frown reaching down his face nearly to his double chins. He bore a striking resemblance to Jonathan Winters but hadn't nearly the same sense of humor.

Bryan raised his eyebrows and stepped back from Rachel, breaking the tension that had enveloped them both. Suddenly a hand reached around from behind the deputy and a finger thrust forth.

"There she is!" Addie's voice was muffled by the deputy's bulk. "She's the one."

The deputy lumbered forward, his dark gaze pinned on Rachel, whose expression was the very picture of stunned surprise. "All right, angel face, the jig's up," he said, his voice a flat, comical monotone that could have belonged to a detective in a movie from the forties.

"I beg your pardon?" Rachel squeaked, her gaze darting from the deputy to her mother and back.

Addie gave her a cold, hard look. "She's the one, Officer. The intruder."

"Mother!" Rachel exclaimed, aghast. Embarrassment flamed in her cheeks.

"She looks like my daughter, but she isn't," Addie said. "She's an imposter. She broke in here last night and stole my dentures."

"That's low," the deputy said, shaking his head reproachfully. "I've heard it all before. Desperate times and desperate measures. Makes me sick."

"It's not true!" Rachel insisted emphatically. "I *am* her daughter." She turned toward Addie, her big eyes imploring. "Mother, how could you say that?"

"You're not my daughter. My daughter left me," Addie said flatly. She lifted her slim nose regally and gave a dismissing wave of her hand. "Take her away, Deputy. I'm going to go have my toast. Hennessy, to the kitchen."

With that she turned on the heel of her green rubber garden boot and marched from the room, obviously expecting Bryan to follow her. Bryan cleared his throat and smiled pleasantly at the deputy. "I believe there's been a small misunderstanding here."

The deputy pulled out a pocket notebook and a pencil, prepared to take Bryan's statement. "You were here last night?"

"Yes. I slept on the billiard table. I wouldn't recommend it."

Skreawupp halted his scribbling and pointed at Bryan with his eraser. "Don't get cute with me, bub. I'll clip you like a wet poodle."

Bryan looked shocked. "Please, sir, there's a lady present!"

"Look," the deputy growled, his droopy shoulders slumping further. He gave up on Bryan, directing his questions to Rachel. "I am damned sick of being called out here on all kinds of wild goose chases. Are you Batty Addie's daughter, or what?"

"I am Rachel Lindquist," Rachel said tightly, her chin rising defiantly, her eyes burning with fury at the deputy's attitude. "Would you care to see proof of identification?"

"Skip it." He tucked his notebook back into his breast pocket. "I should have known this would be another waste of my valuable time. Last month she had me out here because she thought a commie sub had washed up on her beach. Before that she was being abducted by a religious cult. I don't need it."

"Well," Bryan said in a tone that belied the anger in his own eyes, "we'll all kick in a little extra on our taxes next time around to compensate." He followed the deputy into the hall and pointed the way to the front door. "I'd show you out, but I have to go make the toast."

"Hippie," Skreawupp muttered, swaggering away. He turned and pointed a finger at Bryan. "I've got my eye on you, Jack."

Rachel pushed past them both and strode stiffly down the hall, trying to find her way through the maze of rooms to the kitchen. She found rooms packed full of dusty old furniture, one room that was crammed full of old wooden church pews stacked one on top of another like cordword. Finally she pushed open the correct door.

The kitchen had once been sunny yellow, but the color of the walls had dulled over the years to a dingy ivory shade. It was a huge room with black and white tiles on the floor and an array of oversize appliances, one of which was an outdated wood-burning cookstove that had been left ostensibly for decorative purposes. Near the window was an oak table that had been haphazardly set with mismatched china. Addie sat at her place, her back straight, her hands folded in the lap of her flowered cotton housedress. She refused to look when Rachel entered the room.

"Mother, we have to talk," Rachel said through clenched teeth.

"I don't want to talk to you. Where is Hennessy? I want my toast."

Rachel pulled out the chair beside Addie's and sat down. She composed herself as best she could. She had read about the kind of behavior her mother was exhibiting, but comprehending a textbook and living the reality were proving to be two very different things. Logically, she knew Addie's behavior stemmed from her illness. Realistically, she knew her mother was probably incapable of manipulation because manipulation required a great deal of careful thought and planning, and those were abilities Addie was losing.

Emotionally, she couldn't help but feel hurt and humiliated and angry. She resented the way she'd been treated since coming to her mother's house. She felt manipulated, because Addie had been a master at it in her day. It had been Addie's machinations that had ultimately driven them apart. That was a difficult thing to forget now, when Deputy Skreawupp's squad car was rolling down the driveway.

"Mother," Rachel said, trying to speak calmly so she wouldn't precipitate another catastrophic reaction like the one she had been greeted with the night before. "I'm Rachel. I'm your daughter."

Addie glanced at her, annoyance pulling her brows together above her cool blue eyes. "Of course I know who you are."

That was her standard reply when she wanted to cover up a lapse in memory, but this time it was the truth. She hadn't recognized Rachel earlier, when she'd seen her in the upstairs hall. Now she was ashamed of having called the police, but it was over and done with and there was nothing she could do about it. She closed her eyes and turned away.

"Mother, I know about your illness. I've come here to help."

"I've been a little forgetful recently, that's all. I don't need help."

"You don't need help or you don't need *my* help?" Rachel asked, her anger lapping over the edge of her control like a pot threatening to boil over. She reined it in with an effort, but the toll it took came through in her voice. "Can't we put the past behind us and deal with this together?"

The past. Addie looked at her daughter long and hard. There were gaps in her past that grew larger by the day, but she remembered word for word the fight that had taken place before Rachel's departure from Berkeley. "You abandoned me. You abandoned everything we'd worked so hard for."

"You forced me out!" Rachel responded without thinking, lashed out. All the hurt, the pain, the bitterness was there just under the surface. The only difference between herself and her mother was the amount of control she exercised over those feelings.

Rachel took a shallow, shuddering breath and pushed herself up out of the chair. The bread was sitting on the counter, and she methodically undid the twist tie and reached into the bag.

"We're going to see Dr. Moore today to talk."

Addie made a face. "He's a Nazi. I don't want anything to do with him."

Rachel's hands shook as she placed two slices of bread in the toaster. The urge to explode made her tremble from her emotional core outward. "We're going."

"You can't tell me what to do, missy," Addie began. Her movements very deliberate, she rose from her chair and pushed it back. A flush stained the whiteness of her cheeks. Her daughter was trying to wrest her independence away from her. Well, she wouldn't take it lying down! She wouldn't take it at all! Simply because she was getting older and a little forgetful didn't give Rachel the right to waltz in and take over. "Who do you think you are, coming back here after all these years and thinking you can just walk in? Terence put you up to this, didn't he? That no-account, whining little weasel."

"Terence is out of this, Mother," Rachel said softly, her throat tight with a building flood of emotion.

A triumphant gleam flared in Addie's eyes. "That's the first sensible thing you've done in years. I warned you about him. I told you—"

Suddenly, the kitchen door was flung wide open, and Bryan danced in, singing "I've Got a Crush on You." Seemingly oblivious to the tension in the room, he grabbed Addie and danced her around, hamming it up outrageously as he sang the song to her. Addie blushed like a bride and giggled. Almost instantly her anger was diffused.

"Hennessy, you big Irish rascal," she said, batting a hand at him as he left her by her chair and danced away. "You don't know the meaning of decorum."

Bryan halted in the center of the room, cleared his throat, and began to orate: "Decorum: conformity to the requirements of good taste or social convention; propriety in behavior, dress, et cetera; seemliness."

"Did you catch any of that, Rachel?" Addie wondered dryly.

Rachel slammed the butter knife down on the countertop. "Your toast is ready."

"Hennessy makes my toast. I won't eat yours. You're probably trying to poison me."

"The thought has crossed my mind," Rachel muttered to herself, then was assailed with guilt, even though no one else in the room had heard her and she hadn't meant it.

"Let me handle this," Bryan whispered, bending down near her ear as he lifted the plate of toast from the counter.

"No," Rachel said forcefully. She grabbed the plate back out of his hand, nearly sending the bread to the floor.

The fact that Bryan, an outsider, could deal better with Addie was like salt on an open wound. And it was yet another reason she couldn't allow him to stay. She and Addie had to square things between them now, or at least establish their new roles. She was the one who was going to be taking care of her mother, not Bryan Hennessy. Lord knew, men like Bryan Hennessy opted out the minute the going got rough.

He was Terence in spades—a dreamer, a coaster,

a man who ignored reality with an idiotic grin on his face. Abruptly, the comparisons overwhelmed her and coupled with her need to take care of Addie.

"No. I don't need you. *We* don't need you," she said, glaring up at him. "Take your stupid card tricks and your stupid roses and get out of here!"

Bryan backed away as if she'd slapped him. He really didn't need this, he told himself, echoing Deputy Skreawupp's line. He didn't need the kind of trouble Rachel Lindquist was facing, and he sure as hell didn't need to get kicked for his efforts to help.

Without a word he turned to leave the room, but the door from the kitchen to the hall wouldn't budge. He put a shoulder up against it and heaved his weight into it, but it held fast. Drawing a slow breath into his lungs, he stood back and planted his hands at the waistband of his jeans. Behind him, he could hear life going on at the Lindquist family breakfast table. Rachel was trying to give Addie her toast, and Addie was refusing to touch it, her voice rising ominously with every word.

"I have to be the world's biggest glutton for punishment," Bryan mumbled to himself, shaking his head. He turned around, his sunniest smile firmly in place. "Did you say you're going to town? I'll ride along; I need to go to the library."

"I didn't invite you, Mr. Hennessy," Rachel said. A perverse thrill raced through her at the thought that this man did not take no for an answer. He was like a human bulldozer. And that innocently pleasant face he presented the world was nothing more than a very distracting mask.

"No, you didn't," he said affably, taking his seat at the table. "What time do we leave?"

"Two," she answered automatically, then halted her thinking process. Her eyes narrowed and her lush mouth thinned. She wasn't going to be bullied. She wasn't going to let Bryan Hennessy worm his way into her life. "Be sure to pack your toothbrush," she said, rising and going to the stove to start a pot of coffee. "We'll drop you off at the nearest hotel."

"The truth is, it may already be too late, honey." The memory of Dr. Moore's gentle, fatherly voice played through Rachel's mind as she sat behind the wheel of her decrepit Chevette.

"For all the research being done, we know very little about the disease. It progresses differently in different people, depending upon what areas of the brain are attacked. Some people lose the ability to read, while others can read but not comprehend what they've read. Some can understand a conversation in person but not over the phone. Some can remember everything that happened in their lives ten years ago, but they can't remember what happened ten minutes ago."

"She seems to remember everything that happened five years ago," Rachel said ruefully.

Dr. Moore, who had the wisdom of decades in medicine and in dealing with people, had reached out to take her hand, knowing that small comfort might soften the blow. "But she may not be able to comprehend what happens today or tomorrow. I'm not saying it can't happen, sweetheart. At this point in Addie's illness, it's anyone's guess. I just want you to realize that you can't pin your hopes on a reconciliation, because it might never come about."

Rachel rested her forehead against the steering wheel and closed her eyes against a wave of despair. A reconciliation with Addie was the one thing she had wanted, needed, to pin her hopes on. What else was there? Certainly not a cure for Alzheimer's; no one knew yet what caused the disease, let alone what would cure it.

"Are we going to sit here all day, or is there some other vile place you intend to force me to go to?" Addie asked imperiously.

"We need to stop at the drugstore," Rachel said.

"I don't want to go to the drugstore." The drugstore was a confusing place, aisle upon aisle of items and millions of brands from which to choose. Addie never went there if she could help it. She gave Rachel a shrewd look. "I suppose you're going to force me to go in there nevertheless."

"You don't have to go in. You can wait in the car if you like."

Too distracted to notice her mother's sigh of relief, Rachel started the engine and pulled out of the clinic parking lot and into the flow of tourist traffic. The fog that had blanketed the coastal village in the early morning had long since burned off. The day was bright with a blue sky. Anastasia's quaint streets were clogged with people browsing and window-shopping and admiring the carefully restored Victorian architecture of the town. Through the open windows of the car came the sounds of the traffic, the calling of gulls, and the distant wash of the ocean against the shore.

It all seemed comforting, Rachel thought. So normal and sane. She could easily grow to love Anastasia. Unfortunately, she would never have the chance. She had a job waiting for her in San Francisco when the fall school term began. A call to a former vocal instructor who was now an administrator at the Phylliss Academy of Voice had landed her a position. As soon as she had sorted out Addie's affairs, and they had sold Drake House, they would be moving south to the city. Anastasia would be a place to visit on weekends if they were lucky.

By some small miracle of fate there was a parking spot opening up in front of Berg's Drugstore just as Rachel piloted her car across the intersection at Fourth and Kilmer. She pulled into it and cut the engine.

"I'll only be a minute," she said as she grabbed up her purse and slipped out of the car.

Addie smiled serenely, her eye on the keys dangling from the Chevette's ignition.

"So, Addie has a daughter," Alaina Montgomery-Harrison mused, seizing instantly upon the one significant thing Bryan had said since she'd walked outside her office with him to enjoy the sun. She leaned back against the sun-warmed side of the building that housed her law practice, her smart red Mark Eisen suit a startling contrast

against the white stucco. Her cool blue eyes studied her friend intently. "What does she look like?"

Bryan shrugged uncomfortably. He stuck his
nose into one of the library books he'd borrowed
on the history of the area and mumbled, "Like a
woman."

Alaina gave him a look. "Oh, that narrows it
right down. So she falls somewhere between Chris-
tie Brinkley and Roseanne Barr?"

"Hmmm . . ." Glancing up with bright eyes and
a brighter smile, Bryan attempted to derail her
from her line of questioning. "How's my beautiful
goddaughter?"

"She's perfect, of course," Alaina said, idly
checking her neatly manicured nails. "What a
lame attempt to throw me off the scent, Bryan,
really. Why so secretive?"

"I'm not being secretive," he protested. "There's
simply not that much to tell. She's Addie's daughter. She's young, she's pretty, they don't get
along." *She cried on my shoulder, and I haven't
wanted to kiss a woman so badly in ages*, he
added silently, turning the pages of his book without seeing them.

"That's putting it in a nutshell. You should get a
job with *Reader's Digest*. Think of the money they
could save on paper if they had you to condense
books for them," Alaina said. She reached out and
gently closed the book Bryan was using as a prop
to evade her questions. Her gaze searched his face
with undisguised concern. "Where do you fit in at
Drake House?"

Bryan held his expression carefully blank. "I'm there to find a ghost."

"And?"

"Sometimes I really despise your keen insight," he complained. Alaina was characteristically unmoved by the remark. He heaved a sigh. "All right. It's a tough situation. If I can in some small way help Rachel and Addie—"

At that instant a car horn blared and a rusted orange Chevette squealed around the corner. People on the sidewalk leapt back, shrieking as a wheel jumped over the curb and a trash can went sailing. Bryan's eyes rounded in horror as he caught sight of the driver.

"Addie!" he shouted, dropping his books and taking off after the car.

The Chevette veered across the street, eliciting a chorus of horn-honking from cars in the oncoming lane, and jumped the curb into Kilmer Park. People and pigeons scattered. Addie stuck her head out the window of the car, waving and shouting for people to get out of her way.

Bryan caught up with her as she cranked the steering wheel and began driving in circles around the statue that immortalized the late William Kilmer, an obscure botanist who had grown up in Anastasia and gone on to relative anonymity. He jogged alongside the car until he managed to get the passenger door open, then he executed a neat gymnastic movement and swung himself into the moving vehicle. All he had to do then was reach over and switch the ignition off. The Chevette rolled to a halt.

Bryan heaved a huge sigh of relief. The park was full of tourists now gathering around to satisfy their morbid curiosity. Addie might have ended the earthly outing for any one of them and sent them on to a more permanent sort of trip.

"There's something wrong with the brakes," Addie grumbled, scowling, completely unwilling to admit she had forgotten how to work them.

Rachel ran up beside the car, her face as pale as milk. Bryan climbed out, rounded the hood, and took her by the arm. He dangled the keys from his forefinger, then closed his fist gently over them as he guided Rachel a short distance away.

"Addie isn't allowed to drive," he said softly, managing a half smile at the look on her face.

Rachel was too petrified to speak. She merely stared up at him, horrified at what had happened and what might have happened.

"It's all right," Bryan said, easily reading her feelings. "No one was hurt."

Without thinking, he leaned down and pressed a soft kiss to her lips. Golden sparks of electricity burst through him, stunning him.

"I'll drive us home," he said breathlessly, not quite certain how he had managed to speak at all. His heart was pounding like a jackhammer.

Dazed, Rachel lifted a hand to her lips. He'd kissed her. He'd kissed her and immediately the icy terror that had filled her had melted away. She knew she was supposed to tell him he wasn't coming home with them, but she couldn't begin to form the words in her head. For one of the few times in her life she was rendered completely speechless. It was amazing.

"We'll go home. You can have a nice brandy and lie down for a while," Bryan went on as he led her back to the car. "Dinner is at seven." He opened the door to the backseat and helped her in, then leaned down into the open window. "By the way, we dress for dinner at Drake House."

"Dress?" Rachel questioned dumbly.

"Hmmm. Black tie or the closest you can come."

"You're serious?" she said, trying to read his expression. "You're not joking?"

Bryan smiled. "Quite and no. At any rate," he said, his eyes crinkling attractively at the corners, "I'm hardly ever more serious than when I'm joking."

He straightened then and took the ticket Deputy Skreawupp handed him without saying a word. His look warned the deputy to follow suit. Opening the driver's door, he slid into the Chevette beside Addie, saying, "Scoot over, beautiful, and let a man handle this machine."

Addie giggled and punched his arm. "You big Irish rascal, you."

He piloted the car slowly out of the park, leaning out the window, waving and smiling to the crowd as if he were driving in a parade. Addie joined in his enthusiasm and leaned out her window, throwing out old Life Savers she had found in her handbag.

And in the backseat, Rachel sat staring blankly into space, marveling over the power of a simple little kiss.

FIVE

Rachel checked her watch and frowned. Ten of seven. She hadn't meant to fall asleep. On returning to Drake House from Anastasia she had taken Bryan's advice and modified it slightly, trading his suggestion of a brandy for a hot bath. She had shut herself in the upstairs bathroom and soaked in the deep old claw-footed tub until the tension of the day had all washed out of her. It had taken a concerted effort on her part to push it from her mind, and the effort had left her feeling drained. When she returned to her room at last, wrapped in an old terry-cloth robe, she had curled up on the creaky old bed, intending to rest for just a few minutes.

Two hours later she had awakened abruptly from a deep sleep with the distinct feeling that she was being watched. She had sat up, clutching her robe to her chest, and stared all around the bedroom she had moved into that morning. It was located in the turret on the south side of the house. The walls curved; there were no dark corners to hide in. The room had been quiet and empty, but someone had been there. It wasn't just the lingering tension that had told her. Laid out across the foot of the bed had been a dress. A dress she had never seen before.

Rachel ran her hand down the front of it now in a gesture of uncertainty. It seemed strange to be wearing it when she didn't know where it had come from or whom it belonged to, yet she hadn't quite been able to resist the urge to put it on. If Bryan had been telling the truth about dressing for dinner, then she didn't own anything suitable to wear—nothing that came close to this dress anyway. Most of her skirts and dresses were comfortable cotton fabrics in styles that leaned toward a Gypsy or prairie look. She had never had the occasion or the money to buy an evening gown during her life on the road with Terence.

The whole idea of dressing for dinner seemed absurd. It was a custom from a bygone age and a class of people she had only read about or seen on television. No doubt it was one of the little eccentricities Addie had developed since her illness. In light of all that had happened since she had arrived, Rachel thought it best to go along with the odd dictate. If it would make her mother happy, if it might somehow help Addie to open up to her, then it would be worth the effort.

She stared at her reflection in the freshly polished mirror above the vanity. The dress was burgundy silk decorated with black jet beads. The thin straps flowed into a V neckline in both the front and the back. The fully pleated skirt fell from a dropped waist to swirl about her calves. It was pure 1920s, an antique in its own right. It was the most beautiful thing she'd worn in ages. And Bryan Hennessy had brought it to her.

Her chest tightened at the thought. He must have slipped in and put it across the foot of the bed while she'd been sleeping. What if she had opened her eyes and turned to look up at him. Her robe might have fallen open, and his gaze would have lowered deliberately—

Rachel gasped in embarrassment. The woman who looked back at her from the mirror wore an expression of uncertainty. Her wide eyes were pansy-purple in the dim light of the room. Soft color rose on her cheekbones. There was a decidedly vulnerable look about her mouth. She didn't have time to put up her hair again, so she left it to fall down her back in luxurious golden waves. She wondered if Bryan would like it down.

"Oh, Lord," she said with a groan, squeezing her eyes shut and rubbing at her temples, "what am I going to do about Bryan?"

Somewhere a gong sounded.

"A dinner gong?" she questioned on a laugh. "Well, I suppose I shouldn't be surprised. There isn't anything ordinary about this house or anyone in it."

Slipping into a pair of black high-heeled shoes,

she gave her reflection one last glance in the mirror and left the room.

She caught sight of Bryan as she began to descend the grand staircase, and her heart vaulted into her throat. Her hand gripping the mahogany banister, she halted on the stairs and stared down at the scene below, where Bryan stood sipping a drink and chatting with a woman Rachel had never seen before.

She had thought him attractive in a rumpled, all-American way. Big and cute with his earnest blue eyes and his tawny hair falling every which way and notes sticking up out of all his pockets. But in a tuxedo he was devastating. Handsome with a capital H. The black jacket hugged his shoulders in a way that nothing off the rack could have. The wings of his shirt collar framed his strong, freshly shaved jaw. His hair looked as if he had actually taken a comb to it. The overall effect was one of intelligence, authority, and money.

He looked completely at ease in formal attire, and that threw Rachel off balance. Would she ever get a handle on who Bryan Hennessy really was? Was he charlatan or scientist? Buffoon or bon vivant? The only thing she knew for certain was that he believed in ghosts and magic, and she would be far better off steering clear of him.

As she resumed her descent of the stairs, she forced her gaze to the woman with the wild mane of dark auburn hair. The light from the chandelier brought out the red in her tresses, surrounding her pixie face with extraordinarily rich color. She had enormous black eyes and an infectious, mischievous smile that seemed vaguely familiar. She was quite lovely despite what she was wearing—a man's white dress shirt and black necktie over a wildly flowered dirndl skirt and paddock boots.

She glanced up suddenly and grinned with pure delight. "You must be Rachel," she said, her voice honey-rich with the sounds of the South.

Bryan jerked his head up and stared openly at the woman on the stairs. He felt awed, paralyzed, thrilled—as if he were witnessing some kind of vision. The studs on his shirtfront strained as he tried to take in a deep breath.

Rachel stood on the landing, staring uncertainly back at him, her eyes wide, her hair spread out behind her in a fall of softest gold. The old-fashioned dress she wore bared her angular shoulders and hugged her small breasts just enough to hint at their fullness. With its straight lines and long skirt it was hardly a revealing garment, yet it emphasized her femininity and her own innate sense of class.

Jayne gave him a quick, practiced elbow to the ribs, her smile never wavering. "Bryan Hennessy, I know your mama taught you better manners than this."

"What?" he asked, looking confused, then he snapped out of it. "Oh, yes. Jayne, this is Addie's daughter, Rachel Lindquist. Rachel, this is Jayne Jordan Reilly, a friend of mine from college, and a friend of Addie's as well."

"I'm so pleased to meet you," Jayne said, extending her hand. "I've heard so much about you."

"But I arrived only last night," said Rachel, a little taken aback by the stranger's warm welcome.

Jayne shrugged, winding an arm through Rachel's and leading her away from the stairs. "It's a small town. News travels around here at the speed of light. What a lovely dress. Wherever did you find it?"

"Laid out on my bed," Rachel said pointedly, her gaze meeting Bryan's head on. He had the gall to look innocent. "Things have a funny way of turning up in my room."

"Oh, honey, I'm not at all surprised." Jayne waved a dainty hand, her purple fingernails flashing in the light from the chandelier. She leaned close to Rachel, her expression intensely serious, as if she were about to confide an enormous secret. "This house is haunted, you know."

"So I'm told," Rachel said, managing a polite smile. Her gaze darted to Bryan, flashing her disapproval his way.

"You haven't been lucky enough to see Wimsey, have you?"

"No, I haven't had the pleasure."

Jayne frowned her disappointment. "Too bad. Addie's the only one who's actually seen him. My theory is their consciousness coexist on a single plane of understanding, while ours is on a dual plane, which is why we never see him. What do you think?"

Rachel stared at her for a moment, not quite sure how to respond. Jayne, while undeniably sweet, was apparently just as batty as everyone else in Drake House.

"Rachel doesn't believe in ghosts," Bryan said, handing her a glass of white wine. His eyes sparkled like sapphires. "Rachel is practical." He said the word as if it were the name of a strict religious order.

Jayne's dark eyes widened. She looked from Bryan to Rachel and back. "Oh, my."

"I'm sorry I didn't come down earlier," Rachel said, changing the subject. "I'm afraid I dozed off. I meant to help Mother with the meal."

"Oh, Addie doesn't cook," said Bryan.

Her brows pulled together as she looked at him. "What do you mean? Mother used to work nights at a very nice restaurant when we lived in Berkeley. She's a wonderful cook."

"Not since the infamous incident of the fish-head soup and chocolate-laxative cake," Bryan said.

Jayne rolled her eyes in dismay at the memory. "Reverend MacIlroy was indisposed for a week."

Bryan sighed. "Thankfully, the soup filled me up, and I passed on the cake."

"You ate fish-head soup?" Rachel asked, both incredulous and nauseated at the thought.

"I prefer to think of it as a variation on bouillabaisse. It was hardly the strangest thing ever to cross my palate. A particular dinner in China comes to mind. They do things there with snakes—"

"That shouldn't be discussed before dinner," Jayne said firmly, giving him a look of disgust. She took Rachel by the arm again and steered her toward the dining room, interrogating and commenting all the way, her conversation flowing from one topic to the next without pause. "I think it's just wonderful that you've come back to take care of Addie. We all try to check in on her from time to time, but it's not the same. I hear you're a singer. Will you look for work here in Anastasia?"

"I have a job lined up at the Phylliss Academy of Voice in San Francisco," Rachel said, seeing no reason to hide the fact from them. At any rate, she needed to practice saying it. She was going to have to tell Addie soon, so they could make plans to sell Drake House and move.

"San Francisco?" Jayne said it as if it were a place totally foreign to her.

Bryan merely stood silent, his expression carefully blank.

"Yes. As soon as I get my mother's affairs in order, we'll be selling the house and moving to the city."

"Does Addie know about this?" Bryan asked, taking great care to sound more neutral than he felt.

Rachel nibbled at her lower lip. She couldn't quite meet his eyes. "Not yet."

At that moment Addie made her grand entrance into the dining room. Her style of dress was even more incongruous than Jayne's. Over her flowered housedress she wore a filmy pink robe trimmed in pink ostrich feathers. On her feet, her ever-present green rubber boots. She took in the group with one regal, sweeping glance.

"Hennessy, my G and T, please."

Rachel grabbed at Bryan's coat sleeve. He turned

toward her and her concern momentarily fled. He was so close. His mouth was no more than inches from hers as he leaned down toward her. She moistened her lips nervously as the memory of his kiss came flooding back. Beneath her fingertips and the fine wool of his jacket his arm was a rock of muscle.

"Don't worry," he whispered, easily reading her mind. "There's almost no G in Addie's G and T. I just splash some on the ice so I'm not really fibbing when I give it to her."

He turned toward the sideboard to mix the drink. Rachel sighed, helpless to stop the sweet warmth flooding her chest. It would be so very easy to let herself fall for him. He was handsome and charming in a rather bizarre sort of way. He was so kind and solicitous toward Addie. She watched him hand her mother the weak drink. He winked at Addie and pretended to pull a quarter out of her ear.

"You're an idiot, Hennessy. I don't know why I keep you on," Addie blustered, shooing him away, but there was a rare twinkle in her eye and a bloom in her cheeks that hadn't been there when they'd returned home after the incident in the park.

How Rachel envied him that easy rapport with her mother. He didn't have the burden of a past full of pain and mistakes weighing down his every word. He didn't have the burden of a future full of heartache and sacrifice holding him back. He could walk away anytime he liked, and no one could ever fault him. He didn't have to deal with issues like selling Drake House. All Bryan had to worry about was pulling quarters out of people's ears.

They sat down to a meal of thick, aromatic beef stew and hot biscuits. It wasn't exactly a five-course dinner to go along with the china and silver on the polished walnut table, but it was hearty, healthy fare and required only one utensil to eat it—an important consideration for Addie, who was slowly losing her ability to deal with a full complement of flatware.

"Hennessy is quite an adequate cook," Addie said, dipping her biscuit into the gravy on her plate and nibbling at it delicately. "He's an impudent rascal, insisting on eating at the table with the rest of us, but I tolerate him."

Rachel frowned. Bryan wasn't the butler, and she didn't see any reason for him to be treated like one. But when she opened her mouth to set her mother straight, Bryan caught her eye and shook his head ever so slightly.

"That's very big of you, Addie," he said. "Not everyone is as generous and forgiving as you are."

Addie gave him a shrewd look. "Remember that, young man." She tossed back the last of her gin and tonic and thrust the glass at him for a refill. Lifting her nose slightly, she glanced askance at Rachel. "Some people don't appreciate generosity and sacrifice, and look what happens to them."

Rachel ground her retort between her teeth and choked it down with a piece of potato.

"Did I mention how stunning you look tonight, Addie?" Bryan said affably, handing her glass back to her filled with tonic water and a slice of lime. "I can't think of another woman who could wear that outfit quite the way you do . . . unless it might be Jayne," he added, grinning across the table at his friend, who stuck her tongue out at him.

Addie beamed and fluffed her ostrich feathers.

"And didn't Rachel find a beautiful dress?" Bryan said, not realizing the way his voice dropped and softened. Nor did he realize the longing that shone in his eyes.

Rachel sat directly across from him, between Addie, at the head of the table, and Jayne. A tiny smile of gratitude canted the corners of her lips.

Addie gave her daughter a hard, assessing look. "Yes, it's very suitable. For once you don't look like some cheap, wandering Gypsy."

The smile faded away as Rachel closed her eyes and counted to ten.

"Rachel," Jayne said brightly as she picked around the meat in her stew. "Tell us all about your career as a singer. My, how exciting that must be. I couldn't carry a tune in a bucket."

"That's not much to tell," Rachel said, bracing her shoulders. She kept her head down, her eyes trained on her plate as she tried to extricate herself from the subject as quickly as she could without being rude. "We played a lot of clubs, managed to get on a couple of PBS folk music shows."

"That's wonderful." Jayne smiled. "I just love folk music. It's very spiritual. So visual and honest in its images. Don't you agree, Addie?"

Addie's lips pinched into a white line. "Drivel. Opera is the only pure form of vocal music."

Jayne never missed a beat, turning back to Rachel. "You said 'we.' I take it you have a partner?"

"Had," Rachel said shortly. Her fingers tightened on her fork in anticipation of the comment her mother would surely make.

"Feckless little ferret."

"Mother, please . . ."

"Addie, I love your hair in that style. What do you call it?" Bryan asked.

Addie scowled at him. "A braid. Honestly, Hennessy, there are times I wonder if you aren't mentally deficient."

"Well, the color is marvelous," he went on, grinning as he speared vegetables with his fork.

Addie's attention shifted between Rachel and Bryan, between unpleasantness and inanity. Bryan's wink won her over, and she turned toward him with a pleased look. "You think so?" she asked, stroking the frazzled braid that lay over her shoulder. "I've been thinking of dying it. I saw a color on television called Sable Seductress."

"Oh, no. Blondes have more fun. Take it from me," Bryan said, winking at her again.

Addie blushed and turned toward Jayne. "He's such a flirt."

"Always has been, Addie," Jayne said. "His whole family is that way. Why, it would make you swoon to see all those men together. They look like something out of *Gentleman's Quarterly*."

"Where is that Australian tonight?" Addie demanded, her mind already drifting from the topic of Bryan.

"Reilly's in Vancouver shooting a movie," Jayne

said, automatically glowing at the thought of her husband.

Bryan managed to steer the conversation in Jayne's direction for the remainder of the meal. He coaxed her into speaking at length about her husband's acting career and her own budding career as a director. As curious as he was to learn more about Rachel and her past, he wasn't eager to have Jayne prize the information out of her there at the dinner table, where Addie could carve it all up for ridicule.

He'd been willing to do the carving himself less than twenty-four hours earlier, he reminded himself. But that had been before he'd had the chance to observe Rachel. That had been when his only knowledge of her had come from Addie's cutting remarks and the obvious pain behind them. Now he had seen Rachel. He'd seen—and felt—the turbulent tangle of emotions she was struggling with. He'd watched her look for the slightest sign of forgiveness or approval from her mother, and he'd seen the hurt flash in her lavender eyes when her hopes had met with cold disappointment.

He had accepted his own decision to help Addie and Rachel as best he could. And with that acceptance had come a subtle shifting in his feelings toward Rachel. The beginnings of protectiveness were coming to life inside him. Every time Addie inflicted another small cut with the razor edge of her tongue, the faint urge to take Rachel in his arms washed through him. He ignored the feeling on a conscious level, on a level where he was still not ready to involve himself completely, but it was there just the same.

Finally, Jayne scraped her chair back from the table and gave everyone an apologetic look. "I hate to say it, but I've got an important meeting tonight. I really have to be running along. Thanks so much for inviting me, Addie."

"You invited yourself," Bryan said, a grin teasing the corners of his mouth as he rose from his chair.

Jayne made a face at him. "Don't get snippy. I brought the biscuits, didn't I?"

"So you did," he conceded graciously. "And they were delicious."

Jayne bent, kissed the parchmentlike skin of Addie's pale cheek and bid all good night.

"Where's that Australian?" Addie asked.

"He's working," Jayne replied patiently. She leaned down and impulsively gave Rachel a hug around her shoulders. "It's been such fun, Rachel. You'll have to come over to the farm one day soon for a visit."

Rachel managed a genuine smile for her new friend. It was impossible not to like Jayne immediately. "I will. It was nice meeting you, Jayne."

"Same here," Jayne said sincerely. "By the way, what's your sign?"

"Um . . . Aquarius, I think," Rachel mumbled uncertainly, knocked off balance again by Jayne's sudden change of subject.

Jayne's dark eyes took on a considering gleam as she looked from Rachel to Bryan, a secretive smile on her lips. "Bryan, honey, walk me out, will you?"

Leaving the Lindquists in the dining room, Bryan took Jayne's arm and strolled down the hall with her. Neither spoke until they were on the wide porch.

"She's very pretty."

Bryan put on his blank, amicable smile and stuck his hands into his trouser pockets. "Who?"

Jayne frowned prettily. "Don't play that role with me, Bryan Hennessy. I know you too well to be fooled by it. Really," she said in a huffy tone, toying with the dainty gold bracelet that circled her left wrist. "I ought to be offended."

"But you're too busy recapping the dinner conversation and condensing it for analysis to bother."

"I'm sure I don't know what you mean," she said, pouting.

Bryan grinned openly at that. He reached up and tugged playfully at the end of her necktie. "Tell me, does this miraculous turn of events warrant a conference call or an all-hands-on-deck type meeting?"

Jayne's eyes twinkled. "Faith has baked a cake for the occasion."

"And what occasion is that?"

"Alaina thinks you're falling in love."

Bryan wouldn't have been more stunned if she'd suddenly smacked him between the eyes with a hammer. He literally staggered back a step. "That's absurd! I only just met her last night—"

"Ample time for you."

"—and she's done nothing but try to throw me out of the house ever since. That's hardly romantic," he argued, doing his best to tamp down the memory of holding her.

Jayne just shrugged. "Monica Tyler hit you in the face with a peace pie, and you fell in love with her."

"You're taking that pie thing completely out of context," Bryan said, shaking a finger at her. "That was an entirely different situation. I'm not in love with Rachel. You may report that to the rest of the joint chiefs of staff. I'm not in love. I'm not going to fall in love."

"Don't say that, honey," Jayne whispered, all teasing aside. She reached up a hand to touch his flushed cheek. "I know how it hurts to lose someone. I also know a very wise man once told me we can't orchestrate our lives, that we have to take our happiness where we can get it."

Bryan scowled as Jayne threw his own words up to him. "I'd forgotten how that photographic memory got you through art history." He heaved a sigh and stared out at the unkempt lawn and the fog that draped it all in a dreary cloak of gray. "Yes, we have to enjoy our lives while we can. I want to help Rachel and Addie do that. But I'm not ready for anything more." He gave a derisive half laugh. "Besides, I'm the last man Rachel wants to get involved with."

Jayne watched him closely. "How do you know that?"

"Just a feeling," he murmured absently, recalling very clearly the way he had heard Rachel's own inner voice state that fact earlier that morning.

Jayne's eyes widened slightly. She opened her

mouth to comment, but thought better of it. Instead, she offered him a soft smile and rose up on her toes. "Kiss me good-bye."

After Bryan had complied dutifully, Jayne adjusted the strap of her enormous canvas purse on her shoulder and trotted down the steps and across the yard to her little red antique MG, whistling softly to herself all the way. Her dear friend Bryan hadn't had a "feeling" about anyone else since Serena had died . . . until now. Until Rachel Lindquist.

"In love," Bryan muttered in disgust as he let himself back into the house. Of course he wasn't in love. He was attracted to Rachel, yes. Any man with eyes in his head would be attracted to Rachel. He was sympathetic toward her, naturally. Any caring human being would have been. But in love with her? No. It would be a long time before he felt ready to make that kind of emotional commitment again.

He made for the dining room, intending to excuse himself for the rest of the evening. He had a lot of reading to do about the history of the area and about Drake House in particular. If Wimsey had lived here, the fact would likely be documented someplace. Wimsey was, after all, his main reason for being there—work, getting back his professional instincts, getting back on track. Falling in love was not on the agenda.

The dining room was deserted. He hadn't been on the porch for more than ten minutes, yet the table had been cleared of china and linen. The room looked as undisturbed as if dinner had never been served. He was about to count himself lucky and escape to hit the books when a sound drew his attention toward the kitchen. It was soft, muffled, like a cough or a sniffle . . . or crying.

Quietly he stole across the room and cracked open the door to the kitchen. Rachel stood near the sink, which was full of suds and dirty dishes, her arms crossed in front of her and one fist pressed to her lips. Her bare shoulders lifted stiffly as she sucked in another shaky breath and valiantly fought the urge to cry.

Bryan's heart dropped to his stomach. It took every ounce of strength he had to keep from rushing across the room and scooping her into his arms. Instead, he backed away from the door and began humming loudly. He gritted his teeth and forced his frown upward at the corners, then burst through the door into the kitchen.

"What ho! This looks like a job for the butler," he said cheerfully.

Rachel swallowed down the last of her unshed tears and cleared her throat. She took the chance to speak but didn't turn to face him, afraid her eyes might betray the overwhelming emotions she had been struggling to keep at bay. "We haven't got a butler."

"I suppose I could take that as an insult, but, being such a sweet-tempered soul, I won't. At any rate, I suppose it's a matter of opinion."

"It's a matter of money," Rachel said firmly. "Which is something I haven't got much of."

"That's all right," Bryan said, taking a position

beside her and eyeing the dirty dinner dishes. "I work cheap. Find me a ghost or two, and I'll be as happy as a clam. Where's Addie?"

Rachel gave a short, humorless laugh. "She chose to retire to her room rather than spend another minute in my tainted company." The tears threatened again, but she lowered her head and fought them off with a tremendous burst of will.

"I see," Bryan said quietly. Then, coming to a decision, he waved a hand at the sink in a gesture of dismissal. "These dishes can wait. Come along."

Rachel started to protest as he took her by the hand and led her from the room, but the set of his jaw told her it would be pointless. For all his pleasant manner, the man had a stubborn streak a mile wide. She trailed along after him, marveling instead at how strong his hand was, and yet how gentle.

He towed her into a study, a masculine room with cherry paneling and a fireplace. After depositing her on a leather-covered camel-back love seat, he knelt on the hearth and put flame to the kindling already lying beneath the andirons. Warmth bloomed outward from the blaze as Bryan went around behind the desk, withdrew a cut glass bottle from a drawer, and poured amber liquid into two of the glasses that sat on a tarnished silver tray on one corner of the desk. He returned to her then and pressed a glass into her hand.

Rachel scooted back into one corner of the love seat as Bryan settled at the opposite end. She watched him, taken by surprise by his sudden air of authority. He was regarding her through his spectacles with serious eyes.

"Rachel," he said with utmost gravity. "I think it's only fair to warn you: I'm going to help you whether you like it or not."

"Help me?" she questioned, eyeing him suspiciously. "Help me what?"

"Deal with Addie. I get the distinct impression you're not good at accepting help."

"Probably because I haven't had much practice recently," she murmured candidly as she stared down into the liquid in her glass.

"Are you going to explain that rather cryptic remark, or I do get to make use of those interrogation methods I'm not supposed to talk about?"

She glanced up at him sharply, completely unable to tell whether he was joking or not. He wore a pleasant expression—the mask again, she decided.

"I know this much: you and Addie had a falling out five years ago, you left with Clarence somebody-or-other and didn't come back," Bryan began, priming the pump for her in hopes that she would jump in with the rest of the story.

Rachel placed her drink on the low butler's table and stood up. "I really don't think there's any need for you to know all the details of my life, Mr. Hennessy," she said, her sense of self-preservation rushing to the fore. "The gist of the story is this: One time in my entire life I defied my mother's authority, and she has never forgiven me."

"You were in love with this Clarence?"

"Terence."

Bryan noted with a certain satisfaction that she corrected him only on the name, not on the past tense he had used in regard to the relationship. "Where is he now?"

Rachel wandered away from the heat of the fire to the cool air near the French doors that led out onto a terrace shrouded in mist. "Chasing a rainbow," she murmured softly. Terence Bretton seemed a lifetime away from her now, so far removed from her situation that even his memory seemed unreal.

"And what about you, Rachel?" Bryan whispered.

She jumped a bit at the sound of his voice. He had come up behind her without her realizing it, but her sudden awareness of him was acute. She could feel the heat of his body, hear the subtle sigh of fabric on fabric as he shifted position. He didn't touch her, but she realized to her shame that she wanted him to. She hadn't known the man two days, and she wanted him to take her in his arms and hold her. She wanted it so badly, she ached.

Her lashes fluttered down, and she was immediately overtaken by the imagined sensation of being held. His arms were hard and strong, but his touch was gentle. . . . She felt herself leaning back, almost as if she were being pushed back, and she caught herself and fought the strange feeling off.

"What about you, Rachel?" he asked. "Where does your rainbow end?"

"You mean this isn't Oz?" she said ruefully, an acute sadness filling her, a sadness that came through in the soft, clear tone of her voice. "I was so sure it was. You're the Wizard and Mother . . ."

Addie was the wicked witch telling her she could never go home, telling her she was destined to be trapped in a surrealistic nightmare, that somewhere over the rainbow was a place dreamers longed for but could never find.

In the silence Bryan could feel her disillusionment as sharply as if it had been his own, and he hurt for her. Whatever she had given up to return to Addie had been better than the future she faced here.

Seemingly of its own volition, his hand rose toward the shimmering fall of Rachel's hair. It spilled down her back, a pale river of moonspun silk. He couldn't quite bring himself to resist the urge to touch it. Like a man trying to touch a dream, his fingers reached out hesitantly to brush against the curling ends. There was something incredibly sensual in the act, something strongly erotic, though he had barely grazed her. He inhaled sharply as desire streaked through him, setting all his nerve endings ablaze.

"And who are the munchkins?" he asked, trying to offset his reaction with a bit of levity. He barely recognized his own voice, it was so hoarse and low.

The absurdity of the question struck Rachel in the tattered remains of her sense of humor, and she managed a soft laugh. There was something wonderful about a man who could make her laugh on a night when her whole life seemed like a bad dream.

She turned away from the window and looked

up into his eyes, so warm and caring behind his glasses. He was much too near. She had told herself to keep him at least an arm's length away at all times, but there he was, no more than a deep breath away, and, while her wary heart told her to flee, Rachel found herself rooted to the spot.

"I never thanked you for this afternoon." She rolled her eyes and smiled wryly. "I never dreamed Mother would try to take off with my car. Thank God no one was hurt. You saved the day."

Bryan shrugged it off, uncomfortable with genuine praise. "Any other magical being would have done the same. See how invaluable I'll be to have around?"

It was the perfect opportunity to tell him he couldn't stay, Rachel thought. But she couldn't bring herself to say the words or even to consider the consequences of allowing him to remain in Drake House and in her life. She couldn't bring herself to say anything at all.

She stood staring up at him as if transfixed by a spell. The light from the fire cast her face in an amber halo, glistened off the vulnerable curve of her lower lip. It caught on the black jet beads adorning the old dress she wore and set each one with a miniature starburst of light.

"Have I told you how beautiful you are in this dress?" Bryan asked softly, something vital trembling deep inside him, something that had lain dormant, like a seed beneath the snows of winter. He felt it struggling to come to life with each shallow breath.

"I think you did," Rachel murmured.

"Oh." His mouth quirked up on the right in sheepish self-deprecation. Again he raised his hand to touch her hair, this time letting his fingers sift through the strands of silk. "Then, have I told you how much I want to kiss you?"

He didn't wait for a reply. He didn't wait to question himself or his vow of nonromantic involvement. He bent his head to hers and brushed his mouth gently across the satin of her lips. She tasted of sweetness and wine and need, a need that called out to her own lonely soul. His fingers threaded deeper into her hair, his hand sliding to cup the back of her head, to tilt her face to a better angle as the first kiss faded and the second began.

Just a kiss, Rachel thought. What harm could there be in a kiss? The solace and warmth and tenderness she found as she let herself melt into Bryan's arms—how could anything bad come of this? She felt so alone, and he was so sweet. She had forgotten what it was like to feel like a woman, and he was so masculine. She had been so filled with misery, and he was magic.

Her hands slid up to grip the solid strength of his arms, her fingers drinking in the feel of his tuxedo jacket as her mouth drank in the taste of him—warmth and whiskey and desire. It was a tender kiss, but not a tame one. There was a hunger in the way his lips rubbed against hers, a barely leashed demand for more. His tongue slid gently along the line of her mouth, asking for entrance, then taking it at the first hint of acquiescence.

Rachel sighed as she allowed him the intimacy.

Her heart raced as her breasts molded against the planes of his chest. She lost all sense of time and place, of who and where they were. She forgot all about duty and practicality. She gave herself over to a kind of sweet, gentle bliss that could have carried her into the night . . . until a crash and a scream shattered the still air.

SIX

Bryan bolted for the door with Rachel right behind him. He took the grand staircase two steps at a time and ran straight for Addie's room. Addie shrieked again as he burst into the room.

"Blast you, Hennessy!" she blustered, shaking a gnarled fist at him. "I ought to pop you one! You startled the life out of me!"

Bryan brushed the reprimand aside. "Addie, what happened? We heard a crash. Are you all right?"

"I'm fine, no thanks to you." She clutched a fistful of nightgown to her chest. Her knuckles were white. "There was a ghost outside my window, trying to get in! Go out there and catch it," she ordered, thrusting a finger at the portal. "You're supposed to be good at that, aren't you?"

For all her effort to appear calm, she was still

116

terribly rattled. She'd been lying in bed, trying to sleep as memories tumbled through her mind all out of order, like the colors in a kaleidoscope, when the apparition had appeared. The shock had thrown her into a mental tailspin. Now fragments of the past mingled with the present so that she couldn't distinguish one from the other. Her heart beat frantically as she tried to sort it all out.

"Mother!" Rachel gasped as she burst into the room belatedly, her shoes having hindered her progress on the stairs. "Are you all right?"

Rachel. Addie stared at her, confused. Love ached inside her. She lifted a wrinkled hand to brush her daughter's hair back from her flushed face. "Rachel," she said firmly but with far more gentleness than she'd used in years. "You ought to be in bed. You're going to ruin your voice, staying up all hours. What will Mrs. Ackerman say?"

Rachel blinked at her. She hadn't had a voice lesson with Mrs. Ackerman in ten years, but she couldn't bring herself to say that to Addie. She didn't want to do anything to ruin this single fragile moment of peace between them. Still, something had happened in this room, and they had to find out what it was.

"Mother, why did you scream?" she asked carefully.

Addie looked at her blankly.

"The ghost," Bryan prompted. "Was it Wimsey?"

Rachel scowled at him. Why did he persist in this ghost business? How would Addie be able to cling to any part of her sanity with Bryan encouraging her hallucinations?

"Of course it wasn't," Addie muttered crossly as she backed up and sat down on her rumpled bed. She couldn't think for the life of her who Wimsey was. It seemed best to lay the blame elsewhere. "It was a ghoul. It was the ugliest thing I've seen since Rowena Mortonson bought that horrid little Chinese dog. Perfectly hideous little thing. You couldn't tell if it was coming or going."

"Who's Rowena Mortonson?" Bryan asked Rachel.

"She was our next-door neighbor in Berkeley."

"Don't speak as if she's dead, Rachel. She's only gone to Los Angeles to visit that effeminate son of hers," Addie muttered, playing with the fraying end of her braid. "There's a boy who needs a can of starch in his shorts."

"What did it look like?" Bryan questioned.

"Oh, he favored Rowena, poor homely boy—pug nose, receding chin, limp brown hair. That pretty well describes the dog too."

"No, Addie. The ghost that was at your window. What did it look like?" Bryan asked, earning himself another glare from Rachel.

"Ooooooh . . ." Addie shuddered. "Pasty white with black eye sockets, and it made the most horrible strangled wretching sound."

"You say this ghost was trying to break in?" Bryan asked.

"The window *is* broken," Rachel said, slightly unnerved but unwilling to admit it. She sat down on the bed beside her mother and took advantage of Addie's confused state, wrapping an arm around her frail shoulders. She wanted the physical contact, to comfort and be comforted, whether Addie was coherent or not.

"The glass was broken from the inside," Bryan said, examining the gaping hole in the window. Shards littered the footwide ledge outside. Carefully, he raised the window and stepped out with one foot. He looked up at the gable peak and around the ledge itself, which was ornamented by a rusting wrought iron railing that had come loose on one end. There was no evidence of Addie's "ghoul," just a mournful howling as the wind swept around the various turrets and gables of the old house. In the distance the ocean roared.

"I threw a rock at the ugly thing," Addie said truculently. Her eyes narrowed with anger and suspicion. "Coming in to steal my bird cages."

Rachel closed her eyes and sighed. She was sure there hadn't been anything at the window except a figment of Addie's imagination. She had read that paranoia was one of the more common effects of Alzheimer's. The person wasn't able to remember where she'd put something and wasn't able to reason that no one else would want it, so she was sure people were stealing from her. Seeing and hearing things that weren't there were also common nighttime occurrences for someone with Addie's affliction. Knowing that, it seemed painfully obvious to Rachel what had happened.

"Well, he's gone now," Bryan said, climbing back inside. He had pulled a screw from the loose base of the railing and stood rubbing the clinging bits of rotted wood from the threads, a thoughtful expression on his face. "I'll take care of this window first thing in the morning. For tonight—"

"You can sleep in my room tonight, Mother," Rachel offered, not only eager to make her mother comfortable, but eager to score some brownie points with her as well.

· Addie looked around the room with a slightly frantic widening of her eyes. This was her room. She knew where everything was—most of the time. She usually remembered how to get from this room to any other part of the house. But if she spent the night in Rachel's bed, she would be lost, and everyone would see it.

"This is my room," she said, her chin lifting. "I shall sleep in it if I so choose."

"Mother," Rachel said wearily, "please don't be stubborn."

"Never mind." Bryan smiled suddenly, bending to take off his shoe. Using the heel for a hammer, he drove the tip of the rusty screw into the thick meeting rail of the window. Then he took a large, gloomy oil painting of a foundering ship off the wall and hung it so that it covered the entire lower portion of the window, blocking out the damp cool air that had flowed in through the broken glass.

"Good as new and more interesting to look at," he said as he dug a crumpled scrap of paper out of his trouser pocket and scribbled something down.

Relieved, Addie's shoulders relaxed as she let out a breath. She slipped out of Rachel's loose embrace and went forward to pat Bryan's cheek. "Good boy," she said as if he were a dutiful spaniel.

"I know how fond you are of your room, Addie,"

.he said. He took her hand in his, but his gaze went meaningfully to Rachel. "We don't want to uproot you if we don't have to."

"Hennessy, you're a treasure," Addie said.

Rachel sat on the bed, running a finger absently across her lower lip, reflecting on Bryan's actions—both there and in the study below. She could still feel his arms around her, could still taste him. He kissed wonderfully. Whether or not she should have allowed him to kiss her, she felt stronger and less alone now than she had before.

Her mother looked relaxed and was happily fussing with the painting at the window, straightening it to her satisfaction, the incident of the ghost apparently forgotten already. Rachel's thoughtful gaze slowly swept around the room with its garish red moiré silk wallpaper. A place for everything and everything in its place. Everything in the room was arranged just so. Not all the items seemed to belong there—like the weird assortment of smooth stones on the white linen dresser runner—but Addie apparently found comfort in having them there, just as she found comfort in being in the room itself.

"Good night, Addie," Bryan said. His gaze was on Rachel as he crossed to the bed and took her by the hand. He smiled gently. "Come along, Rachel. We don't want you to ruin your voice staying up late; what would Mrs. Ackerman say?"

She'd say you were a treasure, Hennessy, Rachel thought, a small ember of warmth glowing inside her, but she kept the words to herself as Bryan escorted her out of the room and down the hall.

"I'll have a look around outside, and I'll keep an eye on her room," Bryan said. "But I doubt anything more will happen tonight."

"I doubt anything happened at all," Rachel muttered. "I wish you wouldn't persist in encouraging these fantasies of hers."

"What makes you think this was a fantasy?"

Rachel gave him a look. "An ill woman looks out her second-story window and sees a ghost she knows is trying to break in to steal her bird cages. You don't have to be Sherlock Holmes to figure this out."

"Well," Bryan conceded grudgingly. "I'll admit the bird cage thing is a little farfetched."

They stopped outside the door of Rachel's room, and Bryan leaned a shoulder against the frame. Rachel looked up at him pleadingly. "Don't you see it, Bryan? She imagined there was something there, panicked, and threw a rock through the window."

Bryan frowned, the corners of his handsome mouth cutting into the lean planes of his cheeks. He looked disappointed. "You didn't see it, therefore it doesn't exist? There are lots of things in this world that can't quite be explained, Rachel. 'The best and most beautiful things in the world cannot be seen or touched, but are felt in the heart.' Helen Keller wrote that. She was blind and deaf. Just because she couldn't see or hear the rest of the world, do you think she gave up thinking it existed?" he asked quietly.

Rachel took a breath, preparing to argue, but it occurred to her suddenly that he had changed the subject, had subtly altered the slant of the conversation so that ghosts were only a small part of it. The man was much more clever than that innocent smile of his let on.

Holding her gaze with his, he reached up into the darkness of the hall, and when he brought his hand back down, he held a tiny white flower between his thumb and forefinger. He tickled her nose with it and gave her a sweet, lopsided smile.

"Explain that, Miss Lindquist."

Rachel laughed and batted his hand away. "You had that up your sleeve, you charlatan."

"You'll never know for sure, unless you get me to take my shirt off," he said, teasing. "And I'm not that kind of boy," he added, squaring his big shoulders and lifting his nose in the air.

"Don't let Mother hear you say that," Rachel said, eyes twinkling. "She'll think you need starch in your shorts."

"Hardly," Bryan muttered dryly, gritting his teeth on the surge of desire that came automatically from just looking at her. He couldn't seem to keep his gaze from wandering to the low V of her neckline. With every subtle movement she made, the silk of the old dress slid sensuously over her creamy flesh. Lord, how he envied that dress! Just the thought of touching her made his lungs hurt from lack of oxygen.

Rachel smiled up at him, unaware of his torment. It was wonderful the way he made her feel relaxed and playful in spite of all that had happened. He had a rare way with people, Bryan did. And he was a heck of a kisser.

As if he had read her mind, he leaned down and
brushed his lips across hers. The kiss caught fire
as quickly as dry kindling, burning hotter and
hotter as Bryan's mouth slanted across Rachel's.
He pinned her between the doorjamb and his own
body, seeking as much contact as he could get.
Rachel's arms wound around his neck, and she
arched into him, swept away by a flood of physical
desire that had leapt out of control before she had
even had a chance to consider damming it up.

Need built inside them and around them in
waves of heat. Rachel gasped at the feel of Bryan's
hand skimming down her side, tracing the outer
swell of her breast, following the inward curve of
her waist and the flare of her hip. His fingers
stroked downward to cup her bottom and lift her
against him. She gasped again at the feel of his
arousal, pressing hard and urgent against her
belly, and succeeded in drawing his tongue deeper
into her mouth.

Somewhere in the dimming regions of her mind
she knew she should have been putting an end to
this instead of encouraging it, but her sense of
logic seemed to have little control over the situation. Her body wanted Bryan Hennessy. She'd
never been one to throw herself at a man, but it
felt as if her body was ready to change that trait
right now.

It didn't make sense, she thought, struggling
against the wanton need rampaging inside her.
Why would she lose control this way with a man
like Bryan, a man who believed in ghosts and
magic, a man who, in the end, would only bring

her more disappointment. She couldn't fall for him. It just wasn't smart.

"Good night, angel," he whispered softly, pushing himself away from her. His chest rose and fell quickly with shallow breaths. There was a sadness in his steady gaze that made Rachel want to apologize, though she wasn't certain for what.

He slipped the tiny white flower into her hair behind her ear and backed into the hall, tucking his hands into his trouser pockets in a vain attempt to disguise his state of arousal. "Put the flower under your pillow and you'll have sweet dreams."

Her confusion plain on her face, Rachel waved to him as she disappeared into her room. And Bryan turned and wandered down the hall, thinking it was going to be another endless night.

In the long, sometimes illustrious life of Drake House, not once had the estate been owned by anyone named Wimsey. Nor had any of the owners had any children with the first name Wimsey. These facts Bryan had managed to discover easily enough, checking old records and browsing through the library books he had found. That left a number of possibilities. Wimsey might have been someone's nickname, or he might have been a servant of one of the families or a friend or an enemy.

Or he might have been, as Rachel had interpreted the name, a whimsy, a figment of Addie's deteriorating mind.

"No," Bryan muttered, paging through yet another book. "I don't believe that."

Addie was too matter-of-fact about Wimsey. She didn't bring his name up to garner attention or to divert attention from herself. Wimsey was real to her, and Bryan wanted badly to prove her right, if for no other reason than to show Rachel that ghosts existed as surely as dreams and rainbows and magic did.

Rachel. So responsible and practical and level-headed. Rachel, who had been avoiding him like the plague for two days—ever since they'd shared that searing kiss at the door of her room. She believed she couldn't have magic in her life when it was what she needed most. He meant to give it to her.

He'd made his decision. He couldn't stop thinking about her, couldn't stop wanting her. It seemed he had no real choice in the matter. He was going to pursue a relationship with Rachel Lindquist whether either of them thought it prudent or not.

A thread of guilt drifted through him, and he sat back in the desk chair with a sigh. Elbows on the arms of the comfortable old chair, he steepled his fingers and his gaze came to rest on the small etched-gold ring he wore on his left pinky. Even in the subdued morning light of the study the ring glittered on his finger, bright and merry and pretty, just like Serena had been.

She would have wanted him to get on with his life. She wouldn't have wanted him to shut himself off from people the way he had been doing. His self-imposed isolation had closed him off from his gift and his magic. And since he had begun to open up again, he had begun to feel again.

He could feel himself standing unsteadily on a threshold with the cocoon of his grief behind him and the rest of his life before him. Already he could feel himself leaning through the portal toward whatever the future held for him. A part of him was eager and a part of him was sad because of it.

He bent his head and pressed a gentle kiss to the ring Serena had given him, the ring that encircled his finger in warmth, and tears rose up in his eyes as he said his final good-bye.

"Bryan?"

Rachel's voice preceded her into the study, giving him enough warning so he could clear his throat and squeeze his eyes shut.

"Bryan, are you—oh, here you are," Rachel said. She stopped uncertainly as she stepped into the study. Her brows pulled together in concern. "Are you all right?" she asked hesitantly.

"I'm . . . fine."

He didn't look fine, Rachel thought. He looked like a man laboring under the strain of some terrible emotion. The idea caught at her heart and squeezed it tight. Bryan was always smiling—except when he was scolding her for not believing in magic. In the short time she had known him, she had seldom seen him be entirely serious. She had never seen him in pain. Until now.

"I was resting my eyes," Bryan lied. He plucked his glasses off and rubbed at the bleary blue orbs. "Too much reading."

He settled his spectacles back on his nose and stared up at Rachel. She was worried about him. He could sense her concern. Warmth stirred inside him, and a soft smile tugged at one corner of his mouth.

"What are you searching for?" she asked, approaching the desk slowly, trying not to appear too curious.

She had been forcing herself to steer clear of him, but discovered she was so drawn to him that she kept dredging up excuses to seek him out. Her emotional tug-of-war was wearing her out.

"Proof of Wimsey," he said.

"You haven't found any, have you?" It was more a statement than a question. She felt the pendulum inside her swing away from him.

"That doesn't mean there isn't any," Bryan said with forced cheerfulness, "only that I'm not looking in the right places."

Rachel sighed, her shoulders drooping with resignation. "Do you really think this whimsy is what Mother keeps seeing at night?"

There had been two more incidents involving Addie's elusive intruder. Both times she had been the only one to see anything. Rachel was no more convinced now than she had been that the apparition was real. Bryan, on the other hand, seemed as sure as ever that it was.

"She says not. She seems to think it's some other entity. Odd that she's never spoken of other ghosts before, only Wimsey," he reflected, clearing a fat book aside so he could stare at his charts. "And there's been almost no activity recorded in the parts of the house where these last three sightings have been."

"So?"

"So," he drawled, beckoning Rachel nearer still. He swept a hand across his blueprint of the house on which he had drawn a numbered grid and jotted down smaller numbers that were circled. "Sightings are almost always concentrated in specific areas. This very room, for instance, and the foyer." He tapped his pencil to two separate grid blocks, each of which was crowded with a cluster of little numbers.

"This looks very . . . scientific," Rachel said, surprised. She might have decided Bryan was no con man, but that didn't mean she had decided to accept his so-called profession.

He gave her a wry look. "Yes, they try to train us properly at Transylvania U."

Rachel felt a blush creep into her cheeks. "You said the other night you and Jayne went to college together."

"Yes." Mischief twinkled in his deep blue eyes. "She majored in witchcraft and druid rituals. Ask her to change a man into a toad for you sometime. She's quite good at it."

"Stop it," Rachel commanded, narrowing her eyes at him. Laughter threatened, and a smile tugged at the corners of her mouth. "I'm trying to extricate myself gracefully."

Bryan winced. "Sounds painful."

"You're not making it any easier."

"Sorry," he said, utterly unrepentant. "Jayne and I and two other friends you will no doubt meet soon attended Notre Dame. I got my master's at Purdue." Rachel's eyes widened comically. Bryan chuckled. "And you thought you Californians had cornered the market on weird."

Her brows lowered ominously, and she tapped a finger to the blueprint. "You were explaining this to me."

"All right," he conceded. Maybe he would be able to convince her with a logical scientific explanation. Somehow the idea didn't appeal to him as much as simply having her believe did. He took a deep breath and began. "Many parapsychologists believe all places are 'haunted' by memories of past events. Some places more strongly than others, naturally, say the scene of a violent death, for instance."

"Why can't I see this whimsy of Mother's? I heard her talking to him in the hall this morning, but when I stepped out to look, there wasn't anybody with her."

Bryan shrugged as he wrote himself a note to check the hall tape recorder. "Maybe you haven't got the right kind of psychic sensitivity. You don't want to believe in him; that doesn't help. People tend not to see things they don't want to see."

"Why doesn't he appear to you? You want to see him."

"I don't know. I don't know why my equipment hasn't picked anything up either, but then, these things are never predictable. If they were, we wouldn't call them 'paranormal,' would we?"

"I'm sorry," Rachel said, shaking her head, "but I still don't believe in ghosts."

"Neither do many psychic investigators. As a whole, we tend to be a very skeptical lot."

"You seem anything but skeptical."

He grinned at her, and Rachel felt her heart lurch. She reminded herself that this was exactly why she'd been avoiding him. He made her body react entirely against the better judgment of her mind.

"I'm one in a million," he declared happily.

That was for sure, Rachel mused, watching him as he leaned toward her. She thought he was going to kiss her again, and her lips buzzed with the memory of the kisses they had shared. But he touched the tip of his nose to hers instead, and smiled the most devastatingly sexy smile. Heat washed through her, and she unconsciously wet her lips with the tip of her tongue.

"Did you have sweet dreams the other night, angel?" he asked in a voice so soft it was like a caress.

Rachel's cheeks bloomed red. *Sweet* was probably not quite the word to use regarding the dreams she'd had. *Erotic* was far and away the most accurate. She didn't understand it. Bryan was hardly the first good-looking man she'd ever known. And she was categorically against getting involved with him. Why then did she continue to go on feeling such a fierce attraction?

It made no sense. But then, little that had gone on in the past few days had made any sense. It was this blasted old house, she decided irrationally. The sooner she was out of it, the better for all concerned. Her life was pointed down a very narrow road. There was no room for a dreamer to tag along.

Bryan drew back, a gleam of satisfaction in his eye. She had dreamed about him. That bit of news was certainly a balm to his bruised male ego. He decided not to gloat; it wasn't his style. Instead, he produced three small red foam balls from nowhere and began to juggle.

Rachel stared at him, bewildered. That was all right, he decided. It would do her some good to be thrown off balance on a regular basis. It was too easy to picture her letting her life settle into a rut of dreary, dutiful routine. If she didn't learn to look around for magic and rainbows now, she certainly wasn't going to start in a year or two. The struggle to cope with Addie's illness would have worn her down and extinguished all belief in dreams and happiness. He just couldn't let that happen.

"Did you have a question?" he asked.

"What?"

"When you came in here, did you have a question, or dare I hope you came seeking out my pleasant company?"

Rachel gave herself a mental shake and gathered her wits. She straightened away from the desk, looking suddenly very purposeful. She was wearing a soft blue prairie-style dress with a simple shirtwaist and gathered skirt. A big turquoise pin was fastened at the throat of the stand-up collar. Her hair, which had flowed like fine champagne down her back the night they'd kissed, was up now, secured in a sensible knot at the back of her head. Wild tendrils curled around her face.

Bryan thought she looked like a schoolmarm—a very pretty, vulnerable schoolmarm.

"Perhaps you've come to discuss our relationship," he suggested.

Rachel nearly bolted. "We—we don't have a relationship," she said, sounding more rattled than resolute.

"I beg to differ," Bryan argued with a charming smile. He caught the red foam balls and clutched them to his chest, his expression turning melodramatic. "Or were you just leading me on when you kissed my socks off?"

"I was not leading you on!" Rachel protested. He made the whole incident sound as if she had planned it.

"Well, then . . ." He shrugged innocently, implying that if she hadn't been leading him on, then she had been seducing him with a purpose.

Rachel ground her teeth and refused to rise to the bait. She wasn't getting involved with him. She wasn't even going to argue about getting involved with him.

"I was wondering if you knew where my mother keeps the books for her antiques business. I've been looking all over for them. I have to get started on them so I can find out exactly where we stand financially."

"Did you ask Addie?" He settled back down on the desk chair.

"Do you honestly believe she'd tell me?" she questioned, unable to keep all the bitterness out of her voice. She and Addie seemed no closer to a reconciliation than they had five years before. It didn't help that Rachel had been to see her mother's lawyer to find out where they stood legally and financially. Talking about power of attorney and conservatorships did not make for ice breaking.

"Have you spoken with her about selling the house?" Bryan asked.

"No."

"She isn't going to like it."

"Then I'll have to deal with her anger, because there isn't any other way," Rachel said stubbornly. The frustration of the past few days boiled up anew inside her. "I have a good job waiting for me in the city. We need the money."

"There's always another way, Rachel," Bryan said, his disapproval of her plan subtle but clear.

"Oh, really?" Rachel arched a brow as her temper flared up. She crossed her arms in an effort to keep from trying to strangle him. "What is this wonderful alternative? Maybe you could enlighten me. So far I've discovered that this house is probably worth less than Mother owes the bank because it's falling down around our ears. The electric company is threatening to discontinue service because she hasn't paid the bill in months. The doctor bills we're going to incur will wipe out my own bank account all on their own."

"You need to have a little patience," Bryan insisted. "Something will turn up."

Rachel felt as if a switch had been flipped inside her, letting anger pour forth unchecked. Something will turn up. That had always been Terence's line. He'd forever been telling her to lighten up, loosen up, that the future would take care of itself. She'd seen firsthand that wasn't the case. Nothing ever just "turned up." She had learned the hard way that the world had two kinds of people: People like Terence who believed in rainbows, and people like her who accepted responsibility.

It made her angry to think that Bryan belonged to the first group, the group she knew better than to get tangled up with. And deeper down it made her angry that she had to belong to the second group. Her life would have been a whole lot brighter with a rainbow in it, but she couldn't have one, and she didn't have time to go chasing it, at any rate. She had responsibilities.

She was angry with him. Bryan could feel the heat of it, he could see it burning in her eyes. He had stepped on a nerve. He opened his mouth to smooth things over, but Rachel didn't give him the chance.

"It must be nice to be able to coast through life believing everything takes care of itself," she said bitterly. "But I wouldn't know, because I've always been one of those people destined to pick up after dreamers and shoulder the realities they can never seem to face."

Bryan shot up out of his chair and grabbed her by the wrist as she turned to storm out. "Rachel, wait—"

"I can't wait, Mr. Hennessy," she snapped, glaring at him. "I've got work to do." She jerked her arm from his grasp and rubbed at it as if to erase the memory of his touch. "I'll let you get back to your juggling," she said with a sneer.

Bryan closed his eyes and heaved a long sigh. Each click of her heels on the wooden floor made him wince until the sound faded away. He turned to stare up at the portrait that hung on the paneled wall.

"Got any bright suggestions?" he asked.

The pleasantly pudgy man in the painting was Arthur Drake III, the last Drake to own the house. He merely went on staring straight ahead, a secretive smile on his small mouth, one hand raised, palm up, as if gesturing to the viewer to behold the room around them. A badly tarnished brass plaque fastened to the bottom molding of the frame was engraved with a quote by Seneca: Gold is tried by fire, brave men by adversity.

"I guess this is adversity," Bryan muttered. "We'll see how acceptable I am."

He sank slowly into the chair and swiveled around, letting his gaze take in the gracious room: the cherry paneling, the built-in bookshelves crowded with musty old leatherbound volumes, the fireplace, which had apparently been renovated at some point because the brick was newer than any other in the house.

What was he going to do about Rachel?

Kissing her seemed like a good idea.

"Right," he murmured wryly in answer to his inner voice. "I'll do it again next time she lets me get within a hundred yards of her."

* * *

Rachel finally found the books for her mother's antiques business squirreled away inside an oak icebox in what was supposed to be Addie's office. It was a sunny room at the front of the house, cluttered with stacks and stacks of old newspapers, and wastebaskets full of splintered glass figurines. The desk contained hundreds of old lace doilies. One drawer was brim full of ballpoint pens. But not one scrap of relevant business information had been housed there. Inside a file cabinet she had found cigar boxes full of buttons of every description, but not until she checked the icebox and looked beneath three dozen old *Life* magazines did she find what she'd been looking for.

She realized, as she eased down into the chair behind the desk, that while she had been looking for this financial information, she had been dreading actually finding it. It had become obvious to her that Addie was in no condition to run a business with anything remotely resembling efficiency. She feared the books on Lindquist Antiques would only confirm what she already knew to be true.

Shoring up her resolve with a deep breath, she brushed the dust from the cover of the old ledger and turned it back. The first few pages of columns were written in her mother's neat, brisk hand. Sales and acquisitions were noted with proper care and detail. The columns of figures added up to the penny.

Rachel checked their accuracy with her calculator, feeling slightly inferior. Addie had always done math in her head as quickly and unerringly as any machine. She had always expected Rachel to be

able to as well, and she had always seemed let
down when Rachel hadn't been able to live up to
that standard. Rachel recalled with a pang the
nights she had sat up in her bed with her covers
over her head to hide the brightness of the flashlight as she worked on her math tables, determined to make her mother proud of her.

The only thing about Rachel that had unfailingly
pleased Addie had been her voice. Addie had been
a demanding taskmaster, forcing her to practice,
practice, practice; correcting her slightest error;
critiquing every note. But when Addie had sat and
listened to a performance, a look of rapturous
longing had stolen over her face. Pride and love
had shone in her eyes. And afterward Addie had
always roused herself, as if from a dream, and
said, "You have the voice of an angel, Rachel. I am
so very very proud of you."

Rachel shook herself now from the bittersweet
memory. She had fought against that pride in an
attempt to gain her mother's understanding, and
she had lost. It had been a foolish thing to do, but
she'd been young and rebellious and longing to
have her mother love her for who she was, not how
she sang. She rubbed at her temples now as she
thought of how it had all backfired on her, how all
her pretty rainbows had melted into grayness.

Maybe if Bryan had had to deal with a harsh
reality or two, he wouldn't be so quick to believe in
magic either, she thought.

A relationship with Bryan Hennessy. She shuddered at the thought, though whether it was out
of fear or anticipation she couldn't have honestly

said. She told herself it was righteous indignation. The nerve of the man insinuating that she had been pursuing him!

Turning another page in the ledger, she noticed that the handwriting had changed subtly. It wasn't quite as neat or strong. A figure or two had been scratched out and written over. The penmanship worsened with every page, until she began to find words misspelled, letters transposed, mistakes in the math. And Rachel realized that what she was seeing was documentation of Addie's decline.

Nearly a year had passed since the last entry had been made in the book, and that final column of figures had never been tallied. The page was wrinkled and dark from a coffee stain, as if Addie had perhaps become upset with her inability and had spilled the cup in her haste to escape the written evidence of the illness that was progressively stealing her mind.

Rachel set the ledger aside and picked up the inventory book, hoping against hope that it was more up-to-date. But what she found was a repeat performance. The entries started out logical and legible, and gradually declined to the point that what little she could make out made no sense. The book was no more up-to-date than the ledger had been, and it was too much to hope that nothing had been purchased or sold in the interim. She was going to have to inventory everything in the house, then they would have to have a sale of some kind to dispose of the bulk of the merchandise.

They would be able to take only Addie's most

personal possessions and a few antiques to San Francisco. Rachel knew they would not be able to afford much in the way of an apartment. There certainly wouldn't be room for the hundreds of pieces of furniture Addie had accumulated, or the bric-a-brac . . . or the bird cages.

"Oh, Mother," she whispered, planting her elbows on the desk and rubbing her hands over her face as a wave of helplessness crashed into her. "What are we going to do?"

Addie stood in the doorway to the office, motionless as she stared at Rachel. Spread out on the desk before her daughter were the books she had come to dread and hate. It was clear to her that Rachel had seen them. A cold knot of panic settled in her stomach.

"What are you looking for?" she asked, trying to sound commanding but sounding uncertain instead. She shuffled into the room, her garden boots scuffing on the worn rug. "Money to give to Terence, the slimy snake?"

"I don't see Terence anymore, Mother," Rachel explained calmly. She wondered how pleased Addie would have been to know her relationship with "the cheap folk singer" had died long ago, that the bloom of love had faded along with her dreams.

"Good," Addie said, taking a seat on a dusty chair that sat beside the desk. "I never liked that boy. He wasn't good enough for you."

Rachel didn't comment on the remark. Terence was in the past. There was no sense wasting energy thinking about the past when the future was going to take everything they had.

"Mother, we need to talk," she said gravely. She was bracing herself for a fight, but when she looked into her mother's eyes, she didn't see the anger she had come to expect. She saw sadness. Somehow that was worse.

"I'm a little behind on those books," Addie said.

"It's all right. We'll get them straightened out."

"Here. Let me, Rachel. You were never good with numbers."

For an instant there was a flash of her old efficient, businesslike self as Addie reached across the desk and picked up the ledger. She sat up straighter, her bony shoulders squared beneath the thin cotton of her housedress. Taking a pencil out of a cup on the desktop, she opened the book.

Gritting her teeth in determination, she began at the top of the page. She saw the numbers, took them into her brain, and tried to put them together, but they scattered and went off in all directions in her mind. She took a deep breath and tried again. She had always been so good at math. Now she could barely comprehend the numbers on the page before her. She tried to add two numbers together, and just before the answer became clear to her, it slipped away.

A terrible chill ran through her. She could excuse her forgetfulness. She was a busy woman with a lot on her mind. So what if she put her car in reverse instead of park once? So what if she went to the mailbox on Sunday? Busy people forgot things all the time. But this, this was something else. She couldn't discount her inability to add these simple numbers together.

She stared at the figures on the page until they seemed to leap out of their columns and spin around one another in a whirlpool of black and red ink. Panic rose up in her throat, and she slammed the ledger shut. She wanted to throw the book aside and run out of the room, but her brain suddenly couldn't separate all the intricacies of each task, and she clutched the book to her breast instead.

"Mother?" Rachel asked softly. Her own sense of panic was growing inside her, and it trembled in her voice. She had never seen her mother as anything other than strong, invincible, indomitable. And before her very eyes Addie was shrinking down on her chair, her face a mask of stricken confusion. Rachel reached out toward her, the fingers of her hand curling over the edge of the musty old ledger. "Mother?"

"Rachel," Addie murmured, her voice straining. She felt too fragile and frail to speak louder than a whisper. She felt as if she might shatter like the many china figurines she had broken over the last few months as the connection between her brain and her fingers had shorted out. The shield of anger and indignation that had held her up so many times was gone, vanished as suddenly as her memory could vanish.

All her life she had been strong. She had stood on her own to raise her daughter when her husband had been killed. She had never asked for help from anyone. But now she turned instinctively to her daughter, her eyes full of anguish and tears. "Rachel, I'm so frightened."

Rachel took her mother in her arms and held her as her mother had held her when she'd skinned her knee or had had a bad dream. And she offered what comfort she could while she shared her mother's pain and felt the pain of her own loss. She was losing her mother. Addie would never be the strong one again. It was Rachel's turn. At that moment both of them realized it.

"I'm frightened too," she murmured through her tears. "But we'll manage. Together, like it used to be. Just the two of us. I'll take care of you. I love you. I love you so much."

Bryan stopped in the doorway, everything inside him going still at the sight. He had intended to barge in and sweep Rachel away from the books for a walk around the grounds. He wanted to show her that there was more to her life than worrying about money. But it looked as if she didn't need him to tell her that at the moment.

He knew he should have stepped back out into the hall and allowed Rachel and Addie absolute privacy, but it seemed important that he see Rachel this way—as a loving daughter, as a caring person, not embarrassed by her mother's illness, but heartbroken for a loss that could never be replaced.

Or perhaps what was truly important was the feeling coming to life inside himself, the feeling he had denied over and over the past few days. He was in love with Rachel Lindquist.

He did step back then, as if the realization had come in the form of a physical blow. He let himself out of the house and strode quickly toward the fence that ran along the cliff's edge, breaking into an athletic lope that ate up the distance. When he reached the rusty iron railing, he stopped, sucking in great deep gulps of sea air. In each hand he grasped a spear point that decorated the top of the wrought iron pickets, twisting at them so that the oxidizing metal flaked against his palms.

Without really seeing it, he stared out at the ocean. The gray-blue waves rolled in, one after another. Fishing boats dotted the misty horizon. Gulls keened and swooped along the rocky beach below.

How had it happened so fast, he wondered. He hardly knew anything about her. Except that she loved a mother who had shunned her for five years, and she'd had dreams broken, and she tasted of need and sweetness. And when the moon shone in her eyes, he could see how badly she needed to believe in rainbows and how afraid she was to reach out for one.

It didn't seem possible that he could have fallen in love when he had just opened up enough to offer Rachel his help. He had meant only to reach out to her, to offer her a little respite from her worries. But in opening up he had not simply given, he had received. He could feel again. Now Rachel's pain would be his pain, her fears would be his fears.

"I don't know if I'm strong enough to go through that again," he whispered.

You are. Love makes you strong.

He thought of Rachel holding her mother, whispering assurances through her tears. Love was the most powerful thing in the world. It could endure time and turmoil, hurt and heartache, pride and pain. Love was magic.

Bryan's broad shoulders rose as he drew a deep breath, filling his lungs with cool air, and a deep, abiding calm settled inside him with the kind of acceptance that comes only from the heart. It might not have been smart or logical for him to love Rachel Lindquist, but love her he did, and if he could give her magic, he would.

SEVEN

" 'I love a maiden fair with sunlight in her hair. Her beauty was so rare, but she did scorn me,' " Bryan sang as he trailed along behind Rachel and Faith Callan like a wandering troubador.

They were systematically working their way through Drake House, making an inventory. Faith, who had experience with antiques, was identifying each piece, then Rachel looked the item up in a dealer's catalog, and they tried to arrive at a fair market value. Bryan tagged along behind them, jotting down their findings in the inventory book. Addie followed them to each room, then stood in a strategic spot and glared at them as they went about their business.

She wasn't taking it well at all, he thought, stealing a surreptitious glance at the older woman. The peace mother and daughter had made the day

146

before had already been wrecked. Addie was sulking in the corner of the room near the window, her mouth pinched into a line as she twisted the end of her braid. She dug a hand into the patch pocket of her cotton housedress, pulled out a long stalk of celery, and began to munch on it angrily.

Bryan knew Rachel had explained to her that the antiques would have to be inventoried and sold because they needed the money, and Addie had seemed to comprehend the situation, but that didn't mean she had to like it. He couldn't blame her. Her independence was being taken away from her bit by bit. A proud woman like Addie wasn't likely to accept it with a smile.

Still, Bryan thought with a sigh, he had promised to try to ease this transition for both Addie and Rachel. Drawing in a deep breath, he broke into song again.

" 'She was a maiden fair with sunlight in her hair. Her name was Addie.' "

Addie scowled at him and gave him a loud raspberry, spraying bits of celery out at him.

"I think she likes me." Bryan grinned, and winked at Faith. "What do you think?"

Faith giggled, dark eyes twinkling. The sun streaming in the window caught in her mop of burnished curls, turning them more red than gold. She poked Bryan in the ribs with the eraser end of her pencil. "Behave yourself, Hennessy, or we'll send you out to do some real work."

"You could have brought along my darling godchildren," he said with a hint of reproach. "They would have kept an eye on me."

"No doubt. Lindy would make you toe the line. You know how she bosses Nicholas around."

"He's just biding his time," Bryan said. "In another few years he'll be towering over her. We'll see who the boss is then. I can give him some pointers on diabolical brother-type revenge."

Rachel listened to their good-natured bantering. It was clear that Bryan and Faith were as close as brother and sister. There was a special understanding between them, evident when they smiled at each other. She envied them that. She had never felt that kind of kinship with anyone, not even with Terence.

As she was thinking it, Bryan turned and regarded her with the same warm expression, the same keen knowing in his blue eyes. There was an invitation in his gaze, an invitation for her to share that kind of special friendship with him.

Temptation pulled at her. A part of her wanted badly to accept. It would have been nice to have a friend to lean on, but another part of her flatly denied her that option. She had to take her responsibilities on her own shoulders, because she knew from experience she couldn't count on a man like Bryan to give support forever.

Not that she blamed him. She couldn't see how anyone in his right mind would want to take on the task she was facing if he didn't have to. Why would anyone ask to share that kind of pain?

The word *love* passed fleetingly through her brain, but she dismissed it. She had given up on the idea of romantic love, just as she had given up on the notion of rainbows and happy endings. She couldn't afford romantic fantasies any more than she could afford to lose sleep over the erotic dreams she'd been having lately.

Bryan Hennessy was proving to be one big distraction from the things she needed to concentrate on most. One big, handsome distraction . . .

She stared at him as he made a note in the book he cradled on his right arm. He wore faded jeans that hugged his lean male body in all the right places. A polo shirt clung to his strong shoulders. The color matched the blue of his eyes in a way that made Rachel's breath catch. Glossy strands of tawny hair fell across his broad forehead.

His glasses were slipping down his nose. Without looking up from his work, he reached up and pushed at the wire bridge with the middle finger of his left hand. It was a gesture she'd seen him perform a hundred times, and yet, for some inexplicable reason, this time she thought it was curiously sweet.

Her gaze focused on his hands, and longing rippled through her. Those big hands were strong, yet so gentle, almost as gentle as his lips had been against hers. She'd dreamed of those hands caressing her every night. It seemed like eons had passed since he'd touched her, kissed her. It had been three days. She probably could have said how many hours and minutes had passed.

It irked her that she'd spent so much time thinking about it. She had told herself she couldn't get involved with Bryan Hennessy. That should have been the end of the longing. Since their argument, she had avoided him as best she could, considering they were living in the same house. She had been as cool toward him as possible without being out and out rude.

And still he was sweet to her. The growing bouquet of roses on her dresser was testimony to that. There was one waiting for her on her pillow every night when she went up to bed. It seemed only a sweeter gesture when he denied knowledge of it.

She couldn't stop thinking about him. If she had been the fanciful sort, she might have thought he'd cast some kind of magic spell on her. Instead, she blamed it on the flowers. She had always been a sucker for roses.

"Rachel?" Faith asked for the third time.

Rachel snapped out of her musings with a start. "I'm sorry. What?"

A gentle smile turned the corners of Faith's mouth, setting her heartshaped face aglow. "I was just going to suggest a coffee break."

"Oh, yes, of course," Rachel stammered, embarrassment heating her face. She stifled the urge to rub at the spots of color blooming on her cheekbones, winding her hands more firmly around the book she clutched against the front of her baggy pink T-shirt.

Suddenly Addie stamped her booted foot. "You're thieves, the lot of you! You're going to steal my bird cages. I won't stand for it, I tell you. I'm going to call the police!"

"Mother!" Rachel wailed, at the end of her emotional rope. She had been over this with Addie a half dozen times. It was difficult to tell herself that Addie had undoubtedly forgotten every one of

those conversations, that she wasn't being difficult deliberately. "Don't go dragging that horrid
deputy out here again."

"He'll get to the bottom of this business," Addie
said. "He can find that ugly ghost while he's out
here, too, and haul you all away together."

"If he hauls anyone away, it'll be you, Mother.
He's angry enough with you as it is."

Addie tossed the last of her celery stalk at her
daughter and stomped toward the door. Bryan
headed her off.

"Hennessy, get out of my way," Addie commanded.

"Not a chance, beautiful," he said with an amicable grin. "You know you have the most lovely
complexion, Addie. How do you keep it that way?"

Addie blushed like a schoolgirl. She had always
been vain about her flawless skin. Bryan's compliment bolstered her flagging ego and easily derailed
her thoughts from calling the police.

"All the Gunther women have beautiful skin,"
she said coyly, patting a hand to her pale cheek.
"It's an old family secret."

"Ah, a secret," Bryan said with great relish. He
took her arm and tucked it in his. "I've got one
too. I'll tell you mine if you tell me yours. Then
we'll dance the tango on the lawn."

Rachel watched, bemused by the strange mix of
feelings inside her as Bryan led her mother away.
"Is he ever serious about anything?"

"Oh, yes," Faith said on a long sigh of remembrance. Heedless of the layer of dust, she settled
herself on an old desk and folded her hands in the

lap of her worn jeans. "We went for a long time without seeing Bryan smile after he lost Serena."

"Serena?"

"His wife," Faith said gently. She paused then to let Rachel absorb the information, compassion welling inside her at the look of shock on the woman's face. "She passed away about a year and half ago. Cancer."

"I—I didn't know." Rachel felt as if she'd been hit by a truck. Her knees wobbled, and she sat down on a huge square iron bird cage.

Bryan had been married. He had been in love with a woman who had died. Oh, Lord, she thought, unable to stop the tears that flooded her eyes, what a disservice she'd done him, thinking he had never had to endure pain or accept responsibility.

"So if we seem a little overindulgent of his silliness," Faith went on, "it's only because we missed it so much. Besides," she added, summoning up one of her sunny smiles, "there's a lot more to Bryan than meets the eye."

"I'd already guessed that," Rachel mumbled.

Dammit, she thought, she felt completely off balance. She felt utterly guilty and mean and self-centered. Anger struggled to life inside her. She didn't need this. She had enough emotional baggage to deal with. She couldn't afford to spend her energy on dealing with Bryan's as well. It was just one more reason she shouldn't get more deeply involved with him.

If they'd met at some other place and time in their lives, things might have been different. But the facts remained: she had her mother to take care of, Bryan had his own wounded heart to heal, and they wanted to deal with those issues in two completely different ways. She could see no answer other than practicality, no matter how unpleasant it might be. He chose to gloss everything over with magic and foolishness.

Rachel looked up suddenly, and in the next instant Bryan danced through the door with Addie in his arms. Her mother's cheeks were flushed, and she held a rose between her teeth. He deposited her in a high-backed chair and strode toward Rachel purposefully, stopping before her with an earnest look on his face.

"Dorothy," he said. "I believe the munchkins have arrived."

"The what?" Faith asked.

Rachel, however, knew exactly what he was referring to. She had spoken of this place as Oz. But who exactly the munchkins were, she didn't know. Her eyebrows lifted in question.

Bryan glanced back over his shoulder to make sure Addie wasn't listening. She was twirling her rose by its stem and softly singing a snatch of something from *Aida*. He turned back to Rachel. "There are two rather remarkable-looking gentlemen at the front door, asking to speak to you about purchasing Drake House."

"But I haven't put it on the market yet," Rachel said. "How did they know it was for sale?"

"I wonder," Bryan said, stroking a hand back through his sandy hair. Behind his glasses his eyes took on a faraway look. "I wonder."

Rachel excused herself and went out into the hall, wondering why she wasn't eager to meet these prospective buyers. She'd been worried that they would have trouble unloading the house, it was in such a sad state of disrepair. She should have been bubbling over about this turn of events, but she wasn't.

Swinging the heavy front door back, she immediately saw what Bryan had meant by "remarkable-looking." One of the men was about five feet tall and nearly as wide. His head was as round and bald as a bowling ball. His companion was a few inches taller, built like a rail, and had a face with sharp, sly features and deepset eyes. There was a fading blue bruise on his left cheek.

Rachel cleared her throat delicately and offered her visitors a polite smile. "Can I help you? I'm Rachel Lindquist."

The rotund one stuck out a dimpled hand. "Miles Porchind, Miss Lindquist," he said with a smile, "and my partner, Felix Rasmussen. May we take a few moments of your time to discuss some business?"

Her immediate reaction to the men was dislike, but she reminded herself beggars couldn't be choosers, and invited the prospective buyers inside. She led the way to the study, the skin on her back prickling as she felt their gazes on her.

Once in the room, Porchind and Rasmussen looked around with hungry eyes, taking in the paneling, the old furniture, the bookshelves—particularly the bookshelves, with their dusty old tomes. Their expressions were like those of starving men who had stumbled into a bakery. Rachel half expected them to start salivating. Grimacing in distaste at the thought, she seated herself behind the desk and motioned the men to help themselves to seats. Oddly, they chose to sit side by side on the leather love seat, with Porchind taking up more than half of it.

Bryan wandered in then, jugging two apples and an orange. "Hello again," he said, sending the men his most innocuous grin. He caught two pieces of fruit against his chest with his right arm, caught the remaining apple in his left hand, and promptly took a bite out of it.

"We're here to discuss business with Miss Lindquist," Porchind said with a trace of annoyance.

"So you said. Care for a piece of fruit?"

They merely stared at him, then turned to Rachel, clearly hoping she would toss Bryan out on his ear.

"It's all right," Rachel said. "Mr. Hennessy is the family retainer."

She supposed she shouldn't have, but she wanted Bryan there with her, and, for once, she gave in to her desire. He shot her a wink that seemed inappropriately intimate, and immediately heat streaked through her body. She had to force her mind back to the business at hand.

"Bryan tells me you're interested in purchasing the house," she said. "May I ask where you heard it was for sale?"

The men glanced sharply at each other and answered simultaneously. "In town."

Porchind went on. "We heard you had come back

to settle your mother's affairs and close up the house. Perhaps it was nothing more than small-town gossip."

"Gossip, perhaps," Rasmussen echoed.

"No, I have been considering it," Rachel said cautiously.

"But it's nothing definite, by any means," Bryan interrupted.

Rachel scowled up at him. "I thought you wanted to help," she muttered between her teeth.

"I am helping," he said, ignoring the anger he felt rolling off her in waves. He turned back to their visitors. "There are so many things to consider. The ghosts, for example. You must have heard by now, the house is haunted."

The strangers exchanged another glance. "We're not put off by ghost stories," Porchind said.

His partner shook his head. "Don't believe in ghosts."

Immediately, two huge drops of water fell from the ceiling—one landing squarely on the head of each man. Before they had a chance to recover from the surprise, two more drops fell, followed by two more. Porchind looked up and caught one in the eye.

"And then there's the plumbing," Bryan said. It was almost impossible to contain his excitement. It churned inside him as he looked up at the ceiling, which showed no evidence of a water spot. Wimsey. He knew it. He could sense it. This was his first physical sign of Addie's ghost.

"The plumbing is fine," Rachel insisted. "That's just humidity."

"Humidity from hell," Bryan said dramatically.

Porchind looked past him to Rachel. "My partner and I are interested in the house, Miss Lindquist. Have you set a price yet?"

"No, I haven't," Rachel said, trying to keep her anger out of her voice. She was going to skin Bryan Hennessy alive when this was over. "I need to discuss the matter with my mother."

"Mrs. Lindquist doesn't want to move, you see," Bryan explained cheerfully. "She's attached to the place. Hard to figure, isn't it? But you know how elderly people are. They get something in their heads and there's no telling them otherwise. She wants to stay here forever."

Bryan tossed his apple core into the wastebasket beside the desk, then resumed his juggling, adding a paperweight to the apple and orange. From beneath lowered lashes he watched the two men scowl at him.

"Perhaps we should come back at a more convenient time," Porchind said, heaving himself to his feet.

"When it's more convenient," Rasmussen muttered, rising and trying to straighten his suit over his bony frame.

"Once you've had a chance to speak with your mother and determine a price," the round man said as he and his partner moved toward the door. "We only thought it prudent to let you know of our interest."

"Interest." Rasmussen nodded, smiling at Rachel in a way that made her skin crawl.

She managed a thank-you as she walked them

to the door. When she returned to the study, she was seething. Bryan had seated himself behind the desk and was absorbed in one of his history books.

"How dare you interfere!" she snapped, releasing the pent-up anger not only over the house issue, but the anger and frustration that had been building inside her for days. She kicked a sneakered foot against the handsome walnut desk. "How dare you! Those men may be the only people in the free world strange enough to buy this house, and you practically chased them away! And even if they do come back, I'll be lucky to get enough out of them to pay off the mortgage, thanks to you and your infernal ghost stories and your candor about the plumbing."

"Addie isn't going to want to move," Bryan said calmly.

"It isn't a question of whether or not Addie wants to move," Rachel said, planting her fists on the desktop. "It's the way it has to be. Will you face reality for once? I have a job waiting for me in San Francisco. I'm going to have to support my mother. Her medical bills alone will probably put me in debt for the rest of my life. Insurance would be a great help, but Addie doesn't have any because she lined a bird cage with her premium notice and let the policy lapse. Are you comprehending any of this, Bryan?" She snatched up a pen and pad of paper and thrust them at him. "Maybe you should write yourself a note. I have to sell this house!"

Bryan looked up at her and sighed. "I know it's a cliché, but you're beautiful when you're angry."

Rachel clamped her hands to her head as if to keep the top of it from exploding off. She counted to ten and took deep breaths. Blessed, infuriating man! He could be every bit as impossible to deal with as her mother.

"I don't think you should be too hasty about selling, Rachel."

"Bryan, this house is as expensive to keep as a herd of elephants, and there's no chance of me finding a job around here that would pay more than peanuts. You're allegedly an intelligent man—you do the math. I have to sell this house. I haven't got a choice."

"We always have at least two choices, angel. You're just too stubborn to look for yours."

"*I'm* stubborn?" Rachel went red in the face as a hundred scathing retorts clogged her throat and cut off her air supply.

Bryan had turned back to his book. "I've got a bad feeling about Messieurs Porkrind and Rasputin. I think they're up to something."

Rachel didn't like them either, but she was too angry to agree with him about anything. She regarded him with narrowed eyes. "I suppose now you're going to tell me you're a mind reader."

"Not precisely." Bryan pressed his lips together to fight off the smile that threatened.

He studiously avoided looking at Rachel, concentrating instead on his book. His eyes brightened suddenly, and he tapped a finger to the page before him. "Edmund Porchind, alias Pig Porchind, alleged bootlegger during the Prohibition era, resided in Anastasia until 1931." He pushed his glasses up and stared across the room. "I wonder what one of the late Mr. Pig's long-lost relatives wants with Drake House."

"I'm sure I don't care," Rachel said crossly. She turned to start for the door, but Bryan caught her wrist, and with one deft tug pulled her into his lap.

"Bryan!" she squealed. Her fury was instantly overrun by surprise and a giddy kind of desire that kept her from trying too hard to get away. She squirmed just enough so Bryan had to wrap his arms around her.

"Don't you know when a woman is furious with you?" she asked, fighting to maintain her scowl.

"Yes, but I also know when she's having to work at it." A wicked grin split his features. Rachel was angry with him, but she would recover. In the span of a few short minutes he had had a bounty of clues dropped in his lap. It was as intoxicating for him as was any liquor.

"Look sharp, Watson!" he said merrily. "The game is afoot!"

He covered her frown with an exuberant kiss. He had meant only to give her a quick smack on the lips, but as soon as he tasted her, his intentions melted away on a groan of pure male need. She tasted so sweet. Even angry she tasted sweeter than anything he'd had in his life for a long time. And beneath her initial resistance he could taste a dozen other emotions—longing, hesitancy. He could taste a woman who wanted to believe in his brand of magic but wasn't going to allow herself to.

He slanted his mouth across hers in warm invitation as his left hand slid up the supple lines of her back to tangle in her hair. Pins slipped their moorings and dropped to the floor as the mass of pale silk tumbled loose. Her lips softened beneath his, and she yielded to temptation with a moan.

She shouldn't have been giving in to him this way, Rachel thought dimly. But she didn't seem to have the will to pull away. She felt safe in Bryan's arms. She felt womanly in a way she hadn't experienced in ages. She felt her troubles drift to the back of her mind. That alone was worth the lapse in behavior. What would it hurt to let go of reality for just a moment or two, she rationalized as desire surged through her veins in a hot stream. What would it hurt to take what Bryan was offering, so long as she realized it couldn't be permanent?

His tongue gently traced the line of her lips, and she invited him inside before her brain could summon an objection. She framed his face with her hands as she took his tongue into her mouth, and reveled in the textures her heightened senses experienced—the softness of his lean, clean-shaven cheeks against her palms, the velvet rasp of his tongue against her own. She could feel his arousal press against her thigh, and an answering heat pulsed between her legs. She twisted in his embrace to press closer, flattening her breasts against the solid wall of his chest.

She slid her hands up the sides of his face, hooking her thumbs under his glasses and sliding them up out of the way, so she could kiss him even harder. At the same time, Bryan traced a line around her rib cage, down to the point of her hip. His fingers snuck under the bottom of her T-shirt and slid up to cup a small, full breast. Rachel's breath caught in her throat at the feel of his thumb rubbing back and forth across her hardened nipple.

Bryan drew back a little, planting tiny kisses along the line of Rachel's jaw, then drew back a little farther so he could look at her face. Fresh air rushed in and out of his lungs, bringing with it a measure of sanity. It seemed an eternity had passed since he'd wanted a woman this badly. His hormones were screaming for him to press his advantage and take Rachel right there and then, but as he looked into her violet eyes he saw not only desire, but vulnerability and uncertainty.

She might want him, but she wasn't clear on the reasons why, and for him it had to be something more than an act to obliterate the present and push away the specter of a lonely future. He'd been down that road himself. He wasn't willing to go down it again, even with Rachel. When they made love, it would be just that—love.

He smoothed down the hem of her soft pink shirt and gave her a gentle smile as he dropped his glasses back into place. "For someone who doesn't believe in magic, you do a pretty good job of weaving a spell," he said.

Rachel stared at him as if he had just materialized before her, taking in his tousled tawny hair, the gleam of residual desire in his blue eyes, the slight puffiness of his sexy lower lip. She could still feel him, rigid and ready against her thigh, and a bolt of heat shot through her.

Magic, he'd said. Illusion. That was all this was, she told herself, her heart sinking. She could lose herself to the illusion she found in Bryan's arms, but the reality of her life would still be there waiting for her when the smoke cleared.

She tried to bolt off his lap, but he held her there, his hands firm but unyielding.

"Love isn't the trick, Rachel," he said softly, his earnest gaze holding hers, "believing is."

Awareness shivered through her. Almost immediately panic closed her throat. She couldn't be in love with Bryan Hennessy. She just couldn't be. Fate couldn't be that cruel to her again, to make her fall in love with a man who believed in magic. Love would make her weak when she most needed her strength. It would hand her disappointment when she already had a wagonload of it.

This time when she tried to extricate herself from Bryan's hold, he let her go. She straightened her clothes and pressed a hand to her mouth as she looked away from him. Her lips were hot and sensitive and still tasted of him, of apples and man. Longing ribboned through her again, and she squelched it, wincing as she ground out the fragile emotion.

Bryan watched her, hurting for her as he sensed her inner struggle, hurting for himself as she denied them both. But despite the mild setback, optimism brimmed to life inside him, and he smiled. Things were looking up. There was a mystery to unravel, and Rachel Lindquist had just kissed him silly. What more could a man ask for?

"We'd better get back to work," she said, her voice remote. "Faith will be wondering what happened to us."

"You might be wondering that yourself," Bryan murmured as Rachel walked away. He took one last look at the history book open on the desk, then focused his gaze on Rachel's delectable derriere as he pushed himself out of his chair and followed her into the hall.

"Faith, thanks for all your help," Rachel said. She stood on the porch with her arms wrapped around herself as the fog bank rolled in for the evening, obliterating what was left of the sunlight. "Are you sure you won't take anything for your time?"

"Absolutely not." Faith shook her head, her curls bouncing. "I was just lending a hand. That's what friends do. If you're a friend of Bryan's, you're a friend of mine. Remember that." She skipped down the sagging steps and turned around at the bottom with a sunny smile. "I'll expect to see you at the inn one day soon for tea."

"All right."

Rachel couldn't help but smile in return. It would have been nice to nurture a friendship with Faith Callan. For a moment she let herself think of what it would be like to settle there and have the kind of friends she could call simply to chat with or meet for tea. Another thing she wanted but could never have, she told herself as she watched Bryan walk his friend to her station wagon.

"Dear Miss Lindquist," Bryan said as he ambled along with his hands in his pockets, "you are cordially invited to an interrogation at Keepsake Inn, Anastasia-by-the-Sea. Thumbscrews optional."

Faith frowned at him in disappointment. "I like her, Bryan. She probably deserves better than a man who questions the motives of his dearest friends. Besides," she added, "Alaina and Jayne and I are only looking out for you the same way you look out for us."

"Yes," Bryan agreed, "and I love you for it. But I'm a big boy, now; I can take care of myself—more or less."

Faith didn't look the least bit convinced as she opened the door and slid behind the wheel of her car. "You need a haircut, big boy."

A wry grin twisted Bryan's mouth as he ran a hand back through his hair. He was going to have to write himself another note. He bent and kissed Faith's cheek through the open window, then handed her a little blue flower he had produced from thin air. Faith tucked it into a buttonhole on her white oxford shirt and looked at him with an expression as earnest as any he could have mustered.

"Please be careful with your heart, Bryan. You give it so easily. I'm not saying Rachel isn't worthy of it. I'm just afraid that maybe you're falling in love with her because she needs someone to take care of her and you've run out of people to look after."

"That's not it," he said evenly, though he suspected he was fibbing a bit. He did want to look after Rachel, but caring was a part of love. Besides, kissing her this morning had had little to do with her plight and everything to do with the way she felt in his arms.

Faith sighed and told him good-bye. He stood in the yard, watching as she drove down the long driveway, a pensive mood settling over him. He had a lot to think about tonight—Rachel, Porchind and Rasmussen, the possibility that Wimsey had showered those two with disapproval over their opinion of ghosts.

A mournful wail drifted to him on the cooling breeze. He snapped himself out of his musings and listened, holding his breath. The sound came again, faint but real, and he turned and jogged off across the lawn toward it, not at all sure of what he might find.

Addie wandered through the maze with no idea of where she was. All around her were high wild bushes, their branches tangled into an angry mass with leaves that rattled at her in the wind. They towered over her, casting a sinister shadow across the narrow, weed-choked path.

She had left the house because she was angry and frightened and she had thought the fresh air might clear her head, but she had promptly become lost. She had no idea how long she had been gone. It seemed like hours had passed. She had no idea of how far she had wandered. All she knew for sure was that she was cold and that Rachel was going to sell her home and make her move to a place where nothing would be familiar.

She had overheard her daughter's conversation with those strange little men and her argument with Hennessy afterward. She had thought about confronting Rachel, but fear of the future had overwhelmed her, and she had run away instead. Her forgetfulness wasn't such a terrible thing here in Anastasia, where people knew her, and in Drake House, where things were usually familiar. But to go to a place where everything would be strange, where there would be no memories at all to draw on, where she would have to learn new faces and new ways of doing things . . .

Tears welled up in her eyes and in her throat, choking her as she stumbled along the path, her garden boots catching on the rough ground. How could Rachel betray her this way? How could the daughter she had sacrificed so much for treat her so badly?

Addie stopped and looked around her, her eyes wide with fright. No matter which way she turned, everything looked the same. She pressed her bony hands to her cheeks and sobbed aloud as she sank down on a cracked stone bench.

Suddenly a man burst through the shrubbery. She looked up at him, terrified, and sobbed again.

"Addie," he said, stopping in his tracks. He was out of breath and his hair was disheveled. "Are you all right?"

"Who are you?" she demanded.

"It's me, Addie. Bryan Hennessy."

"I don't know you," she said vehemently, swatting at him as he came nearer and knelt down at her feet. "I don't know you. Go away! Go away or I'll scream!"

"It's all right, Addie," Bryan said in a soft voice. He never broke eye contact with her as he reached out and captured one of her frail hands in his. "It's all right. It's me, Hennessy."

"I don't know you!" she shouted, panic rolling through her like a tidal wave as she stared at him. She fought the horrible fog that clouded her mind, searching for a memory of this man's face. A part of her thought she should know him, which only made her more desperate to find something there that she couldn't quite grasp. Tears spilled down her cheeks, and she slumped on the bench in abject misery, mumbling, "I don't know you. I don't know you."

Bryan settled himself on the bench beside Addie and pulled her thin, trembling body into his arms. Cradling her against him, he stroked a big hand over her hair, and, rocking her gently back and forth, he began singing to her. It was a soft, sweet song he'd learned in Scotland about a girl named Annie Laurie, who was fair and lovely with a voice like a summer wind's sigh. His voice rose and fell with the melody, and trembled a bit as he ached with Addie's pain and confusion. But he sang on, the gentle notes coming from his heart, just as they had when he'd held Serena and sung to her.

Rachel stood at the edge of the clearing in the maze, her body shaking. She had gone into the house, intending to speak with Addie about selling the place, but her mother had been nowhere around. She'd run out into the yard to get Bryan to help her look for Addie, and the sound of crying had drawn her to the overgrown maze.

She stood there now, unable to move or breathe. She stared at the scene before her: Bryan, his eyes closed, but a lone pair of tears escaping the outer corners, holding her mother and singing to her; and Addie rocking back and forth within the embrace of his strong arms, crying.

"It's all right, Addie," Bryan murmured, kissing the old woman's temple. "It's all right if you don't know me. I'll still help you."

It struck Rachel then. As she stood there with her defenses stripped away by raw emotion, with her heart laid bare and the truth confronting her with nowhere for her to hide. She was in love with Bryan Hennessy. And it wasn't a question of whether or not he was the kind of man she needed, it was a question of whether or not she deserved to have the kind of man he was.

EIGHT

"Is Addie asleep?" Bryan asked, looking up from the papers he had spread out on the desk. A small brass lamp illuminated his work area. The only other light in the room came from the fireplace. Shadows jumped on the dark paneled walls.

"Finally," Rachel said on a sigh. She leaned a hip against the desk and allowed her shoulders to sag beneath the weight of her worries. "She wouldn't let me in her room, but I managed to peek inside once it got quiet. She wore her garden boots to bed. I could see them sticking up under the coverlet. I wanted to go in and take them off for her, but I'm sure she would have hit me in the head with a rock and called the police."

Bryan frowned. "Back to square one, eh?"

"I'd do handsprings if we were that far along," Rachel said dryly. "I tried to explain to her that selling the house is the only practical thing, but she didn't want to hear it." She held up a hand as Bryan opened his mouth to speak. "Please refrain from saying you told me so. In fact, a change of subject would be warmly welcomed."

"You're an absolute vision in that dress." He gave her a wicked smile and forced all thoughts of the mundane from his mind.

Rachel beamed as if his words had injected new energy into her. She was wearing the beaded burgundy gown, the same gown that had so mysteriously appeared on her bed that first night she'd had dinner at Drake House. Addie claimed it was Wimsey who insisted they dress for the evening meal, but Rachel didn't see the difference. It was Addie who became upset if she showed up underdressed, so it was Addie she dressed for—most nights.

Tonight she had chosen the burgundy dress without a thought about her mother. She had chosen it because she wanted to feel special and feminine and alluring. She had laid it out on her bed before her bath, and when she had returned, there had been a white rose lying on it.

"How did you know that was the perfect thing to say?" she murmured, settling her hip more comfortably against the desk.

"I'm psychic," Bryan admitted with a smile. "I'll go out on a limb and say that you're probably a vision out of that dress as well."

His voice was dark with desire. The rich quality of it stroked her senses like the caress of the silk she wore.

"Have you been spying on me in the bathtub?" she asked, conjuring up a teasing note to cut through her own sudden rush of yearning.

"Not exactly," Bryan mumbled cryptically. He fixed his gaze on the steaming cup she held, breathing deep of the aroma and sighing in appreciation. "Coffee."

"Would you like a cup? I'll go back to the kitchen—"

"Don't bother," he said, not wanting to lose sight of her. "Just let me have a sip of yours."

Warmth curled inside Rachel as if he had just made a terribly erotic suggestion. She bit the inside of her lip and offered him the mug, sucking in a breath when his fingertips brushed hers. Her senses were so heightened, the slightest glance or touch from him set her nerves sizzling. She had spent her entire time in the bathtub reliving the few kisses they had shared and imagining what it would be like to make love with him, fantasizing until she had hardly been able to stand the brush of the washcloth against her skin.

She had come to a decision about Bryan, about the desire that burned inside her. She had a long, hard road ahead of her. Her future didn't look particularly bright, but for the present she had Bryan. She would have been a fool not to take what happiness she could while she had the chance.

Bryan looked up at her, his blue eyes sharp with awareness. He could sense the shift in Rachel's feelings toward him. They had been changing gradually, constantly, since they'd met, but tonight she had taken a giant step in his direction.

He wasn't sure what had pushed her over the edge in his favor, but he wasn't inclined to question his good fortune either. He was a conscientious man, but he was a man first. A man with needs.

It was a cold, rainy night. The kind of night a man wanted to spend curled up in bed with the lady of his heart, making love to her until they both drifted off into exhausted sleep. He hadn't been able to get that image out of his head all evening. Nor had he been able to stop picturing her in the bathtub, sliding a bar of scented soap over her slick skin. That image still seemed particularly strong. He could see the gleam of light on her wet skin. He could smell the soap. Even now the vision played through his mind, and heat coiled in his belly.

Never taking his eyes from Rachel's, he sipped at the coffee and set the cup aside. Her eyes darkened from violet to deep purple, and a flush crept along under the surface of her fair skin.

"You must be cold," he murmured, pushing himself up from his chair. He pulled his tuxedo jacket off and draped it around her shoulders before she could object. In a move he'd perfected as a teenager, he let one arm slide down her back and fastened his hand on the curve of her hip as he herded her toward the love seat.

Rachel gave him a look. "That's an old trick, Hennessy."

"I'm an old guy," he quipped, and then winced. "I shouldn't have mentioned that. You may not have noticed."

"I'm not concerned. You seem able-bodied to me."

"You don't know the half of it," he muttered, gritting his teeth at the surge of anticipation that stirred in his loins.

"But I guess I'll find out, won't I?" Rachel said softly, lowering her gaze in genuine shyness as they settled on the love seat.

Bryan was so stunned, he felt as if he'd taken a punch to the gut. He hooked a finger beneath her chin and tilted her head up. The sight of the firelight glowing on her face nearly made him forget what it was he'd meant to ask. Holy Mike, she was lovely, and, unless he'd completely lost his ability to read women, she wanted him. After all the fighting she'd done against the attraction that pulled between them, she was admitting she wanted him. Wasn't she?

"Rachel," he began, his voice low and hoarse, "just what are you saying?"

She made a little face. "I was hoping I wasn't going to have to say it. You're a perceptive man—can't you figure it out?"

"Yes, I guess what I need to know is why."

"Does it matter?"

"Yes."

Rachel looked toward the fire, her expression pensive. She couldn't bring herself to tell him she was in love with him. Not when she knew what they could have was only temporary. Not when she wasn't certain of his feelings for her. He had mentioned love in passing that morning, but that didn't mean anything. In her meager experience, love was a word some men tossed around too casually. And Bryan was by nature so openly giving of himself, she might have been reading too much into his attitude toward her. She suspected he had strong feelings for her. She knew he wanted her. But love . . .

Besides, it was so soon. They had known each other such a short time, he was liable to think she's lost her mind if she told him she was falling in love with him.

But none of that seemed to matter. What was left of her mind had made itself up as she'd stood in the shadows of the maze, watching Bryan comfort her mother. It had all struck her with a force so powerful, she'd nearly fallen to her knees. She loved him. There was no future in it, but that didn't seem important now. As she'd stood there, watching her mother cry, she had realized just how suddenly tomorrow could slip away.

Over the past five years she had told herself that one day she would return and make things right between herself and Addie. One day. Tomorrow. Now tomorrow had come and it was too late, and all those days that could have been were nothing more than wishes that would never come true. She didn't need any more regrets haunting her life. She would take what Bryan could give her now, love him while she could, and deal with the consequences later.

She turned back to him with pleading in her eyes. "Bryan, please don't—"

"Shh." He pressed a finger to her lips as he leaned close. A soft, secretive smile curved his mouth, and his blue eyes shone like lapis lazuli. "It's all right," he whispered. "It's all right."

He lowered his mouth then, and kissed her slowly, sweetly, deeply. It was a kiss not of possession, but of sharing. It was a kiss that stirred the hunger in them both and sparked the desires banked inside them to flare into full flame. Questions and motives slipped away, were burned away by needs. He needed to love her. She needed to feel his strong arms around her.

Bryan slipped his coat from Rachel's shoulders and spread it out on the rug in front of the fire. Kneeling there, he reached a hand up to her in invitation. She smiled as she settled her hand in his and joined him on the floor.

"This is romantic," she whispered, cuddling against him knee to knee, thigh to thigh, happy just to be close to him.

He brushed her long hair back, baring one shoulder. "Romantic, hell," he murmured, lowering his mouth to nibble kisses along the creamy line of flesh. The ache in his groin made him pause to grit his teeth, and he shook his head in amazement. He was as eager as an untried kid. He chuckled and nipped at her chin. "I'm just afraid you'd change your mind on the way upstairs."

Rachel laughed softly, marveling at this man's ability to lighten her mood. Even now, when she was trembling with nervous anticipation, Bryan was able to tease a giggle out of her. It was one of the things she loved most about him.

She raised her hands and tugged loose the bow tie that perched crookedly on the collar of his shirt. Her fingers moved down the neatly pleated shirtfront, revealing a V of hard flesh where the snowy white fabric parted and fell away from the contours of his chest. He held still as she peeled the garment back from his broad shoulders and let it fall to the floor behind him.

She paused a moment to simply look at him, to drink in the sight of his solid chest and the ridged muscles of his belly. Firelight caught in the curls scattered across his chest, turning them gold. Her breath caught as her gaze rested on the small brown mole above his left nipple. Somehow she had known it would be there, but she had no time to wonder how, because Bryan was reaching for her.

His thumbs hooked under the loose straps of her gown and drew them down over her shoulders. He traced his fingertips along the line of the bodice, gently pulling it down, slowly uncovering her. Her small, full breasts plumped themselves into his hands as the dress slipped away, her nipples tightening instantly as his thumbs brushed across them. The gown pooled at her knees in a wine-colored drift studded with sparkling black stars.

"So lovely," he whispered, gazing at her in open admiration. "So soft."

He drew his hands downward, following the indentation of her slender waist and the outward slope of her hips, drawing her lace panties down as his exploration moved on to her thighs. Rachel struggled for air as his fingers traced delicate patterns on the satin-soft skin on the inside of her legs. She moaned and bit her lip as he delved into the tender warmth between them, his fingers parting the feminine petals and stroking the aching bud hidden there.

Heat flared through her hotter than the flames that lit their makeshift bed. She leaned into him, gasping at the feel of his flesh against hers, her feminine softness against the hard contours of his masculine body. It was wonderful. It was like coming back to a place she belonged. She rubbed herself against him in a sinuous caress, her hands sliding up his arms to knead the tight muscles in his shoulders and neck. She tangled her fingers in his hair, then brought her hands forward, pulling his glasses off and setting them aside on the low butler's table.

"You don't need these to see, do you?"

"That's okay," he murmured, bending his head to kiss her ear. "I'm good with my hands."

Rachel's giggle turned to a sensuous purr as his big hands slid down her back to cup her buttocks, his fingers kneading her flesh in a way that made her breath flutter in her throat. "So I noticed."

He pulled her hard against him then, letting her feel the strength of his arousal as he took her mouth once more. This kiss was hotter and wilder than the last, hinting at the passion he was struggling to keep in check. His tongue stroked over hers, teasing, tasting, claiming possession.

Rachel pulled her mouth from his and dragged her lips down the strong column of his neck to his chest. Her tongue darted out to tease one flat brown nipple. His flesh beaded into a tight knot;

Rachel impulsively took it into her mouth and sucked on it gently, excitement shooting through her when Bryan groaned in appreciation.

She had never felt so uninhibited with a man. She had expected to feel shy with Bryan; instead, she felt strong and right and so very turned on. She wanted him with an intensity she had never known. She wanted to please him in ways she had never dreamed of. The desire swept through her, overwhelming her normally practical, sensible self, and she let go of that drab cloak of responsibility like a butterfly shedding its cocoon.

Her kisses followed the faint line of downy hair that bisected Bryan's flat abdomen as her hands undid the front of his trousers. Her tongue dipped into his navel. She lowered his trousers and briefs in one motion and another hot flame of desire coursed through her as she revealed his manhood.

He was eager for her. She brushed her thumb across the velvet flesh, drawing another groan from him.

Bryan's control broke with a snap that was almost audible. In the next instant, Rachel found herself on her back, staring up at him as he peeled away the last of her clothes. He stood and shucked his pants. Notes flew from the pockets like confetti as he flung the trousers aside.

He settled himself beside her then, his gaze flowing over her with a heat that seemed scorching in its intensity, and his hand followed the path his gaze had burned along her skin. He caressed her breasts with exquisite care, teasing them to a sensitivity that was nearly unbearable. Only when she began to beg him did he lower his head and take one taut peak into his mouth. At the same instant he swept a hand down over her quivering belly to the apex of her thighs and eased a finger inside her.

Rachel's hips leapt off the floor, arching into his touch in rhythm to the tug of his mouth on her breast. She moaned, but didn't recognize the sound as her own. The sensations building inside her were incredible and overwhelming as they intensified. The coil of desire tightened in her belly with each hard pull of his mouth on her nipple, with each deep stroke of his finger. When his thumb moved to rub against her most sensitive flesh, she was certain she would explode, but still the feelings built. She tangled her fingers in his hair and tugged, frantic in a way she had never experienced.

"Bryan, please," she said with a gasp. "I want more. I want all of you. Please."

He needed no more invitation than that. His own body, so long denied, was screaming for release. He knelt between her parted thighs, struggling to draw breath as he looked down at her. She was everything a man wanted in the woman he loved—open to him, eager for him, her hips arched up toward him in invitation. Grinding his teeth, he fought for some measure of control, reached for her hand, and closed it around his throbbing shaft.

"Guide me, Rachel," he whispered.

He kissed her as she led him into her body, his

tongue delving into the dark warmth of her mouth as his maleness slid into the tight warmth of her womanhood. He groaned as she took him into her measure by measure, her breath catching at each small thrust until he was fully embedded inside her.

Again Rachel felt that sense of coming home, which seemed odd considering she was on the verge of shattering into a million shards. She thought she should have been terrified, teetering on the brink of something she knew instinctively would be overwhelming, but she wasn't. With Bryan she felt safe. He would be there to catch her. He would be there to gather the pieces together again. He might not be there over the long haul, but he was there now. Oh, was he there now!

"Oh, Bryan," she moaned in rapture, rolling her hips into his. "You're so . . ."

"I know," he managed to say through his teeth, gasping as her body tightened around him. "Am I too ... ?"

"No. It's wonderful." Oh, so wonderful. But it was nothing compared to what she felt when he began to move.

He eased nearly out of her, then thrust deep and hard. His chest heaved like a bellows as he levered himself above her on his arms and repeated the process. Sweat beaded on his forehead and chest as he struggled with the effort to hold back. It had been so long, and he wanted her so badly. He could feel his climax rushing toward him like a freight train. He eased out of her again and reached between them as he began what he knew would be his final thrust, teasing her already sensitive flesh as he buried himself inside her.

Rachel bit her lip, fighting back the cry of completion as her hips strained upward against his and he took her over the brink. The explosion that rocked her went on and on. Her consciousness dimmed as she clutched at Bryan's back. He had collapsed against her, spent, and she hung on to him as the sensation of floating filled her with a sweet golden bliss.

This was making love. This was magic.

Magic, she mused, a tender smile curving her lips. Maybe there was such a thing after all.

Bryan rolled onto his back, holding Rachel to him so that she ended up sprawled on his chest. Their bodies were still joined, and he savored every aftershock of the shattering climax she had experienced. He ran a hand over the pale silken curtain of her hair.

"I'd break into song, but I think I'm beyond words," he murmured.

He pressed a kiss to her temple and hugged her tight, a fierce sense of rightness surging through him. Fear came close on its heels. He felt so certain about this love growing within him for Rachel, but did Rachel feel that way about him? Had she merely given in to the feelings overwhelming her? After the day she'd had with Addie and with the prospective buyers for the house, had she simply not possessed the strength to fight the attraction? Or had she needed a chance to escape it all for a few glorious moments? Perhaps the thing that frightened him most was that he wasn't so sure he cared what her motives had been. The love he felt for her was growing so that he was ready to accept her on whatever terms she wanted.

The seed of love was there in her heart. He knew that. Or was it just what he wanted to believe?

"Rachel," he murmured, his heart pounding. "If you're going to regret this, tell me now."

Rachel lifted her head, brushing her hair back behind one ear. She stared down at him, her heart aching at the vulnerability she saw in his eyes. "No," she whispered. "No regrets. I have too many of them already. I don't regret making love with you, Bryan."

She regretted that it wouldn't last. She regretted that her future wouldn't include him and his crazy magic tricks and his contagious optimism. But she wouldn't regret anything that passed between them. She would take what time she had with Bryan and make the most of it, and she would cherish the memories afterward, but she wouldn't regret a minute of it.

Bryan looked up into her dark eyes and smiled sadly. It didn't take a mind reader to see what she was thinking. He barely had to make use of his special gift, the gift that had slowly been returning to him in the time since he'd met Rachel and become a part of her life. She still didn't believe in the magic they shared, but she would. Come hell or high water, she would. He would see to it.

"What?" she asked, startled by the sudden fierceness of his expression.

"I was just thinking," he said, willing himself to relax. He pulled Rachel's head down to his chest and stroked her hair as he might stroke a cat, rhythmically, absently, soothingly as he dredged up the courage to tell her what was in his heart.

"The first time I went to bed with a woman after my wife died I went into the bathroom afterward and threw up for half an hour. She was a nice lady, a colleague of mine, pretty. She . . . expressed an interest, and I . . . needed to." He forced the words out, still uncomfortable with the memory. "It seemed harmless enough. We were taking care of each other's needs. But when it was over, I felt so empty and so disgusted with myself, it literally made me sick. I told her I had the flu, but she knew better. I decided then and there that there wasn't going to be a next time until I could honestly call it making love."

"Are you telling me I shouldn't get too comfortable?" Rachel asked with forced lightness. She pulled away from him a bit, raising her head, bracing herself.

For once Bryan didn't grin or answer with a joke. He reached up and tucked a strand of hair behind her ear. "I'm telling you I love you, Rachel. I'm telling you I'm feeling something I didn't expect to feel again for a long, long time." He rolled her beneath him again and stared down at her with undisguised hunger in his eyes. "I'm telling you I want to take you upstairs and make love to you until the sun comes up. What do you have to say about that?"

Say? She was supposed to say something? With her heart in her throat and her brain suddenly numb, she was supposed to think of something to say? She swallowed hard and raised her head as his mouth descended toward hers, and whispered just before their lips met. "I'm praying for an eclipse."

Flowers. What a lovely dream. There were flowers everywhere. Rachel sighed and burrowed deeper into the soft mattress of the old bed, a smile curving her mouth. There were flowers of every kind and color, delicate wild blossoms with the softest, sweetest scents clinging to their petals. She could feel them against her, cool and dew-damp. They rained down on her and fluttered over every exposed inch of her skin like a hundred silken kisses. And Bryan was the magician responsible for this wonderful illusion.

She couldn't see him in her dream, but Rachel knew he was the one responsible, just as she knew he was the one who had left a rose on her pillow every night since she'd come to Drake House.

Bryan. Her smile widened and she purred in almost feline appreciation as she stretched on the bed. As he'd promised, he had made love to her all night. While the rain had fallen outside the windows of her turret bedroom and the cold wind had howled, Bryan had warmed her with kisses and caresses. He had awakened in her a woman she had scarcely realized existed, a woman of uninhibited passion. He had taken her to heights she had only imagined and set her soul free from the past and the future.

The future. A cloud scudded across the surface of her dream. Now that she knew what real love was, it hurt worse to think of a future without it, but she pushed the thought aside. She had vowed to take no regrets with her when she left for San Francisco, so she concentrated instead on her dream and the flowers.

"Rachel." His voice came to her through the soft fog of sleep. "Rachel."

Stretching, she raised her eyelids to half mast and rolled onto her back. The light in the room was dim, but one thing was clear—it was snowing. She could see Bryan through the flakes falling down all around her. He was standing beside the bed, wearing his jeans, his glasses, and a wickedly sexy smile. She wondered why he didn't look cold, bare-chested in the snow.

Snow? Her drowsy brain struggled to function. They were in Drake House. It couldn't possibly be snowing, not even in this strange place.

"Bryan?" she asked, coming more fully awake. She pushed herself up in bed, looking around, puzzlement creasing a little line between her eyebrows. "What in the . . . ? Flowers!"

She laughed out loud in delight when she realized what he was doing. He was showering her with flowers! The petals covered the bed in multi-colored drifts—pink and blue and violet and yellow and white. They clung to her skin and hair and to the ivory lace bodice of her nightgown. The cloud of fragrance rising from them was intoxicating.

Bryan dropped the last of the blooms and joined her on the bed, scooping her into his arms and rolling through the fragrant cloud, laughing as petals stuck to the lenses of his glasses. He leaned down and kissed her with enthusiasm and rising passion.

"Since you keep accusing me of bringing you flowers, I decided I might as well go all out," he murmured, nuzzling her neck. "Mmmm . . . they smell almost as good as you do."

Rachel scooped up a handful and rubbed them down his bare back. "Where did you get them?"

He smiled as he rose up above her, but his gaze was hot as he lowered the thin straps of her peachy-pink negligee, baring her breasts. "Magic," he said, his voice turning low and velvety as desire flared anew in his eyes.

As Rachel had done, he scooped up wildflowers in his hands and caressed her with them, crushing them as he cupped her breasts. He lowered his head and took one nipple into his mouth, sucking at that tender bud of flesh and the pansy petal that clung to it. His hands swept down her hips, tugging her nightgown up out of his way.

He turned onto his side and admired the view as he showered a handful of flower petals down on the bare skin of her belly and thighs. Sliding down on the bed, he blew gently across her abdomen, sending the buds skittering. With a purposeful look on his handsome face, he parted her legs and settled himself between them, planting kisses on the petals that clung to her inner thighs.

Rachel raised herself up on her elbows, her hair tumbling around her as she watched him, wrapped in sensual fascination stronger than any narcotic. With gentle fingers Bryan parted her most tender flesh and caressed her intimately with the bud of a wild rose. She gasped at the feel of velvet brushing her, cool and damp against her heat. He caressed her again, then lowered his head and tasted her, kissing her softly at first, hesitantly, increasing the pressure slowly, opening his mouth over her and stroking her with his tongue until she was sobbing at the intensity of her pleasure.

He kneeled then, and lifted her into his arms, pulling her against him and kissing her deeply. His lips trailed to her ear, where he traced the danity shell with the tip of his tongue and whispered, "And they taste almost as good as you do too."

Rachel purred and arched against him. A languid smile lifted one corner of her mouth as she reached between them and undid Bryan's zipper. She tugged the denim down his lean hips, scooped up two handfuls of flowers, and encased his manhood in cool soft petals, wringing a gasp from him. She stroked him with them as she planted kisses across his chest. Then it was her turn to gasp as he lifted her against him. She dropped the flowers, her hands going up automatically to his broad shoulders as he pulled her hips to his and joined their bodies once more.

The light in the room was considerably brighter when Rachel awoke for the second time. Bryan's tousled head was on her breast, one of his long, hairy legs was thrown across both of her considerably smoother ones. He was humming the Notre Dame fight song in his sleep.

"Bryan," she murmured softly. "Wake up."

He grumbled and growled, finally lifting his head and pushing his glasses up on his nose. "What time is it?"

Rachel reached to the nightstand for his wristwatch and peered at it, shaking her head. "Three-ten, Bryan Hennessy time. Do you ever intend to set this thing correctly?"

"Oh, sure," Bryan said, hauling himself up to lean back against the ornately carved headboard. "I'm sure I wrote myself a note to do it." He scratched his kneecap through the sheet, looking puzzled. "I wonder what became of that note."

"It's quarter to seven," Rachel said, consulting her travel alarm.

Time to get up and face the day, she thought. Her gaze roamed over the tangle of sheets and flower petals, and she smiled. With a night like this last one to remember, the day wasn't going to be quite so hard to face.

She yawned, stretched, and scratched her arm. Snuggling against Bryan's hard shoulder, she said coyly, "Thank you for the flowers. I loved them."

Bryan turned his head and kissed her temple. "And I love you."

Rachel's heart jumped. She couldn't get used to hearing him say that. She was afraid to say it back for fear the spell would be broken somehow, afraid she would be putting too much pressure on him, expecting too much of him.

She sifted a handful of petals through her fingers and scratched absently at her left hip. "Making love in flowers is the most romantic thing I can think of."

"Flowers are romantic," Bryan agreed absently. He shoved the sheet down and stared, frowning at his belly as he scratched it. "Ants aren't."

"Ants?" Rachel questioned, scratching her shoulder.

"Hmmm, yes," he said. "It seems we have a bed full of them. They must have ridden in on the flowers," he ventured, but his explanation was lost on Rachel, who shrieked and leapt from the bed, shaking herself like a wet dog. He watched her grab up her robe, thrust her arms into the sleeves, and bolt for the door.

"Have a nice shower!" he called, laughing, then he found a scrap of paper and a pen on the nightstand and he wrote himself a note—Beware of Ants.

NINE

Rachel stood outside the door to her mother's bedroom, as nervous as she had been at fifteen when she had needed to ask permission to go on her first date. She was freshly showered, debugged, and looked as presentable, in her black dirndl skirt and lavender cotton blouse, as any voice teacher she had ever encountered. Her hair was secured in its knot at the back of her head and only a few tendrils had as yet escaped to frame her face.

It occurred to her that she shouldn't have had to go to such pains to see her own mother. A mother wasn't supposed to care about appearances. A mother was supposed to be accepting of her children whether they were in rags or designer wear. But it was that line of thinking that had caused the problems between her and Addie in the first place, so Rachel stopped that train of thought before it ran out of control.

It was a new day, a day for beginnings. She felt fresh and strong, rested despite the precious little sleep she'd had. Spending the night in Bryan's arms had revitalized her, recharged her. She was brimming with energy and ready to take on whatever the day had in store for her. As she had showered the flower petals and ants from her skin, she had come to the conclusion that she would redouble her efforts to solve the problem with Addie.

Rachel raised her hand to knock at the door, but it suddenly fell open as if someone on the other side had jerked it back. Addie, however, was standing across the room in a yellow flowered housedress, scowling into her mirror as she struggled with the task of braiding her hair. She crossed one strand over, twisted it around again, pulled another across, then swore and let go the entire mess to start again.

It was clear to Rachel that her mother had either forgotten how to braid or the message from her brain to her hands was getting lost somewhere along the way; apraxia was the term the doctors used for it. In either case, it was sad, and it reminded Rachel yet again of how their roles were being reversed. She could easily remember Addie painstakingly plaiting her long hair on her first day of kindergarten, how she had sat very still on the wire vanity stool in her mother's bedroom, staring wide-eyed into the mirror as her mother's fingers had magically tamed her wild locks.

"Mother?" she asked softly, forcing herself to step into the room before her memories could steal her courage from her. "Can I help you with that?"

Addie stared at her daughter, wondering just how much Rachel had seen. "Don't you know how to knock?"

"It was open."

Addie muttered, "Wimsey. Meddling old coot."

Rachel ignored the odd remark. Taking a brush from the cluttered dresser, she went to stand behind her mother and began working on the hair that had once been as golden as her own, but had now paled to silver.

"I can do my own hair," Addie said, staring at their reflections in the mirror.

"I know you can. I just want to help. Like you used to help me."

Their gazes met in the glass, and Addie's heart lurched. She had done everything for Rachel. She had been both mother and father. She had raised her daughter without help from anyone. She had held down two jobs at a time and had never run out of energy or drive. Now that daughter was standing behind her, braiding her hair because she suddenly wasn't able to manage so simple a task herself.

"I believe I'll wear it down today," she said, moving away from the dresser. In the mirror she could see Rachel standing with her hands still raised, the hairbrush in one, reaching out toward her. Her daughter's eyes were filled with hurt. Rachel let her arms fall to her sides as Addie moved another step out of reach.

She found a black sweater lying at the foot of the bed and put it on inside out. "I'm going down to breakfast. Hennessy should have the toast done by now."

Rachel stood by the dresser, twisting the hairbrush around in her hands. Every ounce of that newfound strength had drained out of her. "Why won't you let me help you?" she asked softly, hurting in a way that is peculiar to mother-daughter relationships—a deep, sharp hurt, like a needle piercing her heart.

"I don't need any help," Addie replied, squaring her bony shoulders with stubborn pride. "Not from you or Wimsey or anyone. I have managed quite well on my own for some time now, as you well know."

With that she clomped out of the room, her boots thumping on the wood floor. Rachel closed her eyes and counted to ten, wrestling her temper and her tears under control.

"No luck?"

Startled, she looked up to find Bryan standing not two feet away. She shook her head, at a loss for words. She wasn't sure she would have trusted herself to say them anyway. Her emotions were running dangerously close to the surface, muddied and churning like floodwaters. She had the strange feeling that if she let them out, they would swell up and drown her.

"You'll work it out," Bryan said gently, taking the hairbrush from her fingers and setting it aside. He gathered her into his arms and hugged her close, pressing soft kisses to her hair. "It'll all work out. You'll see."

Rachel let her hands sneak inside the old cardigan he wore unbuttoned. Her arms slid around his lean waist. She nuzzled her cheek against his Chicago Cubs T-shirt, taking comfort in the solid muscle beneath the soft gray fabric. She noticed he didn't say "give it time." Time was not on their side. A little bit of Addie slipped away with every grain of sand in the hourglass. But he offered her his strength and his comfort, and she loved him for that.

"Here now, enough of this," Bryan said, standing her back from him. There was a devilish twinkle in his eye. Rachel realized with a start that he was wearing a bedraggled black top hat. "I know you can't get enough of me, but I won't spoil you—unless you beg me to," he added with a wicked grin.

"Conceited man," she said, fighting back a chuckle. "I should beg you to have your head examined. Why are you wearing that ridiculous hat?"

"Ridiculous?" he questioned, highly offended. "I'll have you know this hat was given to me by Anton Figg-Newton, master magician of England."

He rolled the hat down his arm Fred Astaire–style and presented it to her upside down.

"Just reach in there and see what you find, girlie."

Cautiously, Rachel leaned over and peered into the hat, narrowing her eyes in suspicion. "There's nothing in there."

Bryan made a great show of looking into the hat himself, turning it over, and shaking it.

"I think you got taken on that one, Merlin," Rachel quipped.

A gleam came into Bryan's eye. "Oh, ye of little or no faith. I merely forgot to say the magic word."

"The magic word," Rachel parroted flatly. She crossed her arms over her chest and tapped her foot in mock impatience.

"Marshmallows!" he intoned dramatically, and tapped the brim of the hat three times with the fingers of his left hand. This time he reached inside, and when he withdrew his hand, he was holding a brooch of intricately worked silver fili-gree set with a translucent stone of deep purple.

Rachel's mouth dropped open as he handed it to her. It was an exquisite thing that looked to be very old and very valuable. The stone gleamed as it caught the morning light that streamed in through the window.

"Bryan, it's beautiful," she whispered reverently. "Where did you find it?"

"In my hat. Jeez, Rachel, I think your memory is worse than mine."

"Really," she insisted, fingering the brooch lov-ingly. "I've never seen anything like it. Is it an heirloom or something?"

He cleared his throat and looked uncomfortable. "I came across it in a country that frowns on exporting such things. You're probably better off not knowing."

She gave him a suspicious look, wondering, not

for the first time, just who Bryan Hennessy really was.

"Legend has it that when a man gives this brooch to the lady of his heart, she'll love him into eternity," he said, taking the gift from her and pinning it carefully to the throat of her prim blouse. The stone picked up and intensified the color of her eyes, making Bryan's breath catch. A crooked, self-deprecating smile tugged up one corner of his mouth. "It's a custom also known as hedging your bets."

"Thank you," Rachel whispered, smiling at him. She rose up on her toes and kissed his cheek. Practically in the blink of an eye he had lifted her mood out of the doldrums. He was amazing and wonderful, and if she could tell him nothing else, she could at least tell him that. "What an extraordinarily sweet, bizarre man you are."

Remarkably, he blushed, and Rachel's heart swelled a little more with love for him. Grinning, she plunked his magic hat upon his head, grabbed his hand, and pulled him toward the door.

"Come on, Hennessy. Let's go get some breakfast. I'm starved."

"What's your hurry?" Bryan asked, patting her bottom with a loving hand. "Ants in your pants?"

"Very funny."

They sauntered down the grand staircase together, hand in hand, smiling at each other the way only lovers do, arguing amicably over how they would spend the day. Rachel insisted there was no time for anything other than marking prices on the antiques that would be offered at the tag sale in two days. Bryan insisted there was more than enough time for a stroll along the beach. But as they neared the kitchen, he broke off in mid-rebuttal and held a finger to his lips, suddenly alert to something going on in the next room. Together they inched toward the door, listening.

"You're a meddling, bone-headed Democrat, Wimsey," Addie said. "Just keep that long nose of yours out of my affairs. I don't need you. I don't need anybody."

There was silence then. Bryan held his breath as he tried to tune in, hoping for anything—a sigh, a vibration in the air, anything.

"Keep your opinions to yourself, you blithering British idiot," Addie snapped.

The rattling of pots and pans blocked out whatever response she might have gotten, and Bryan frowned in frustration. Rachel rolled her eyes in impatience.

"She's just talking to herself," she insisted in a harsh whisper.

Bryan ground his teeth. If only he had enough equipment to monitor every room in the blasted house. He had chosen to concentrate on the study and the foyer. Of course, Rachel wouldn't have believed Wimsey was in the kitchen if the ghost had walked up to her and kissed her on the nose.

"This is ridiculous," Rachel muttered. "Every sensible person knows there's no such thing as ghosts."

As soon as the last word left her mouth, the kitchen door swung inward so quickly neither of them had a chance to brace themselves, and they both went sprawling across the cracked linoleum. On the far side of the room Addie stood staring at them, a gray cloud billowing around her.

Bryan's eyes widened at the sight. "An apparition," he whispered.

"Apparition nothing," Rachel said, clambering to her feet. "The kitchen's on fire!"

Smoke rolled out of the old cookstove, an appliance that hadn't seen action since Thomas Edison was in short pants. Rachel grabbed her mother's hand and jerked her away from the thing while Bryan, who had scrambled to his feet, grabbed the fire extinguisher and blasted the blaze with white foam.

"Hennessy! You're ruining my eggs!"

"Mother," Rachel said between her teeth, "you were ruining the house. That stove doesn't work."

"Of course I know that," Addie grumbled, but there was uncertainty in her eyes as she looked around the room as if seeing it for the first time.

"You should have waited for us to come down," Rachel said, her temper rising like steam in a pressure cooker. Why couldn't Addie accept her help? Was she going to cling to that damned stubborn pride of hers until she burned the house down around them?

Addie bristled like a cat. "I don't take orders from you, missy!"

She hauled back to punch Rachel on the arm, but Bryan caught her fist in his hand and pulled her into his arms.

"Come on, beautiful. Let's go dance in the fresh

air while Cinderella cleans up the kitchen. Maybe we'll run into Wimsey."

"Pompous, presumptuous pinhead," Addie said with a snarl, though it wasn't clear whether she was referring to her invisible friend or to Bryan. She dug the heels of her rubber boots into the floor and gave him an amazed look. "Why on earth are you wearing that ridiculous hat?"

"There's a rabbit in it," Bryan said, coaxing her toward the door as Rachel began flinging pots off the stove in a rage. "I thought you might want hasenpfeffer for breakfast."

"You're an idiot, Hennessy," Addie declared, but followed him out of the room nevertheless.

"I'll second that," Rachel grumbled, poking at the debris inside the cookstove with a tongs. "Ghosts. What intelligent man with degrees from two major universities believes in ghosts? What intelligent woman falls in love with a man who believes in ghosts? Ghosts. The man must have been hit over the head with something when he was young."

She bent over to look inside the oven, and an enamel pot tipped off the cooking surface and bounced off her skull. She stared at the pot as it rolled across the floor, sure she had knocked it over during her initial burst of fury. Dismissing it, she turned her attention to the mess her mother had made.

"Oh, no . . ." she said on a long groan.

With her tongs she fished out a stack of half-burned mail. She flipped through the ruined envelopes, her heart sinking. Bills. Bills that had never been opened. Bills that had certainly never been paid. She bent over again and tugged out another long envelope, this one only slightly charred, and her heart dropped from low to the pit of her stomach, where it lay like a rock.

"Ooooh, noooo . . ."

"What is it?" Bryan asked, returning to the kitchen without his dancing partner.

In a daze, Rachel handed him the envelope. "You know how you keep saying something will turn up? Something just did."

Bryan took the letter out, pushed his glasses up on his nose, and began to read to himself. He paled a bit beneath his tan and handed the piece of stationery back to Rachel, muttering, "Oh, no . . ."

Feeling as if all her bones were dissolving, Rachel sank down on a chair at the kitchen table and stared across the room in a trance. It wasn't the first time she had seen a letter like this one. It was, however, the first time she had felt dizzy because of it.

The IRS was going to audit Lindquist Antiques

Visions of Leavenworth danced in her head.

She looked up at Bryan and forced the corners of her mouth into a parody of a smile. "Got anything in your magic hat for this one, Mr. Hennessy?"

"I am not moving from this house." Addie pressed her lips into a thin line and crossed her arms over her meager bosom. She leaned back into the worn red velvet of an enormous thronelike Victorian chair, settling in for the battle.

Rachel and Bryan had spent the day working their way through the huge maze of rooms that made up Drake House, tagging the antiques that would be offered at the sale. It had been a long day of building tension. Addie had trailed after them, pulling the tags off the furniture and complaining incessantly about the way Rachel was treating her. Twice she had called the police to tell them she was being robbed. Twice Rachel had had to call them back and tell them it was another false alarm. Meals had been stilted affairs seasoned with sharp remarks. Addie's mood had darkened with every hour, and Rachel's control on her temper had worn down to the last frayed threads.

Bryan watched both women with a terrible sense of foreboding. He could feel Rachel's tension, the hurt and anger that had been simmering just under her lovely surface for days. Her jaw was set at a mutinous angle and trembled with the emotion she was struggling to keep in check. And Addie, who had been on a rampage all day, showed no signs of backing down.

He pulled his glasses off and rubbed at his eyes. He was exhausted from intercepting Rachel's feelings all day and from running interference between the two Lindquist women, but it was clear there would be no rest for the weary this evening.

"Addie, you look like a queen in that chair," he said, flashing one of his inane smiles. "Did I ever tell you about the time I met the queen of Sweden?"

"Could she sing?" Addie asked. "Rachel used to

sing, you know. She had a voice like an angel, but she wasted it, and now we're destitute."

"Addie, that's not fair—"

"No, she's right, Bryan," Rachel said with a frightening smile. She threw her hands up in the air in a gesture of surrender. "I screwed up the whole flipping world because I didn't become an opera singer. I'm sure they would have found a cure for cancer by now if only I had gone on to perform *Aida*. And anyone with a brain in her head knows, there would have been an end to world hunger long ago if I had toured with the Metropolitan Opera. Certainly, Mother and I would be wealthy beyond our wildest imagining, living in a state of bliss if only I had played Carmen."

"Rachel, don't be flip," Addie snapped. "Carmen was never a role for you."

"I'm sorry, Mother," she said without a hint of remorse. "How could I have been so foolish?"

"You take after your aunt Marilyn. She never had any sense of responsibility either."

Rachel staggered back as if she'd been struck a savage blow. No sense of responsibility? She had always been responsible! She had given up much of her childhood and adolescence to her responsibilities for her singing talent. She had given up her dreams to take on the responsibility of managing Terence's career. Now she was giving up all hope of a happy future, taking on responsibility for the very person who sat in judgment of her.

"Rachel," Bryan said softly, reaching out for her.

She could see him out of the corner of her eye, could easily read the concern in his expression.

She could have gone to him for comfort, but she didn't. The pain she was feeling was too personal. It went too deep for comfort, too deep for tears. She stepped away from Bryan and nearer her mother, isolating the two of them in the aura of her pain. She stared into Addie's pale eyes and spoke softly in a voice that trembled with the strength of the emotions underlying it.

"I'm sorry, Mother. How many times do I have to say it? I'm sorry for the disappointment I caused you. I'm sorry I wanted something more in my life than training and practice and performance. And most of all, I'm sorry I wanted you to love me regardless of what I did, because obviously you weren't capable of it."

It was Addie's turn to look stricken. Her thin, lined face turned ashen, and she pressed a hand to her chest, as if to see if her heart was still beating.

"How dare you?" she said, her voice as soft as Rachel's had been, as full of pain. "How dare you say I didn't love you! I did everything for you."

"You turned me away. You exiled me. That's an awfully funny way of showing love."

Addie said nothing. She struggled to sort through her feelings. They seemed to assail her from all sides and from within—anger, guilt, resentment, regret, disappointment. The present faded, and she suddenly found herself in the past, wishing back the words that had forced Rachel to leave, wishing Rachel hadn't pushed her into saying them. They were in the little house in Berkeley, and Rachel was backing away from her, moving toward the door with a terrible look of hurt in her wide eyes. It was too late. Her daughter was leaving her. She had pushed too hard, expected too much, laid down one law too many. Her sweet Rachel was leaving her.

"This is all your fault," Addie said bitterly, turning on Bryan. "You good-for-nothing, god-awful folk singer!"

She pulled a man's shoe out of the patch pocket of her housedress and flung it at him. Bryan caught it and stared at it, frowning, not quite sure what to say. A cherry tomato sailed through the air and caught him unaware, bouncing off his forehead.

"Mother, stop it!" Rachel ordered. "That's not Terence, it's Bryan."

"Bryan—" The word caught on the end of Addie's tongue, and she bit it back, but her confusion was already apparent and she knew it. Panic left her only one option—escape.

She pushed herself up out of her throne chair and backed toward the hall. She pulled half of a cheese sandwich from her sweater pocket and held it out in front of her as if it were a gun.

"Stay back or I'll shoot!" she demanded. "I'm going to call the police!"

"Mother!" Rachel started after her, but Bryan caught her by the arm and pulled her back.

"Let her go, honey. I unplugged the phones after the last call."

Rachel shook her head and sighed, what little strength she had left draining out of her. This time when Bryan tried to gather her close, she let him. Bryan squeezed his eyes shut and pressed a kiss to her temple. He could think of nothing to say that would ease her pain. Words from him were not going to mend her past with Addie. All he could give her was his support and his love, and he gave them both without reserve, wrapping her in his strength and pressing her head to his heart.

They stood there for a moment in silence, letting the tension settle into the dust around them. Finally, Rachel stood back a little and scrubbed at the few tears that had managed to escape the barrier of her lashes to slide down her cheeks. She took a deep, cleansing breath, gathering herself together, dredging up a little more determination from the deep well inside her.

"I shouldn't have lost my temper," she said evenly. "I know it doesn't do any good. It only upsets Mother."

"You can't always keep it all in." Bryan reached out a hand to toy with the whisper-soft tendrils of hair that framed Rachel's face. "Look on the bright side: In ten minutes Addie is liable to have forgotten you had this conversation."

Rachel managed a wry smile. "That's true. Too bad she can't forget the phone number for the police department."

Bryan's heart welled with pride and love. She was some kind of lady, his little Rachel. Life wasn't exactly being kind to her, but she took it on the chin and came back smiling. That she managed to keep a sense of humor through all of this was a real indication of the depth of character she possessed.

He stared down at her in the gloom of the poorly lit room. All around them stood dark, dusty, neglected furniture. The striped paper on the walls was stained and buckling, the draperies, heavy with mildew and age, drooped from their hooks. It was a grim setting, and yet Rachel shone like a gem, so bright, so pretty, her amethyst eyes smiling up at him, echoing the glow of the old brooch he had given her.

"I love you," he murmured, leaning down to kiss her.

She melted against him, all warmth and willingness. She slid back into his arms, fitting there as if she were a part of him. Rachel gave herself over to the kiss, trying to communicate the words that were locked in her heart. She couldn't bring herself to say them. Somehow she thought that if she said them aloud, it would only hurt worse when the parting came.

"I want you," Bryan whispered, trailing his lips down the ivory column of her throat as he bent her back over his arm.

"Oh, Bryan," she said, all the longing she felt dragging the words out on a moan of need.

His hand slid up between their bodies to cup her breast, his gentle fingers kneading her swelling flesh, his thumb brushing across her nipple, teasing it to hardness. Desire surged through her like an electric current, converging in the most feminine parts of her body and intensifying there into pools of heat. She didn't try to stop the sensations from overwhelming her. There were too many things in her life now that needed rigid control and discipline and self-sacrifice. In these few stolen moments with Bryan she was going to be selfish. She was going to take his passion, as much as he wanted to give her. She was going to revel in the strength of this desire. It was so unlike anything she had ever known, and she knew nothing would ever compare to it.

They sank down onto an old fainting couch, coughing at the cloud of dust that enveloped them but not letting it interfere in the proceedings. Rachel purred her contentment as Bryan settled himself on top of her, his manhood prodding at her from behind the snug barrier of his jeans. She loved the weight of his trim, hard body bearing down on her, loved the masculine sounds of frustration that rumbled in his throat as he tried to get closer to her. Wantonly, she arched up against him, her legs parting so he could press against her more intimately.

"Oh, Rachel." Bryan groaned. "Oh, Rachel."

A scream rattled the chandeliers above them.

"Oh, hell." He uttered the words through gritted teeth, feeling as if he might start sobbing at the agony of thwarted passion. "Oh, hell."

He levered himself up off Rachel and staggered to his feet, gritting his teeth at the throbbing in his groin. "If there isn't a ghost upstairs, there will be when I'm finished."

"If you get violent, can I help?" Rachel asked dryly as she forced herself off the couch.

"Absolutely."

The second scream kicked them into action. They ran down the hall and bolted up the grand staircase, turning in at Addie's room only to find it empty. They found Addie at the back of the house, standing in the hall in her nightgown, her face as white as paste.

"Mother, what happened?" Rachel asked, going to her mother's side but hesitating to put an arm around her.

"It was that terrible ghoul again!" Addie said, panting. Her hair was in a wild tangle around her head. She looked as if she had stuck her finger in a light socket. "It was standing down there at the end of the hall with this weird white mist all around."

All three peered down the corridor, but nothing was there.

"What happened to it?" Bryan asked.

"Poof!" Addie said, flapping her arms at her sides. "He just disappeared."

Rachel ground her teeth as she followed Bryan to the end of the dark hall. "People don't just disappear."

"Ghosts do."

"There're no such things as ghosts."

" 'Asserting a statement an infinity of times does not in itself make it true,' " Bryan quoted. "Abel J. Jones."

Rachel scowled at him. " 'No matter how thin you slice it, it's still baloney.' Alfred Smith."

Bryan met her look with a determined one of his own. " 'There is nothing so powerful as the truth—and often nothing so strange.' Daniel Webster."

He stopped at the spot Addie had pointed to, letting his gaze roam over the area, letting his

sixth sense listen for any kind of sign. It was one
of his ordinary senses, however, that picked up a
clue. He held himself very still and sniffed the air
like a bird dog.

"Ammonia," he mumbled, his eyes taking on a
faraway look.

"Ammonia?" Rachel questioned, making a face
as the scent burned her nostrils. "What does ammonia have to do with anything?"

"Magic," Bryan said flatly, almost angrily.

"A ghost that does housecleaning," Rachel
mused, leaning back against the paneled wall and
crossing her arms over her chest. "I love it. Do you
think we could get him to do windows? There are
about ninety of them in this dump that all need a
good scrubbing!"

She squealed the last of the word as the wall
shifted behind her. Startled, she bounded into the
middle of the hall, and then did her best to not
look embarrassed, straightening her lavender
blouse and smoothing her hands over her skirt as
if yelping and leaping were not the least bit out of
the ordinary.

Bryan was too absorbed in his inspection to
notice the instinctive flame of fear that had burst
to life in Rachel's eyes. Following his nose, he
moved toward the wall, where he stopped and
stood staring down at a smudge of dirt on the
wooden floor. His heart sank a little, but he
stemmed the rush of disappointment. Ghost or no
ghost, there was a mystery to be solved, and solv-
ing mysteries was his forte.

With a look of grim determination on his face,

he opened the door in the wall, flipped on the light, and followed the scent of ammonia down the dusty servants' stairs. The step with dry rot was cracked through, and he skipped it altogether, frowning harder. He slipped out of the cabinet in the pantry, careful not to make a sound.

The kitchen was dark, illuminated only by the reflection of moonlight on the fog that hung outside the windows, but his eyes adjusted quickly. He eased along the wall, keeping to the deepest shadows, his gaze taking inventory of every object as he moved toward the back door. Nothing moved. The only sound was the wind outside and the metallic screech and clang of the vent for the stovepipe of the old appliance Addie had set ablaze earlier in the day.

He let himself out the back door and stood on the porch with his hands on his hips. He looked out across the grounds of Drake House, solemn and silent. There was nothing to see but overgrown bushes shrouded in fog. There was nothing to hear except the roar of the wind and the sea. But there was something out there. He could feel it. He could sense it—a menace, a threat. There was something out there, and he was determined to find out who or what it was.

After locking up and thoroughly checking the downstairs for any sign of an intruder, Bryan climbed back up the servant's staircase, going slowly in hopes of picking up some sense of who their uninvited guest had been. Rachel met him at the door in the second-floor hall.

"I got Mother to go back to bed," she said quietly,

wrapping a sweater around her shoulders. "Did you find anything?"

Bryan shook his head. "No, but I have an idea or two."

"Casper the Cleanly Ghost?" she suggested with an irrepressible smile.

"Very funny," he drawled, sliding an arm around her and steering her down the hall toward her bedroom.

"Ammonia and hydrochloric acid. It's an old magic trick," he explained. "You soak a wad of cotton in ammonia and one in hydrochloric acid. Forcing air through the cotton produces volumes of white smoke. Very eerie-looking stuff. My dad taught me how to do it when I was ten. You can't imagine the trouble I got into in Sister Agnes's religion class when Mark Tucker and I engineered a surprise reenactment of the Ascension, using that trick."

Rachel had a fleeting impression of the adorable little boy he must have been with his serious expression and his glasses sliding down his nose, his bag of magic tricks tucked under one arm. A little more of her heart gave itself over to him.

"So," she said, forcing herself to stay on the topic, "you're admitting what Mother saw wasn't a manifestation from the spirit world after all?"

"Reluctantly. I'm not saying Wimsey isn't legitimate, but I think our other visitor is a ghost of a different color."

They stopped at the open door of Rachel's room. Bryan leaned back against one side of the jamb and Rachel leaned back against the other. He gave her a serious look. "I think someone is trying to frighten Addie into leaving Drake House."

An automatic shiver ran through Rachel at the thought, but she dismissed it. "Why would anyone do that? It seems to be common knowledge that we're going to sell the place. Why would anyone bother?"

"Why, indeed," Bryan murmured, combing a hand back through his hair. He had his theories, but they were only beginning to form. For the moment he had nothing concrete to share with Rachel, and heaven knew she had enough on her mind already.

A sexy smile curving his mouth, he pushed himself away from his side of the door frame. Bracing his hands above Rachel's head, he leaned close and brushed his lips across hers. "I think we ought to sleep on that."

"Really?" she whispered, heat sweeping through her. She ran her hands under his open sweater and up his sides, following the outward slope from his lean waist to his solid chest. "I was going to suggest we sleep on the bed."

"Were you?" He chuckled, a low, masculine sound that rumbled deep in his throat as he pinned Rachel to the door frame with his hips.

"Mmmm . . ." she sighed, forgetting all about ghosts and goblins as her body melted into his. "Clean sheets, no ants."

"Sounds inviting," he said, nibbling at her earlobe. "Can I make one more suggestion?"

"What?"

"Let's skip the sleep. I can think of better things to do in a bed."

TEN

"Thieves! Thieves! We're being overrun by thieves!"

Addie stamped her foot on the hall floor, causing several more people to turn their heads and stare at her. She glared back at them. The gall. For all these people to simply walk into her home and steal her things! She couldn't imagine what the world was coming to. No good, that was for certain.

One of the strangers, a pudgy, middle-aged woman in a brown pants suit and a bad blond wig, emerged from the parlor, cradling a large white wire bird cage in her arms. Addie gasped in outrage, her narrow gaze boring into the woman. She recognized the culprit as being the receptionist for the intolerable Nazi doctor, Moore.

"I should have known you'd be a thief!" Addie snapped, launching herself at the woman.

She grabbed at the bird cage, her fingers threading through the wire. The startled receptionist hung on to the other side of the cage and the two women jerked each other around the hall like children fighting over a new toy.

"Mother! For heaven's sake!" Rachel exclaimed, pushing her way through the crowd of bargain hunters. She grabbed Addie by the shoulders, halting the tussle.

"She's stealing my bird cage!" Addie accused the receptionist as she gave her the evil eye.

"She's not stealing it, Mother," Rachel explained patiently, even though her patience had pretty much worn out an hour into the tag sale. She pried her mother's fingers away from the now-bent wire cage. "Mrs. Anderson is *buying* this bird cage. We're having a tag sale, Mother. We can't take all this furniture with us to San Francisco, so we're selling it."

She turned to the receptionist, whose wig was askew, and mustered an apologetic smile. "I'm sorry, Mrs. Anderson. Mother is a little . . . confused about all this."

"It's all right, Rachel," the woman said, composing herself like a plump pigeon whose feathers had been ruffled. "I understand."

"Oh, I get it," Addie said, turning on her daughter. "You're in on it. It's a conspiracy."

"It's a tag sale, Mother," Rachel said through her teeth as she bit back her temper and her feelings of guilt.

It *was* a conspiracy. There was no getting around that fact. She had conspired to usurp her mother's authority over her own property. The fact that she didn't have a choice, that what she was doing was perfectly legal, that Addie wasn't competent to handle these affairs, didn't make it any more palatable. Not even thoughts of their dwindling finances and the upcoming visit from the IRS could make her feel justified.

"I'm calling the police," Addie said flatly.

Rachel's shoulders slumped, and she heaved a weary sigh as she watched her mother stomp away. She debated whether it would take more strength to stop her from calling or to deal with Deputy Skreawupp's ire after the fact. Suddenly Bryan bounded into the hall, blowing a party horn. His magic hat was perched on his head.

"Hennessy!" Addie said. "What is the meaning of this?"

"It's a party, beautiful!" Bryan declared, flashing her his most brilliant smile. He removed his hat with a flourish and pulled another party horn out of it for Addie. "Let's go dancing on the lawn."

Addie scowled at him, uncertainty flashing in her eyes. She didn't like what was going on here. She didn't like that she seemed to have no control over it. And all the strange faces in her house frightened her. There were so many of them, she had trouble distinguishing one from the next. But Hennessy, she knew. Hennessy, she trusted.

"I love your hair that way, Addie," he commented. "It's very . . . carefree."

She raised a hand to pat at the hairdo, blushing like a schoolgirl. She had hacked off her long tresses with a pinking shears because she hadn't been able to remember how to braid it. Now it fringed her face in a kind of frenetic pixie look. "You're such a flirt, you big Irish rascal."

Bryan tucked her arm through his and led her down the hall toward the front door, shooting a wink at Rachel as they went.

Rachel smiled her appreciation and mouthed a thank-you. Clutching her clipboard to her chest, she sighed up into the limp curls that had long ago escaped her sensible hairstyle. What would she have done without Bryan here these past few days? What would she do without him when she and Addie moved to the city?

"He's something, isn't he?"

She turned in surprise toward the voice that had suddenly sounded beside her. Alaina Montgomery-Harrison stood there, looking cool and immaculate in her Pierre Cardin ensemble of a black pleated skirt and cream-colored sweater. Tall, angular, elegant, she was just one of Bryan's many friends who had volunteered to help with the tag sale.

Rachel wondered how the woman managed to appear so unfrazzled. They had all been run ragged in the four hours the sale had been going. She decided Alaina was just one of those few lucky women who got out of bed in the morning looking like an ad for ageless beauty.

"Bryan," Alaina prompted with a wry smile.

"Yes." Rachel shook her head. "He's something."

They were alone in the hall for the moment. Alaina fixed her with a sharp, intuitive stare that made Rachel feel as if she were suddenly under a very powerful microscope.

"May I ask what exactly he is to you?"

Rachel's eyes widened, revealing most of the information Alaina required.

"It's not that I have designs on him," Alaina said, deliberately softening both her look and her attitude. Her translucent blue eyes glittered with warm affection. "My husband is the only lunatic I need. It's just that Bryan is a very special friend. I don't want to see him get hurt."

"I don't want to hurt him," Rachel said carefully.

Alaina bit her tongue on the words *but you will if you have to*. A little worry line formed between her eyes, then her gaze came to rest on the brooch Rachel wore at the throat of her white blouse.

"Did he, by any chance, give you that?"

Rachel lifted her fingers to the heavy pin and brushed them across the smooth surface of the stone. "Yes, he did. Why?"

A soft, knowing smile curved Alaina's mouth. "No reason," she said softly. Changing gears smoothly, she motioned toward the empty hall. "There seems to be a lull in the storm. Can I buy you a cup of coffee?"

Rachel had the distinct impression she had just passed some kind of test. Relief poured over her, and she smiled at the dark-haired woman, glad, though she wasn't quite sure why. "I'd like that."

They walked outside, onto the porch, where Alaina's husband, Dylan, was overseeing the group of children running the refreshment stand. Dylan's son, Sam, who Rachel guessed to be about eleven, seemed to be in command of everything. He was a very serious boy with sandy hair and a mind-boggling vocabulary. His assistants included his younger sister, Cori, a dark-eyed, dark-haired charmer; and Faith Callan's daughter, Lindy, an adorable little six-year-old moppet with burnished gold curls. Lindy appeared to be in sole charge of the brownies—there was a telltale smudge of chocolate frosting on her cheek and a dot of it on her button nose. Dylan was lounging on a folding chair with his feet up on the porch railing and a chubby baby girl on his lap.

"Hardly working, as usual, I see," Alaina said dryly, an affectionate light in her eyes as she mussed her husband's unruly chestnut hair.

Dylan flashed her a lazy smile. "I know how to delegate authority."

"That's one explanation."

Alaina scooped the baby up in her arms and cuddled her, making a comically disgusted face when the baby squealed in delight and wiped chocolate frosting on her immaculate sweater. Alaina dabbed ineffectually at the stain with a napkin.

"I swear, they gave us the wrong baby in the hospital," she said mildly. "They gave us the dry cleaner's child; it was a plot." She kissed her daughter's nose and grinned. "But I won't trade you back, will I, sweetheart? No way."

The baby squealed again and bounced in her mother's arms.

Rachel smiled and sipped at her coffee. Alaina didn't strike her as the baby-cuddling type, which made the display of affection all the more touching. Her gaze fell on her own mother, who stood with Bryan near a set of lawn furniture they were trying to sell—a wooden glider and three chairs. Addie had never been the cuddling type either. Still, they had been close once. Rachel had hoped they would be close again, before Addie's illness stole away all familiarity. But they didn't seem to be able to manage it. The past stood between them like a wall, and the present, with the conflict about the move and their changing roles, was only reinforcing that wall.

"Excuse me, Miss Lindquist."

Rachel nearly bolted out of her skin. Her coffee sloshed over the rim of her cup, and she had to hop back to avoid getting it on her plum-colored slacks. "Mr. Porchind. You startled me."

To say the least, she thought as she looked down at the man. Mr. Rasmussen stepped out from behind his partner, where he had been almost completely obscured from view. The bruise had faded from the thin man's cheek, but he still looked creepy with his sunken eyes and sharp features.

For just a second Rachel tried to picture either of them as Addie's ghost, but she dismissed the idea. Bryan was being overly dramatic thinking someone was trying to get her and Addie to leave Drake House. She was convinced it was just some local kid playing a prank, if indeed anything *was* going on. The last incident, which had happened several days before, had faded enough from her memory to seem almost as unreal as Addie's whimsy.

"Mr. Rasmussen and I thought we would stop by and do a little bargain hunting."

"Bargains," Rasmussen echoed, steepling his hands in front of him like a preacher giving a blessing.

"Yes, well," Rachel said with a smile that looked more pained than pleasant, "there are plenty to be had here today. I see you've found some things already."

Porchind held a small stack of old books in his dimpled hands, the bindings pressed back into his enormous belly. "Indeed." He gave a nervous little laugh. "Have you had a chance to speak with your mother?"

"No, I haven't. No, not yet. I'm sorry."

As if on cue, Addie, standing down on the lawn, shouted, "I'm not leaving this house! Get that through your thick head, Hennessy! I am not leaving this house!"

Rachel felt the color drain from her face as all eyes turned toward her mother. There had to be close to thirty people on the lawn, browsing at an assortment of sale items, and another ten on the wide porch. Addie stared back at them, a truculent gleam in her eyes. She pulled her party horn out of the pocket of her sweater and blew it at them.

Jayne Reilly saved the day, bravely stepping forward to comment on the attractiveness of Addie's new hairstyle, thereby distracting her from Bryan, who had suddenly fallen out of favor.

"Well, there you have it," Bryan said, shrugging as he mounted the steps to the porch. A particularly inane smile graced his handsome face as he regarded Porchind and Rasmussen. "Addie's not moving. Looks like you're out of luck, gentlemen. How about a consolation prize?"

He flipped off his magic hat, reached into it, and pulled out a bouquet of red carnations. The children paused in their work at the refreshment stand to applaud. Their cheers broke abruptly into laughter as Bryan offered the flowers to Porchind and a fountain of water suddenly sprayed up out of the silk blossoms, drenching the man.

"Gee, I'm sorry about that," Bryan said, thoroughly unrepentant. He tossed the flowers aside. "I didn't know they were loaded."

Rachel glared at him as she grabbed a handful of napkins. "Bryan, must you be so *helpful*?"

"Helpful is my middle name," he said pleasantly. He took the books from Porchind's hands and handed them back to young Sam Harrison, who wrapped them in a towel to dry them while the fat man dabbed at his eyes and his dripping double chins with cocktail napkins. "Bryan Liam Helpful Hennessy. It's on my confirmation certificate."

"I'm sorry, Mr. Porchind," Rachel said sincerely, handing him more napkins. "I hope it didn't ruin your suit."

"Impossible," Alaina muttered dryly.

"No, no, I'm fine, Miss Lindquist," Porchind said, shooting Bryan a malevolent look. "We were just leaving."

"Oh, well, here are your books." Bryan took the stack wrapped in white terry cloth from Sam and handed it back to Porchind. "Keep the towel—our compliments."

The two men nodded to Rachel, glared at Bryan,

and stomped down the steps. Bryan watched them cross the yard toward an old brown Ford Galaxy that was parked among the dozens of cars on the lawn. Out of habit he memorized the license plate. He also noted with grim satisfaction that Rasmussen was limping slightly.

"That was really uncalled for," Rachel said through her teeth when the rest of the crowd had dispersed.

"On the contrary." Bryan regarded her with an earnest look. "It was most necessary."

"Here are the books, Uncle Bryan," Sam Harrison said, handing the little stack over.

"Well done, Sam. Worthy of the Baker Street Irregulars, I'd say."

"Thanks, gov'nor," Sam said, using the dialect of the London street urchins who had come to the aid of Sherlock Holmes on occasion.

The conspirators grinned at each other.

"Bryan!" Rachel gasped, appalled. "You stole those from Porchind!"

"Borrowed," he corrected her.

"And made my son an accessory!" Alaina fixed him with a steely look, turning her body as if instinctively shielding her baby daughter from Bryan's powers of corruption.

Bryan ignored them both, totally absorbed in examining his ill-gotten booty. He singled out one small book from the others and tapped a finger against the title handwritten inside the front cover. " 'The Journal of Arthur Drake III.' " He turned to Rachel and lifted an eyebrow. "Now, what do you suppose Porky and the Rat would want with this?"

"To read it, I imagine," she said tightly.

"What's going on out here?" Faith Callan asked, stepping out onto the porch with her son Nicholas perched on her hip. The toddler rested his dark head on his mother's shoulder, and had his thumb firmly planted in his mouth. His eyelids were at half mast, indicating naptime was at hand.

"Just a little shell game," Bryan said absently, stroking his godson's head.

Alaina tugged Faith aside to give her the play-by-play, and Bryan turned to Faith's husband as he came out onto the porch. Shane Callan was tall, aristocratically handsome with black hair and pale gray eyes, but most important to Bryan at the moment was the fact that Shane had spent sixteen years as a federal agent.

"Shane," he said with a bright smile. "You're just the man I wanted to see."

"I'm glad Addie refused to let this thing go," Bryan said as he and Rachel settled back against the chintz cushions of the old glider.

"Me too."

They had moved the old swing around to the back of the house. It now stood near the fenced edge of the cliff with overgrown shrubbery on either side of it, creating a secret bower from which they could watch the sun sink into the ocean and the stars drop down into the twilight sky. A benevolent weather system had kept the fog bank from rolling in and made the evening lovely and warm.

Waves washed against the shore below in a soothing rhythm. It was such a peaceful scene compared
to the afternoon that Rachel took a long moment
just to savor it.

Addie had gone to bed directly after supper,
exhausted from the day's events. Rachel felt the
same kind of freedom as a mother whose toddler
had drifted off extra early for a change. She and
Bryan were going to have a few extra hours all to
themselves. Bliss.

She had changed into a loose-fitting purple cotton sweater and a comfortable lavender skirt. Her
hair was still up, but the chignon was very loose,
and the evening breeze set all the fine tendrils
around her face fluttering like ribbons. She curled
her bare feet beneath her on the cushion and
sipped at her glass of white wine.

Bryan sat beside her, the picture of relaxed masculinity in old jeans and a faded denim work shirt.
His long legs were stretched before him and
crossed at the ankles. His profile was to her as he
gazed out at the ocean, and Rachel studied him as
an artist studies a subject to be sketched. His was
a strong, handsome face with its high forehead
and solid jaw. His evening beard shadowed the
lean planes of his cheeks. His eyes looked tired,
but intelligent, contemplative as he stared out at
the sea.

A wave of love swept over Rachel, echoing the
surf that surged against the shore below them. It
took her a little by surprise and it frightened her
deep inside. Summer was slipping away from
them.

Bryan turned to her slowly, his eyes mirroring the ache she felt. He lifted a hand to cup her cheek, and his thumb brushed away a teardrop she hadn't been aware of.

"Summer's not over yet," he whispered, and bent to press a sweet kiss against her lips.

When he sat back, he took a deep breath, almost visibly shrugging off the mantle of melancholy that had fallen over them. He smiled gently and sang a line from an old Celtic folksong about a young man who had wandered into Edwards Town unknown, unloved, and unseen, there to meet a beautiful girl he called his County Leitrim queen.

Rachel smiled. He had a lovely voice. "Did you learn that in Ireland?" she asked, suddenly realizing how little she knew about him, about his background.

"No. My father likes to sing that one. It makes my mother furious because the girl in the song is blond and my mother's hair is black. She claims Dad sings it to remind her of one of his old girlfriends. He's allowed to sing it only when he's in the garage making his fireworks."

"He makes fireworks for a living?"

"No. That's his hobby. He designs twelve-meter racing yachts for a living."

"That's . . . unusual."

"We Hennessys are an unusual bunch," he admitted with great pride.

Rachel chuckled. "So I gather. Tell me about them."

Tell me about you, Bryan heard her ask, though she didn't speak the words. That gentle, knowing smile curved his mouth again as he put his arm around her shoulders and she settled against him with her head tucked beneath his chin.

He told her about growing up in the Hennessy household with his three brothers and three sisters, about how they had all been encouraged to be themselves, to pursue whatever dreams caught their fancy. He told her about Catholic school and Sister Agnes, the Iron Nun. He told her about his travels and his work. He told her about Serena. He told her about the Fearsome Foursome and how they had all ended up in Anastasia.

"They're wonderful friends," Rachel murmured. "You're very lucky."

"They're your friends now too," he said, pushing one sneakered foot against the ground to set the glider into lazy motion. "That's the wonderful thing about having friends—you get to share them."

Rachel said nothing. She would have loved nothing better than to stay in Anastasia and have Bryan's friends become her friends. But that wasn't the way things were going to be.

"It'll work out, Rachel," Bryan promised. He lifted her chin and smiled down at her, his blue eyes twinkling like stars in the dusk. "All you need is a little faith in magic."

Rachel shook her head sadly. "You can't pull a happy ending out of that hat of yours, Bryan. Life doesn't work that way."

"We'll see."

She opened her mouth to protest, but he silenced her with a kiss.

"Don't be so practical," he said against her lips as his big hands found their way under her sweater. "Love wasn't meant to be practical. Love is magic."

Rachel didn't try to argue. Bryan seemed intent on showing her the truth of his statement, and she couldn't bring herself to stop him. She didn't want to stop him; she wanted to love him. She wanted to drink in his love and store it up inside her against the promise of a lonely future. She wanted to make love with him there in their secret bower with the ocean sighing below them and the last rays of twilight slipping into the sea.

"Show me," she whispered, leaning back from him. Her fingers caught at the bottom of her sweater, and she slowly drew the garment over her head.

Desire tightened Bryan's expression as he stared at her, his intense gaze lingering on her firm, small breasts and the nipples that hardened with the kiss of the cooling breeze. She was so young and lovely, like an innocent goddess as she sat there on the swing looking up at him with fathomless violet eyes.

With deft fingers he pulled the pins from her hair and the pale tress spilled around her like champagne in the soft light. She reached up to pull his glasses off and set them carefully aside, then her fingers fell to the task of unbuttoning his shirt. Bryan sat very still, almost as if he were afraid to move for fear of breaking the spell. He absorbed every nuance, every subtlety of feeling— Rachel's sadness, her vulnerability, the love she

kept locked in her heart because she was afraid of
how badly it would hurt when the end came.

But there wasn't going to be an end. He swore
that to himself with a fierceness he hadn't known
in years. There wasn't going to be an end to this.
He loved Rachel Lindquist, and he was damn well
going to have her for the rest of his life. He'd been
forced to give up the woman he loved once. It
wasn't going to happen again, not if he had any
power over the matter.

"I love you, Rachel," he whispered, his voice low
and rough as he pulled her into his arms.

Her mouth opened beneath his as she melted
against him. Her breasts were cool and soft
against the searing heat of his chest. Her back
arched as his hands roamed the gentle slopes and
ridges. Her tongue met his in urgent play as each
tried to telegraph feelings to the other.

Bryan eased her down on the cushions of the
glider. His mouth trailed little sipping kisses down
the column of her throat to her left breast, where
he drank his fill of her, rolling the tight bud of her
nipple in his mouth, sucking at it and teasing it
with his teeth. He wrapped his fingers in the hem
of her skirt and dragged the garment up between
them, baring her silky legs to his touch. She
moved restlessly beneath him as he tugged down
her panties just enough so he could tease her.

"Oh, Bryan, please," she whispered brokenly,
desperation consuming her whole.

"Please, what?" he taunted, nibbling at the corner of her mouth. His fingers slid into the dark
silk at the apex of her thighs again and again, only

to withdraw without touching the burning core of
her desire.

Driven by a deep need and an even deeper fear,
he wanted her as wild for his love as he was for
hers. He wanted to possess her completely, body
and soul, with nothing held back, not feelings, not
words.

"Show me," he whispered darkly.

Fire leapt in his veins as her small hand guided
his, showing him exactly how she wanted to be
touched. He complied willingly, growling his satisfaction as Rachel squeezed her eyes shut and
arched up into his caress. He stroked her to the
brink of completion, then pulled away.

Rachel braced herself up on her elbows and
stared at him, her swollen breasts rising and falling with her hard, shallow breaths. Bryan kneeled
on the cushions of the glider with one knee
planted between her bare thighs, the other foot
braced against the ground. She'd never seen him
look more purely male. His bare chest gleamed in
the fading light with the sweat of passion restrained. The button of his jeans was undone, and
his manhood strained against the blue fabric.

Sitting up, she reached out with trembling
hands to lower his zipper. She leaned forward,
pressing hot, open-mouthed kisses against his
quivering belly as she freed him. Her hands closed
around his hard, hot shaft, caressing him reverently. She wanted him with a need that went
beyond desire. She needed him in a way that went
straight to the heart of her, to the essence of what
made her human. At that moment she would

rather have died than deny herself the chance to join with this man in this elemental, mystical act.

Driven by his own desperation, Bryan forced her back down on the glider, his body arching over hers like a bow. He paused at the threshold, the tip of him nudging insistently against her sweet warmth. Bracing himself on his arms, he stared down at her. He had thought it would be enough to know that she loved him. He had thought he could go without hearing the words, but he couldn't. He needed to hear them now.

"Tell me you love me, Rachel," he whispered hoarsely.

She looked up at him, her eyes wide and dark, stark with sorrow and pleading. She was frightened and he knew it, but he was more frightened.

"Say it," he demanded, his whole body trembling with the tension of holding back.

"Bryan, don't—"

He tangled his fist in her hair and arched her head back as he lowered his mouth toward hers. He halted, inches from kissing her. "Say it. Please, Rachel."

Rachel looked up at him, her heart aching. Lord, how she loved him! It wasn't just her own heart she was trying to protect, it was his as well. She didn't want to hurt him. But as she looked up into the tortured expression in his eyes, she knew she was hurting him. Her silence was tearing him apart. He was a good man. He was a dreamer, and there was no room in her future for a dreamer. But there would always be a place in her heart for Bryan and his magic.

Tears welled up in her eyes and slid in a stream down her temples.

"I love you," she whispered, her lips trembling as she leaned up to kiss him. "I love you."

Bryan clutched her to him, a storm of emotion sweeping through him as he eased his body into hers. He made love to her with everything he was feeling—passion, tenderness, anger, and pain. He held her and kissed her. When the end came, he told her again what was in his heart. And she clung to him and cried.

"Hush, sweetheart, don't cry," he whispered, holding her close, pressing kisses into her tear-damp hair. He inched over onto his side and cuddled Rachel against him. "It'll all work out. You'll see."

Rachel smiled sadly against his solid chest. Don't fall in love with a dreamer, the song went. But she had. She couldn't regret it. She wouldn't have traded what she and Bryan had just shared for anything. She only regretted that the world didn't work the way people like Bryan wanted it to.

"I'm all right," she said, dredging up a smile for him. Tenderly, she brushed his hair out of his eyes. "You need a haircut."

"Do I?" he mumbled, marveling at her strength.

She looked so soft and fragile, but under all that exquisite loveliness was a core of steel that would get her through whatever she had to face. It killed him to think of that hardness taking over her life, obliterating the young woman as she sacrificed her happiness and her dreams on the altar of responsibility. If only he could make her see that she didn't have to give up life's magic, that loneliness didn't have to be a part of her penance for past sins committed against Addie. If only he could make her see that his love for her wasn't going to fade away like a rainbow in the mist.

"I love a maiden fair with sunlight in her hair. Her name is Rachel," he sang softly, toying with the tendrils of spun gold that curled around her face. "My love for her is true. Whatever shall I do? She—aargh!"

The glider gave a sudden lurch backward. Instinctively, Bryan's arms tightened around Rachel, pulling her off the thing with him as he fell with a thud to the ground. She gave a squeal of surprise and landed on him, forcing the breath out of him.

"I've heard of the earth moving, but this is ridiculous," he said, coughing and squinting against the pain as he tried to suck air into his lungs.

"Are you all right?" Rachel asked. She sat up and tugged her sweater on over her head.

"Nothing wounded but my pride."

Bryan's attention was riveted on a spot behind the bench. He fumbled for his glasses and pulled them on, squinting into the darkness as his sixth sense hummed inside him.

Rachel's suddenly startled gaze followed his. "Did you see someone?"

"No," Bryan said evenly. It was what he hadn't seen that was important, but he knew Rachel wouldn't want to hear about it.

He stood up, straightening his clothes, then offered Rachel a hand. "I guess that was just a sign that it's time for us to go back to the house."

Rachel scooped up their wineglasses and they walked back across the yard arm in arm. Rounding the corner of the house, they stopped in their tracks at the sight that greeted them.

There was a woman sitting on a stack of suitcases on the front porch. She was a thin, birdlike creature with a wild nest of gray hair on her head. The tip of her cigarette glowed red in the dim light of the porch.

"Bryan!" She shouted his name and popped up off her perch like a jack-in-the-box. "There you are! I must have rang the bell a hundred times! A hundred times!"

"It's broken," Bryan mumbled, momentarily stunned. He mounted the stairs in a daze.

"My stars, it's good to see you, sweetheart!" The woman had a voice like sandpaper, and her cigarette bobbed up and down on her lip as she spoke. She threw her arms around Bryan in an exuberant hug which he started to return, but he quickly jumped back as she burned a hole through his shirt.

He plucked the smoldering fabric away from his skin, pain putting a brittle edge to his grin. "Aunt Roberta! It's so good to see you!" he said with genuine affection, but his brows pulled together in confusion. "What are you doing here?"

Roberta cackled like a crazed chicken and waved a hand at him. "Making the rounds of my nieces and nephews. I wrote you, sweetheart. I know I wrote you."

"You did?" Bryan searched his brain for any memory of such a letter but came up blank.

Roberta's glassy green eyes took on the same kind of absent look as she shrugged her thin shoulders. "I meant to."

Rachel cleared her throat discreetly, drawing both their attention. Bryan looked at her as if he had never seen her before, then jumped to introduce her.

"Rachel, this is my aunt, Roberta Palmer. Aunt Roberta, this is Rachel Lindquist."

Roberta's eyes seemed to bore right into Rachel. "My gosh, Bryan, she's a doll! A *doll*!" She grasped Rachel's hand in a death grip. "You're just a doll, Raquel!"

"Rachel," Rachel mumbled, completely thrown off by this strange woman who appeared to be drowning in a Notre Dame sweatshirt five sizes too big for her. "Thank you."

"My gosh," Roberta whispered, shaking her head at some secret amazement.

They all stood staring at one another for a long moment. Finally Rachel roused the manners her mother had drilled into her. "Why don't we all go inside? I'll make us a pot of coffee. Decaf," she added, thinking Bryan's aunt didn't need to get any more wired than she already was.

They trooped into the hall, and Bryan dropped his aunt's luggage down on the marble floor at the foot of the grand staircase. The stuff weighed a ton and a half.

"How long will you be staying, Aunt Roberta?" he asked.

Roberta shrugged, her face alight with excitement as she set off after Rachel. "A month or so."

With a wry smile Bryan dug into the pocket of his jeans and pulled out a handful of notes. He sorted through them until he found the one he wanted, then he located his pencil and amended the missive.

Beware of aunts.

ELEVEN

September 12, 1931
Great luck at Monte's. Mrs. R. very accommodating.

September 21, 1931
Clement sisters staying with H. Langely. Real gems.
Must call again.

September 25, 1931
Langely off to San Francisco. Golden opportunity.
Thank you, C. sisters.

Bryan shifted his back against the headboard,
sighed, and turned the page. So far Arthur Drake's
journal was providing him with nothing but an
account of the man's rather promiscuous love life.
He couldn't imagine what Porky and the Rat would
have wanted with it, but he figured he had only a

short time to find out. They would be back to claim the thing, of that he was certain.

Why did they want Drake House? What did Porchind's relative, the late Mr. Pig, have to do with it?

Money. That word came to him strongly, but it didn't make any sense. The condition it was in, Drake House wasn't worth anything. The property itself might have had development possibilities, but that didn't strike him as the reason. There was no adjacent development in the works. Anastasia already had its share of inns and hotels. There was some other reason, and it had to do with money and this little black book he held pressed to his bare chest.

It was nearly two A.M. They had settled Aunt Roberta in Rachel's room for the night. Rachel lay snuggled against him, sound asleep. She looked so young when she was sleeping, so pretty, so free of worry. Desire stirred in him anew. He would have liked nothing better than to rouse her with kisses and make love to her again, but she was exhausted and he had work to do.

He turned another page in the diary.

September 27, 1931
Party with A.W. at Garner's. My friend has a dangerous tongue. Worked to my advantage tonight. Caught Cecilia Jonstone unawares while Archie made a friend.

September 29, 1931
Pig getting too fat and sassy. Must roast soon.

October 10, 1931
Stuck pig. Ducky outfoxed the pig! My turn to get fat.

"Stuck pig," Bryan mumbled. He ran a hand back through his disheveled hair. "Stuck pig."

"Mmmm?" Rachel mumbled in her sleep.

She turned over and snuggled closer to him still, kicking the sheet off and using his belly for a pillow. Bryan bit his lip against the groan that rose up in his throat. Her cheek was soft and cool against his skin. Her warm breath swept across his groin as she sighed. As she settled down he forced his attention back to the book.

October 12, 1931
Can't find A.W. anywhere. Worried he said the wrong thing to the wrong person.

Rachel murmured something unintelligible in her sleep and Bryan had to choke back another groan as her lips brushed against his stomach muscles. She nuzzled against him and brought her hand up his thigh to rest it in a spot that made sweat break out on his forehead. A contented smile curved her mouth as she stroked him. Molten heat seared his veins, pooling in the pit of his belly.

His body's reaction was inevitable, which seemed to please the sleeping Rachel. She mumbled something softly and the vibration of her lips against his skin just about sent Bryan over the edge. He tried to ease away from her, but her fingers closed around him and all he could do was close his eyes and whimper. She was giving him a five-star arousal and the little minx was sound asleep!

"Rachel," he said, abandoning the journal on the cluttered nightstand. He stroked a shaking hand over her hair. "Rachel, sweetheart."

Rachel lifted her eyelids just enough to peer up at him. His face was flushed. His blue eyes seemed unusually bright. His expression was pained.

"Why is the light on?" she mumbled.

"The better to see you with, my dear," he quipped, baring his teeth.

"Are you feeling all right?" she asked, concern knitting her brows.

"Wonderful," he said sardonically. "Can't you tell?"

The last fog of sleep drifted out of her head as she realized she was at eye level with his belly button. Her gaze snapped downward, and she gasped. Bryan was roused and ready, and her fingers looked very guilty considering where they were.

"Caught red-handed with the loaded gun, so to speak," Bryan said. He chuckled as he took in the blush that bloomed on her cheeks. "I've heard of sleepwalking, but sleep seducing is a new one on me. What have you got to say for yourself, Miss Lindquist?"

Her initial embarrassment evaporated in the sensual heat that was rolling off him. Beneath her cheek his stomach muscles were like rock. He smelled deliciously male and musky. Desire rippled through her. Scooting down a little farther on the bed, she turned onto her stomach and looked up at him, her hair a wild golden mane around her head and shoulders, her eyes nearly purple with passion.

"I always finish what I start," she whispered in a languid, smoky voice.

"An admirable trait in a young woman," Bryan said through his teeth as she lowered her head. He groaned long and with feeling.

Somewhere below them a scream split the air.

"A man could die from this kind of frustration," Bryan complained as he threw his long legs over the edge of the bed and reached for his jeans. "Cases have been documented. You could look it up."

Rachel wasn't interested. She had already thrown on a robe and was rushing down the hall toward Addie's room in her bare feet.

"Mother? Mother, are you all right?"

"Rachel?" Addie burst out of her room, clutching her pink chiffon robe to her chest with one hand. In the other hand she clutched a rock. "Someone's broken into the house! Call your father!"

Bryan dashed past them, threw one leg over the mahogany banister, and shot down the polished railing to the foyer. Lights flashed at the end of the hall. The alarm on his electronic sensor buzzed furiously. He ran for the study, adrenaline pumping through him.

"Aunt Roberta!"

Roberta stood in the center of the room, her green eyes wide, her hair literally standing on end.

"Oh, my stars, Bryan! I am so glad you're here! I can't tell you. I just can't tell you!"

Bryan flipped off the alarm, pulled off his glasses, and rubbed at the bridge of his nose, heaving a weary sigh. Aunt Roberta had always demonstrated an amazing talent for setting off his machines.

"I came down to fix myself a little snack," Roberta said, pulling a bent cigarette and a lighter out of the pocket of her ratty blue robe. She paused to suck a gallon of smoke into her lungs. "This place is a maze. A maze. I've never seen the like, have you, Regina?" she asked Rachel, smoke billowing out of her nostrils. She patted Bryan on the arm. "I don't know why you'd want such a big place, honey. These old houses are a beast to heat, you know. An absolute b—"

"What happened?" Bryan asked, his normally generous patience wearing thin. He could have been upstairs in the throes of bliss if it hadn't been for his batty aunt.

"I got lost. Lost." Roberta said, waving her cigarette at him. Ash sprinkled to the floor. "So, I'm wandering down the hall, and I decide to ask that pale, thin fellow how to get to the kitchen." She turned to Rachel again, shaking her head. "I hope he's not your boyfriend, Renita. He is one ugly dude. Ugly. My gosh, he's ugly."

Bryan perked up. "A thin man with sunken eyes and white, white skin?"

"White as a ghost. As a ghost! All dressed in white. Pale as death. I guess I startled him. Kind of a flighty guy, isn't he? Well, I followed him in here and all hell broke loose with these crazy machines going off. Just about gave me a heart attack. A heart attack!" She shook her head and crossed herself reverently with her cigarette. "My gosh."

"What did the man do?" Bryan asked as he rewound the film in his camera.

"Grabbed a stack of books off the shelf and ran out that way." She waved her cigarette in the general direction of the French doors which stood open. "Strange time of the day to be going to the library, don't you think? Very strange."

While Bryan went to investigate, Rachel introduced her mother to their new guest. "Mother, this is Bryan's Aunt Roberta. Roberta, my mother, Addie Lindquist."

Addie stared at the woman, obviously confused. "Who is she? The maid? Of course I knew that, Rachel. You needn't introduce me to the maid."

"A little off her rocker, eh?" Roberta whispered behind her hand to Rachel, nodding knowingly. "That's all right, Renée. I understand."

Rachel looked from one to the other helplessly. She honestly didn't know what to say. She felt like Alice must have in Wonderland.

"*Great* hair, Adelle," Roberta rasped, blowing out a jet stream of smoke. She reached out to fluff Addie's pinking-shears special, taking another deep drag on her cigarette. "Did you get it done around here? My gosh, I *really* like that. I do."

"Well, there's no sign of him now," Bryan said, coming back into the room. "I suggest we all go back to bed."

The two older women wandered off together, talking beauty secrets.

Rachel stood in the doorway, hugging her robe around her, watching as Bryan stood on a chair and carefully removed the cassette from the video camera he had mounted in the corner above the door.

"I suppose it's too much to hope for to think they might be having identical hallucinations."

"It's unlikely," Bryan said. He rattled the video cassette. "Just as it's unlikely that a ghost could pull an iron railing loose or track mud into the house or step through rotted wood. I believe we'll have all the proof we need right here to show that Rat is our mystery man."

Rachel shook her head. "I don't understand why Rasmussen and Porchind would try to drive us out. They know I'm interested in selling the place."

"They also know Addie doesn't want to move," Bryan pointed out. "In any case, they could be trying to frighten you into dropping the price, make you so desperate to leave that you'll practically give the place to them rather than put it on the market and let someone else have a chance at it."

He went very still, staring past Rachel, his eyes clear and intense. "Don't let anyone else have a chance at it," he repeated. "Yes."

Rachel ignored his odd trance. She was getting used to such behavior, much to her surprise. "What about Addie's whimsy? Are you finally giving up that ridiculous belief in ghosts?"

"Not at all. I haven't figured out where Wimsey fits in yet, but I will."

Bryan smiled brightly, happy as a clam with his evidence. One mystery was well on its way to being solved. The whole thing would come to a head soon. He could sense it.

Rachel stepped out into the hall. "I'll see you upstairs. I'm going to go make sure Mother and Roberta aren't giving each other crew cuts."

"I'll be right up," Bryan promised.

He reset his equipment on the off chance of a return appearance by their ghoulish visitor, then poured himself a drink from the bottle that still resided in the desk drawer. He had told Rachel he would purchase the desk himself, but he needn't have worried. For some odd reason the study had remained virtually untouched throughout the tag sale. People had avoided the room. He had a strong feeling he knew why.

Now he raised his glass to whatever presence might have lingered in the room and said, "I don't know where you fit in yet, Wimsey, but I'm going to find out." He took a drink, then turned and stared long and hard at the portrait of Arthur Drake. The man was gesturing out toward him with an infuriatingly enigmatic expression on his face. "And I'm going to find out where you fit into this too, Arthur. See if I don't."

The videotape showed the back of a man's head. That was it as far as evidence went. The rest of the show was Aunt Roberta, shouting, screaming, waving her arms. She managed to block the culprit out of the picture entirely. The film in the still camera was no better—mainly photographs of Aunt Roberta getting the bejeepers scared out of her. It was a disappointment, to say the very least.

His call to Shane didn't exactly improve Bryan's morning.

"I didn't turn up anything on either one of them," Callan said. "Porchind was teaching literature at some two-bit junior college in Oregon until this summer. Rasmussen ran a used-book store. They haven't had so much as a parking ticket between them. Sorry."

Bryan managed a smile. Shane apologized as if it would have been infinitely preferable to have discovered the men were notorious serial killers.

"Any clue as to what brought them to Anastasia?" Bryan asked.

"None. But Faith says you should talk to Lorraine at the Allingham Museum on Seventh Avenue. Apparently, she's lived here forever. She should be able to answer questions concerning the history of the place."

Bryan pulled a scrap of paper out of his pocket, located his pencil behind his left ear, and jotted the message down.

"Faith also says to tell you you need a haircut."

"Thanks," Bryan said, scowling at his reflection in the hall mirror.

"Anytime. You know where to call if things get exciting."

Bryan smiled as he bid his friend good-bye. Shane seemed perfectly at ease at Keepsake Inn, working on his music and his poetry. He was a wonderful father and a dutiful, doting husband to Faith, but Bryan sensed Faith hadn't domesticated the agent completely.

Stuffing his notes back into the pockets of his khaki chinos, Bryan set off in search of Rachel, his mind mulling over what little information Shane had been able to give him. He pictured Miles Porchind in an ill-fitting tweed jacket, spraying the students in the front row of his stuffy classroom with spittle as he read aloud from Chaucer. He imagined Felix Rasmussen creeping around the musty stacks of books in a dark little store on some dingy side street.

Literature. Books. Porchind had come to the tag sale for books. Their late-night visitor had snatched an armload of books on his way out. Was it possible they weren't after Drake House at all, but something in it?

"Bryan, they're driving me insane," Rachel said, coming out of the kitchen, wringing her hands in a dishtowel.

"Who?"

Rachel stared at him as if he had completely lost his head. "Who? Who do you think? Tweedledee and Tweedledum. My mother and your aunt."

He waved a hand to dismiss the subject. "They'll be fine once they get to know each other."

"How can they get to know each other? My mother is perpetually confused, and your aunt never calls anyone by the same name twice. They're like squirrels chasing each other's tails!" She did a wickedly accurate imitation of Roberta, substituting a ballpoint pen for the ever-present cigarette. " 'My word, Rochelle, you make good eggs!' Then my mother says, who's Rochelle? 'Your daughter, for heaven's sake, Amelia! Your daughter, Roxanne!' Then they start the whole thing over again! It's worse than having breakfast with Abbott and Costello!"

"Honey, relax," Bryan said with a cheerful smile. He pulled a quarter out of her ear, handed it to her, and patted her cheek. "Buy yourself a cup of coffee. They'll be all right. It'll all work out. You'll see."

Rachel stared at him in exasperated disbelief as he turned and headed for the front door. "Where do you think you're going?"

"To get a haircut!" he called, waving at her over his shoulder.

Rachel ground her teeth. Wasn't that just like him to blithely wander off on some silly errand, leaving her to deal with the problem.

No, she corrected herself as she slumped back against the wall, that was like Terence. Her stomach churned at the thought. Bryan was sweeter than Terence had ever been, and less self-absorbed, but when it came to accepting responsibility, it was looking more and more as if they were peas in a pod, smoothing the rough spots over with platitudes, leaving her to deal with reality while they chased rainbows.

When Bryan returned to Drake House several hours later, he was brimming with barely contained excitement. Unfortunately, Rachel was in

neither the mood nor the position to hear his
latest theories and the history behind them.

Bryan unfolded himself from behind the wheel
of Rachel's Chevette, staring in stunned disbelief
at the scene that greeted him. Addie was hanging
out her bedroom window, flinging Rachel's clothes
out onto the lawn one article at a time. Rachel
stormed around the yard, gathering up undergar-
ments, pulling her bras off bushes, digging her
shoes out of the shrubbery.

"What's going on?" Bryan asked with a quality
of innocence that earned him a scathing glare
from Rachel.

"Mother is upset with me because I let a realtor
into the house this morning."

"Traitor!" Addie shouted, and let fly a pair of
loafers.

"She's taken all my things and locked herself in
her room."

"Oh, dear." Bryan frowned. "Where's Aunt Roberta?"

"She went scuba-diving with someone named
Brutus, an old friend of one of your brothers,"
Rachel said, retrieving one of her shoes from the
hood of her car. "If you want my frank opinion,
the man did not appear to be mentally balanced,
but who am I to judge?" She gave a brittle laugh
that managed to combine fury and hysteria.

Bryan's brows shot up in surprise at the news.

"This is all your fault." Rachel glared at him and
shook a loafer under his nose. "You told Mother we
wouldn't have to move. Naturally, she has no trouble remembering that little gem of information.

Thanks a lot, Bryan," she said, smacking him on the arm with the shoe. "You've made my job *so* much easier."

Bryan winced and rubbed his arm. "But Rachel—"

"You keep saying you want to help me," she ranted, running under a pair of jeans as they floated to earth. "Then you turn around and undermine my efforts to get Mother to accept the inevitable."

"But honey, it's not—"

They both broke off as a brown Ford Galaxy rattled up the drive. The car coughed to a halt and Porchind and Rasmussen emerged from the interior. A rock sailed down from above and richoceted off the grille of the car with a *ping!* All heads turned to see Addie wielding a bra-turned-slingshot.

"It's Porky and the Rat!" she shouted, loading a bra cup and letting another stone fly. "Get away from my house!"

"Please excuse my mother, gentlemen," Rachel said as they all took cover on the porch. "She's been hallucinating a lot lately."

"We've come to retrieve our books, Miss Lindquist," Porchind said without preamble, tugging at his brown vest in a vain attempt to get the garment to cover his protruding girth.

"Books," Rasmussen echoed. He cast a glance at Bryan, his sunken eyes gleaming with restrained temper. Bryan merely smiled at him inanely.

"Oh, yes," Rachel said, giving Bryan her own

fierce look. "I'm so sorry about the mixup. Bryan will get them for you."

"They're in the study," he said, pleasantly unrepentant. Opening the door, he motioned everyone inside. Rachel stomped past him. Porchind and Rasmussen sidled by, reluctant to turn their backs on him. "Wasn't that funny—those two stacks of books getting switched around that way?"

His only reply came in the form of three furious stares, which rolled harmlessly off his shield of innocuous enthusiasm.

"My, that old journal was certainly interesting reading," he said brightly as they went into the study.

The two visitors turned abruptly to each other, their complexions paling from white to ashen.

"I couldn't make head or tail out of it myself," Bryan said with a grin. He fought the urge to chuckle as Porchind and Rasmussen relaxed visibly, letting out a collective breath.

They sank down on the leather love seat, apparently weak with relief as Bryan handed the little stack of books over to them. Porchind's fingers, as stubby and round as breakfast sausages, curled greedily over the bindings as he pressed the books to his ample belly.

"I've spoken to a realtor about the house," Rachel said abruptly, drawing startled glances all around. She leaned back against the desk, crossed her arms over her chest, and gave Bryan a mutinous look.

"We were hoping to save you the trouble, Miss Lindquist," Porchind said with a nervous twitter.

"I had to get a fair idea of the market value," Rachel explained.

"You're certain you're going to sell, then?"

"Yes," she said, avoiding Bryan's intense look.

"There's still the little matter of Mrs. Lindquist," he said pointedly. "It is, in fact, her house."

Rachel reined in her temper and her own feelings of guilt. She hated to have it come down to a competency hearing. She had the ominous feeling that all hope of a reconciliation with Addie would be utterly destroyed by that. But the situation was getting desperate. Their funds were dwindling, and the IRS was breathing down their necks. She could see no way out other than her original plan of selling the house and going on to her new job in San Francisco. Her emotions were only complicated by Bryan's unreasonable opposition. She felt as if he were betraying her.

"And there is the little matter of my contract with Mrs. Lindquist," he continued. With a tremendous effort of will he ignored the fury rolling off Rachel in waves and resurrected his foolish grin. He turned to the gentlemen and began juggling a trio of red foam balls he had produced from thin air. "I've been hired to find the ghost."

"There are no such things as ghosts, Mr. Hennessy," Porchind said as if he were admonishing a ten-year-old.

Immediately both he and Rasmussen gave a little squeal of surprise and leapt forward a bit on the love seat. Their heads swiveled simultaneously, looking behind them as if they expected to see daggers protruding from the back of the chair.

Everyone then glared accusingly at Bryan, who went on happily juggling, ignoring their unspoken accusation that he was somehow to blame.

"Sure there is," he said enthusiastically. "This one's name is Archibald Wimsey. He was staying here in 1931 as a guest of Arthur Drake. Mysteriously disappeared. I'm quite convinced that his spirit inhabits Drake House to this day."

"That's ridiculous," Porchind said severely.

"Absurd," Rasmussen reiterated.

Together they popped up from the love seat, their eyes and mouths round O's of surprise, their hands going to their backsides.

Rachel sent Bryan a withering glare, then stepped forward to console her guests. "The springs must be going in that old thing. No wonder no one wanted to buy it yesterday."

She walked the men to the front door, promising them she and her mother would come to a definite decision about the house very soon. When she returned to the study, she gave free rein to the fury that had been building inside her all day.

"Of all the childish, infantile tricks!" she shouted, standing toe to toe with Bryan. "Booby-trapping that chair with your magic gizmos. Isn't that just like you!"

"Well, yes," Bryan admitted grudgingly. "But I didn't do it."

"Oh, sure," Rachel said with a sneer. She turned and began pacing back and forth in front of him in an effort to burn off some of her anger before she exploded. "What do I have to do to get through to you, Bryan? I have got to sell this house."

"No, you don't," he said. Suddenly he was grinning again with almost boyish excitement. "I think I've found out why Porky and the Rat want it."

"I don't care why they want it. I don't care if they want to set up a nudist colony for the terminally strange."

Bryan grimaced. "There's an ugly thought."

Rachel's eyes flashed. "It's nothing compared to what I'm thinking about you at the moment."

That was true. The signals he was intercepting were more than a little hostile. He cleared his throat, took a deep breath, and took the plunge.

"I think they're after gold."

Rachel halted her pacing and stared at him in disbelief. "What?"

"Porchind's late relative, Pig Porchind, was a big-time bootlegger back in the days of Prohibition," he explained, visibly warming to his topic. "According to the gossip of the time, he had a fortune in gold stashed somewhere around Anastasia."

"What has that got to do with Drake House?" she asked impatiently.

"At that same time in history there was a notorious cat burglar on the loose around here. His targets were the homes of wealthy lumber barons and shipping magnates. There were rumors about the theft of an enormous amount of gold from old Pig. It was apparently never found. Neither was Archibald Wimsey, an old British chum of Arthur Drake's who was visiting during the summer of 1931. By coincidence, all concerned in this story were either dead or gone missing shortly after it all happened, and most everyone forgot about it."

"That's a very entertaining story, Bryan," Rachel said. "Does it have a point?"

"Of course it has a point," he said irritably. "Wimsey is your mother's invisible friend, and Porky and the Rat think the stolen gold is stashed somewhere in Drake House."

"That's absurd," Rachel said. "If there were a fortune in gold in this house, don't you think someone would have found it by now? It's been more than sixty years since Prohibition."

"And almost that long since these rumors were in circulation. Why would anyone look for something they didn't know was there?" he asked reasonably.

"Why would anyone look for something that doesn't exist?" Rachel countered. "Did you find any mention of this legend in that journal?"

"Uh—no," he admitted, "not precisely."

Rachel rolled her eyes. "This whole tale is so farfetched, I can't believe you're telling it to me. Who gave you all this golden information anyway?"

"Lorraine Clement Carthage, who was a debutante at the time and is mentioned—er, fondly in the diary."

"And who is now, no doubt, as senile as my mother."

He couldn't quite meet her eyes after that statement. Lorraine hadn't exactly been in step with the world around her, he had to admit, but to his way of thinking the evidence was all adding up very nicely. Lorraine had thought the dashing

Wimsey was the thief. Apparently Pig Porchind had thought the same thing and had probably had Wimsey done away with, which explained the restless spirit. The fact that the gold had never been recovered meant it still had to be around someplace, and Drake House appeared the likely spot since attention was being focused on it by the late Pig's relative.

"Bryan, don't you see this is all a wild goose chase?" Rachel asked wearily. "All you've got are some moldy old rumors and half-baked speculation. It would be wonderful to find a fortune in lost gold. It would be the answer to my prayers. But life doesn't work that way."

"Not if you don't let it," he muttered.

"What's that supposed to mean?"

"It means you have to believe a little."

Rachel closed her eyes and counted to ten, but the anger was still there afterward, the anger and all the old bitterness. "You think problems can be solved by magic?" she asked. "You think all we have to do is believe in fairy tales and everything will end happily ever after? Magic is for fools and children."

Bryan's head snapped back as if she had slapped him. His jaw tightened ominously. "Well, it certainly isn't for martyrs, is it?" he asked darkly.

Rachel stared at him, her eyes round with hurt.

In a saner moment he would have called himself a bastard, but he had some pent-up pain of his own to vent, and he was only human.

"I think you don't want to believe there could be a painless solution to your problems because you're so damned determined to sacrifice yourself to Addie," he said, leaning over the desk toward her, unconsciously trying to intimidate her with his size. "You've got it all mapped out in that pragmatic head of yours how you're going to make it up to her for wanting a life of your own. You've probably got it figured out to the nth degree the exact amount of suffering you've got to do to redeem yourself."

Silence hung between them like the blade of an ax. Bryan stood on one side of the walnut desk, his chest heaving in the aftermath of his outburst. Rachel stood on the other side, her shoulders stiff with pride, her eyes shining with tears she refused to shed.

After a long moment she said quietly, "I'm not a masochist, Bryan. I'm a realist. In the real world people have to learn to deal with problems in a realistic way. Now, if you'll excuse me, I have to go see to mine."

She turned and went to the door, praying she could make her getaway before the dam burst, but the study door wouldn't open. She grasped the knob with both hands, twisted it, rattled it, yanked on it, but it wouldn't budge.

"Dammit," she swore, sniffling as she yanked on the knob and kicked the door with the toe of her sneaker simultaneously. "Damn this stupid old house."

Bryan watched her, his whole being aching with a ferocious attack of remorse. He'd meant every word he'd said, but he had certainly never meant to say them out loud. He would have done anything to spare Rachel hurt, yet he had just inflicted her with a verbal forty lashes because he was feeling frustrated. It would serve him right if she never spoke to him again, he thought morosely. It would serve him right if she threw him out. Or maybe he should just go . . .

Apologize, stupid.

He hesitated, but suddenly his feet were moving forward. He felt almost as if some outside force were propelling him toward Rachel, who was still struggling with the door. He stopped behind her and reached out to carefully cup her shoulders in his big hands. She jumped and stiffened as if she expected him to become violent. Bryan winced. It wasn't enough that he had to deal with his own pain for what he'd done; now he had to feel Rachel's as well. It was apt punishment, he supposed, but he couldn't help but curse his sixth sense just the same.

"I'm sorry," he whispered, bending his head down so the fresh scent of her hair teased his nostrils. "I'm sorry, angel. I shouldn't have said any of that. I know you're doing what you think is best. I shouldn't have lost my temper."

Rachel tried to hold herself rigid, but she wasn't able to sustain it against the strangely physical pressure to lean back against him. The sting of his words was still bringing tears to her eyes, but she had to admit to feelings of regret herself. She'd been the first one to draw blood, bursting Bryan's bubble of enthusiasm with the pin of practicality. Maybe he wasn't realistic or responsible, but he was trying to help her in his own misguided way.

And she couldn't deny the fact that she loved him, or that it hurt her to hurt him.

She sighed as the fight drained out of her and Bryan wrapped his arms around her. "I'm sorry too."

She was sorry for a lot of things, not the least of which was the inherent differences in their philosophies. She was sorry fate had thrown them together at such an inopportune time. She was sorry she couldn't believe in magic the way he did.

"I don't want us to fight," she whispered, twisting around in his embrace and throwing her arms around his neck. Their time together was going to be too short as it was, she thought, her heart aching. There was no sense wasting it on senseless battles about ideology.

Bryan hugged her tight, closing his eyes against another wave of pain. He had to find some way to show her that her life didn't have to be all sacrifice. He especially had to find a way to show her they didn't need to sacrifice their love, that it would be strong enough to withstand anything if only she would believe.

He gave her a tentative, heart-stealing smile, his blue eyes brimming with vulnerability. "Friends again?"

Rachel nodded. She sniffed, blinked back the last of her tears, and lifted a hand to brush at the errant lock of tawny hair that fell across Bryan's forehead and into his eyes. A gentle smile curved her mouth.

"I thought you were going to get a haircut."

His expression went comically blank, then

guilty. A warm blush colored his high cheekbones. He ducked his head sheepishly. "Um . . . I guess I forgot."

"Come on," Rachel said, chuckling softly. "Maybe we can get Mother to do it for you. She's a whiz with a scissors, you know."

They shared a smile, letting the moment heal the wounds they had inflicted, then Bryan turned the doorknob with suspicious ease and they walked out of the study together.

TWELVE

The term *fool's gold* had taken on a whole new, personal dimension for Bryan. In the three days since he'd discovered the possibility of there being a treasure hidden somewhere in or around Drake House, he had spent nearly every waking moment searching for it. He had inspected the house from its musty, cobweb-filled attic to its dank, dark cellar. He had painstakingly examined every wall and floor in search of hidden compartments. He had experienced considerable excitement upon discovering a secret vault in the basement, only to be visited by crushing disappointment hours later when he finally managed to get the thing open and found nothing inside but some old *National Geographics* and a ship in a bottle.

His search of the grounds had been no less futile. If Arthur "Ducky" Drake had buried his booty, he had certainly left behind no clues in the lawn as to where it was. Of course, nearly sixty years had gone by. Whatever Ducky might have left behind could have been long gone by now.

Bryan heaved a sigh as he went over it all in his mind yet again. He'd spent the entire morning in the study, mostly sitting and staring. This had presumably been Arthur Drake's favorite room. It was where the man had hung his portrait. It was probably where he had written the journal Porky and Rat so coveted—the journal Bryan had photocopied in its entirety before handing it over to them.

He went over the last of the entries again, then pulled his glasses off and rubbed at his weary eyes. The nearest thing to a clue he had found in Drake's writings was mention of his pleasure boat, the *Treasure*. It was on that craft Ducky Drake had met his end on Armistice Day, 1931, when the ship had gone down with all aboard her. The last few notes Drake had made in his journal after the mention of "sticking the pig" were about his concerns over the whereabouts of his vanished friend A.W. and a couple of vague references to having some workmen come to do minor repairs around the house—plumbing and brickwork and the like.

Maybe Arthur Drake and his gold were both now lying at the bottom of the Pacific. Maybe Lorraine Clement had been correct in her hunch that Wimsey had been the elusive gentleman bandit, in which case poring over the Drake journal was a waste of time. But if Wimsey were the thief, why wouldn't he tell Addie where the gold was? Because it wasn't there?

Maybe Rachel was right, he conceded. Maybe it was all a big wild goose chase.

"That's no way to think," Bryan muttered to himself in disgust. Pessimism had never gotten anybody anywhere.

Pushing himself up out of the desk chair, he stretched and cast a cursory glance over his shoulder at the image of Arthur Drake that hung on the wall. He would unravel this mystery as he had unraveled dozens of others over the years. But he needed a clear head to do it.

He had run himself into the ground, spending his days searching for the gold and his nights watching out for signs of Wimsey, not to mention their other nocturnal visitor. What little time he'd spent in bed he'd spent making love to Rachel, trying his best to bind her to him in the most elemental way he could, trying to show her with his body how much he loved her. He couldn't escape the sinking feeling that his message wasn't getting through. Or maybe she was simply ignoring it.

Even though they hadn't argued again, neither had things been the same as before their fight. There was a tension straining their relationship. Bryan could sense the invisible barrier Rachel was erecting layer by thin layer between them. She might have forgiven him for his harsh words, but she couldn't forgive him for believing in things that couldn't be seen or touched. And the harder he tried to convince her that his outlook was a better one, the farther she drifted away from him.

She had been working as hard as he, slaving over the state of Addie's finances and struggling with Addie herself, fighting a futile battle to repair her relationship with her mother before it was too late.

Standing by the French doors, Bryan heaved a sigh. Outside, the morning had turned blue and beautiful. He flung open the doors and drank in the scents. The air was fresh with the tang of the sea and the sweetness of sun-warmed grass and wildflowers.

It was the kind of day meant for playing hooky. It was the kind of day meant for picnics and hand-in-hand walks, for taking leisurely drives along the shore and making love under the afternoon sun. It was the kind of day too many people let pass by, sure that another would come along at a more convenient time in their lives. Bryan knew for a fact that wasn't always true. You had to enjoy life moment to moment because tomorrow was a promise that wasn't always kept. Too many people waited until it was too late, then looked back on their lives with bitterness and regret.

He couldn't let Rachel be one of them.

Determination giving him a fresh burst of strength, he strode to the desk and picked up the telephone.

"My word, that's a lovely color on you, Abbey," Aunt Roberta commented. "Just lovely. And the feathers are really you. Don't you think so, Rebecca? I think they're really *her.*"

Rachel sighed wearily and raised her head, looking past the sea of bank statements, bills, and canceled checks spread out across the dining room table to where her mother sat in a pool of yellow light near the window, glowering at her.

Addie wore another of her nondescript loose housedresses and had an emerald-green feather boa draped around her neck. In her hands she clutched a pottery ashtray the size of a Frisbee, and every so often she thrust it beneath Roberta's cigarette to catch the fallout. Roberta sat in a rocker beside her, pumping the thing as if she were out to set some kind of record. Smoke billowed from her nostrils, giving the impression that her boundless nervous energy came from a combustion engine.

"For goodness' sake, Rowena, you look exhausted!"

"I've had a lot of work to do."

"Stealing my money," Addie muttered.

"There isn't any money to steal, Mother," Rachel shot back. Gritting her teeth, she tamped down her temper. "I'm trying to help you. I came back here to help you."

Addie narrowed her eyes. Her lips thinned to a white line of disapproval. It made her so angry to see Rachel going through her business papers. It made her angry to know she couldn't have gone through them herself because they made no sense to her anymore. She certainly didn't want Rachel sifting through them looking for yet another way to humiliate her and snatch away a little more of her independence.

"She's not my daughter, you know," she said to Roberta.

Rachel rolled her eyes.

Roberta's black brows arched up. "She's not? I thought she was. Bryan said she was. He *told* me Ramona was your daughter."

"Ramona who?"

"Your daughter."

"I don't have a daughter. Pay attention here, Roberta," Addie said crossly, smacking the woman on the arm. "After all the sacrifices I made for my daughter so she could go on to greatness as a soprano, she ran off with a nightclub singer."

"Oh, my gosh, Althea," Roberta whispered in shock, crossing herself with her cigarette. "My gosh."

Rachel tuned out. She really didn't have the energy to deal with her mother today. She had been on the telephone half the morning with a woman from the California Health and Welfare Agency, discussing financial aid for people with Alzheimer's. The bureaucracy was incredible, the benefits negligible in relation to the expenses a chronically ill person faced. She had to consider Addie's loss of income, housing costs, medical costs, cost for in-home help or respite care, the normal costs of living, taxes, miscellaneous expenses. And somewhere down the road she would have to deal with the expense of putting Addie in a nursing home.

As badly as she wanted to care for her mother

herself, Rachel realized that would eventually become impossible. Addie's condition would inevitably decline to the point where she would need constant care and supervision, and Rachel would not be able to provide that and keep a job as well.

She planted her elbows on the tabletop and rubbed her hands over her face. Already the strain was getting to her. What was she going to feel like after months, even years of this? Despair welled inside her at the prospect of a bleak, joyless future.

Bryan.

His name drifted through her mind as if someone had whispered it low and soft in her ear. Warmth cascaded through her, enticing, like forbidden fruit. It was strange, but just thinking about him relaxed her.

"Come along, angel," Bryan said briskly.

Rachel's head snapped up. Cautiously, she turned to look at him as if she didn't quite believe he would be there. But there he stood, looking rumpled and sexy in his snug jeans and faded Notre Dame sweatshirt.

"Come along," he said again, taking her by the hand and tugging her out of her chair.

"Where . . . ?"

He flashed her a brilliant smile. "To play hooky."

Rachel dug her heels in. "Bryan, I don't have time to play hooky."

"I'm not giving you a choice."

There was definitely something steely and predatory about his smile, reminding Rachel that there was a great deal more to this man than what so pleasingly met the eye. A shiver danced through her at the glint of determination in his deep blue gaze.

"Bryan, I would like nothing more than to take a day off, but I have responsibilities."

"They'll still be here when we get back."

"Bryan, honey, what are you doing with Rhonda?" Roberta asked.

"I'm abducting her, Aunt Roberta." He let go of Rachel's hand, quickly bent and put a shoulder to her stomach, and heaved her up, wrapping his arm around her wildly flailing legs. She squealed in surprise.

"Oh, well, fine, dear." Roberta smiled and waved her cigarette at them. "Have a nice time!"

Addie stuck her tongue out at them.

Bryan frowned at her and turned back toward his aunt, balancing Rachel on his shoulder as if she were a sack of potatoes. He gave Roberta a meaningful look. "You and Addie keep each other out of trouble, okay?"

"Trouble! My stars, honey!" She cackled and coughed. "What trouble could we get into?"

"I shudder to think," Rachel grumbled. She wriggled on Bryan's shoulder as he carried her out of the room and down the hall. "Bryan, neither one of them should be left alone."

"Don't be silly. Aunt Roberta is a little unique, but she's perfectly capable of being left on her own."

"Personally, I think it's a toss-up as to which of them is loonier, but the point is: I shouldn't be leaving Mother."

"Rachel, you can't spend every hour of every day

with her. It isn't good for either one of you," he
said, toting her down the porch steps and across
the lawn. "Think about it. You're going to be taking
care of Addie for a long time. Do you want to end
up hating her because you shackled her to you like
a ball and chain and threw away the key?"

She was silent as he deposited her in the passenger seat of her car and went around to the other
side. Any retort she might have made was silenced
by the knowledge that she already had feelings of
resentment toward her mother. Hadn't she wondered herself how bitter she would be in the end?

"Don't worry about Aunt Roberta." The Chevette
started with a squeal of protest that settled into a
pathetic whine. "I explained to her all about Addie's illness."

"When?" Rachel asked in surprise. She thought
he hadn't done much of anything lately except
search for his ridiculous buried treasure.

"When you had your nose buried in work, I
imagine."

"Better submerged in trying to solve my problems than burying my head in the sand or running
off to do Lord knows what—"

"Oh, didn't I tell you?" he said as he turned the
car out onto the busy coastal highway. "We're going ballooning."

Rachel was momentarily struck dumb. For one
terrible instant her heart stopped. When she
found her tongue again, she said, "Going what?"

"Ballooning." Bryan grinned, his handsome face
lighting up with excitement. "Up in a montgolfier."

"Turn this car around right now," Rachel demanded in her sternest voice, proud that none of her sudden panic came through in her tone. She thumped her index finger against the dash. "I mean it, Bryan. Turn this thing around and take me home right this minute."

"Sorry, angel," he said. "I'd rather take you to heaven."

She could tell by the set of his jaw that he wasn't going to back down. The man could be unbearably stubborn. Well, if he thought he was going to get her into the basket of a hot air balloon, he had another think coming. Of all the silly pranks, dragging her away from work for an afternoon of absolute foolishness. The idea was completely . . . tempting.

Settling back into her seat, Rachel crossed her arms over her chest and fumed. This was precisely the reason she and Bryan didn't belong together. He wanted to dazzle her with magic and fun when there simply was no room in her life for either.

They turned off the main road and headed east over the hills. Even this narrow, winding county road was busy, clogged with tourists out for a day of gawking at the beautiful scenery. The lower slopes of the golden hills were speckled with dark fir trees, and the heavier forest worked its way up toward the incomparable blue of the summer sky. They passed sheep farms and apple orchards.

Finally, Bryan slowed the car and turned off the road onto a dirt path where a colorful wooden cutout of a balloon was tacked to a fence post. The sign read SKY DRIFTERS BALLOON RIDES. Rachel swallowed hard.

They parked near an enormous weathered gray barn, beside several cars with out-of-state plates.

Bryan turned and gave her a serious look, though his eyes were twinkling. "Do you walk from here or do I get to carry you some more?"

"I'll walk," Rachel replied in a cool tone, her slim nose in the air.

Still, he took her by the hand when they got out of the car, as if there were some danger of her making a break for it. A loud hissing roar sounded on the far side of the barn. It was a sound that Rachel might once have imagined coming from a mythical dragon. Of course, she didn't believe in dragons anymore, at least not the green, scaly kind.

They rounded the side of the barn, and her heart went into her throat. Some distance away, in a large open field, a balloon was tethered to the ground, its gaily striped bag swaying in the gentle breeze. Several young men in casual dress were leaning indolently against the wicker gondola, obviously having fun shooting the bull. There was another roar as one attendant sent a blast of heat from the burner into the balloon. The striped bag rippled as the air inside it expanded.

"She's all ready for you, Bry!" the slender, bearded man called as they neared the enormous contraption. He pulled his leather gloves off and slapped them against his thigh. "Great day for it!"

"That's what I thought," Bryan said with a grin, tugging a reluctant Rachel nearer the balloon.

Her eyes were riveted to the narrow wicker basket even as the introductions were made. The name of Bryan's bearded friend and the rest of the balloon crew went in one ear and out the other. She'd never been afraid of heights, she reflected, but then, she'd never been asked to go up in a balloon. She could feel her face going pale as Bryan nudged her closer.

"You'll love it, sweetheart," he promised as he lifted her into the gondola.

It didn't seem as necessary to express her skepticism on that point as on the next. "Do you really know how to fly this thing?"

"No," he admitted with a mischievous grin. He pulled on the gloves his friend handed him and swung himself gracefully into the craft. "But I'm pretty sure I can make it land. I managed to do it once near Berlin, and there were people shooting at me then, so this should be a piece of cake."

Rachel stared at him in horror.

His friend took pity on her. "Don't worry, Rachel, he knows more than he's letting on. Besides, you'll be tethered to the ground the whole time. Bryan just wanted a place where the two of you could have a nice, private picnic. Pretty romantic, huh?"

Rachel gave him a blank look, but it was too late to ask questions. Picnic? Who could think about food at a time like this, she wondered as the ground crew moved away from the gondola and the balloon above them tugged the basket up a few feet off the ground. She dug her fingernails into the dry brown wicker and watched in horrified fascination as Bryan attended the burner. Flame roared up into the fabric bag. He shot her a wink as they lifted into the air, but mainly he kept his eyes trained on the instrument panel that hung from the framework just below the burner.

He did indeed appear to know what he was doing, which left Rachel free to experience her first ascent in a montgolfier. The sensation was not unlike going up in an elevator—a wobbly elevator that swayed slightly with their movements, an elevator that had no safe, solid building around it. She braved a peek over the edge, and her stomach fluttered the same way it had on her first roller coaster ride. The crew stood on the ground below, waving happily at her, growing smaller and smaller as the balloon lifted higher and higher. Then the tether lines pulled tight, halting their flight.

"Well, what do you think?" Bryan asked.

She dragged in a deep breath, ready to tell him exactly what she thought of this irresponsible escapade of his, but the words caught in her throat as she took in the view around them. It was spectacular. She could see for miles in every direction. Golden hills, soft green pastures, dark patterns of forest. Northern California in all its rumpled wild charm lay beneath them. In the distance she could see another brightly striped balloon floating free above the countryside. To the west the ocean stretched across the horizon, a ribbon of misty blue between the coast and the fog bank. And the beauty was not only in the landscape, but in the silence—it was exquisite and absolute.

The sudden sense of peace was so startling, it brought tears to Rachel's eyes. For days now she had been feeling worn out and beaten down. Her focus had narrowed to a kind of tunnel vision that allowed her to see only what was wrong with her life. She had been ignoring all this wondrous beauty, had shut it out of her life. And Bryan had given it back to her.

She turned to him now with a tremulous smile and said, "I think I love you."

His wise, warm blue eyes sparkled, and he slid his arms around her and kissed her.

They stayed aloft admiring the view while enjoying a leisurely picnic lunch of fresh croissants, cheeses, grapes, and an excellent bottle of California white wine. They talked about everything they could think of that had nothing to do with Addie or Drake House or money. They stood and enjoyed the silence and the simple pleasure of being alone together. It was a wonderful treat. A perfect way to spend part of a perfect afternoon.

Sadly, Rachel knew they would have to come down to earth, both literally and figuratively. But she held the memory of their golden afternoon in her heart as they drove home. Maybe there was some merit in the occasional burst of reckless frivolity. She felt refreshed, rejuvenated. If that wasn't magic, she didn't know what was. Somewhere up in the sky she had left behind her guilt over abandoning Addie and their troubles for a few hours, and she didn't miss it a bit. Now she felt ready to go back and face her financial troubles, ready to try again with Addie. And she had the man beside her to thank for it.

The real jolt to earth came as they turned up the coast road at the edge of Anastasia and headed north, toward Drake House. On the opposite side of the road a police car and a tow truck sat with their lights flashing. Officers and other assorted folk milled around. Traffic had slowed to a crawl, allowing all passersby a clear view of the trouble.

A rusty powder-blue Volvo station wagon had taken out a roadside vendor's cart, then mushed its nose into a stone retaining wall. There were flowers everywhere—on the road, draped across the car's hood and roof, crushed beneath the wheels of the police car. There were roses and daisies and carnations and tiger lilies, flowers of every color. It looked almost as if someone had strewn them about to make the scene of the accident look less tragic. The vendor's cart had been reduced to a pathetic pile of toothpicks, and the vendor, a huge woman in a Hawaiian muumuu and a tennis visor, stood beside it looking stunned.

Rachel's eyes widened in horror as realization dawned. "Oh, my—oh, my— That's Mother's car!"

Bryan was already steering the Chevette to the shoulder. They abandoned the car and made their way across the road, grim and silent.

"No more gawkers!" Deputy Skreawupp commanded in his gruff monotone. He scowled at them, his jowls drooping like a truculent bulldog's. He pointed an index finger at Bryan as if it were a loaded gun. "This is police business, bub. Now, get out of here, or I'll flatten you like pie crust, and I can do it."

"That's my mother's car!" Rachel said, pushing her way past the deputy's pot belly.

"Humph! Batty Addie's gone and done it this time," he said, flipping back a page in his pocket notebook. "Driving without a license, expired tags, reckless endangerment, destruction of property—"

Rachel wasn't listening to the litany of charges. Her heart was hammering in her ears as she stumbled to the open driver's door of the Volvo, where Addie sat with her legs out, her garden boots planted on the gravel. She was as white as the waxy day lily that was stuck under the windshield wiper. "Mother! Mother, are you all right?"

Addie looked, her eyes wide. She was still stunned from the accident, and the confusion of its aftermath had short-circuited her brain. She stared at the young woman crouching down in front of her and tried to concentrate on the girl's face. She was someone Addie was certain she should recognize.

"Rachel?" she murmured uncertainly. Fear shivered through her. She'd never felt so old or so frail . . . or frightened.

"Mother, what happened?" Rachel asked gently. She took one of Addie's thin, cold hands between hers and held it, both to comfort her mother and to reassure herself.

"I'm . . . not . . . sure," Addie said slowly, tilting her head this way and that, as if the movement might jar loose a memory.

"I am," Roberta said.

Bryan's aunt was still strapped into the passenger's seat. Her hair stood up around her head like an abused Brillo pad. "She can't drive worth a damn, can she? It's a good thing we remembered our seat belts. My gosh."

It was a good thing they had remembered their seat belts, Rachel reflected, shaking her head. Too bad neither of them had remembered Addie wasn't supposed to get behind the wheel.

Deputies came then to take the two ladies' statements and Rachel wandered away from the wrecked car. Hugging herself, she stood beside the retaining wall and stared out at Anastasia, nestled below, picture-postcard perfect with its Victorian buildings and boat-filled bay.

"Nobody was hurt," Bryan said, coming up behind her. He refrained from mentioning that the flower vendor was threatening to sue. He would speak with Alaina about that. Rachel looked rattled enough as it was. "I'm afraid Aunt Roberta misunderstood me when I told her Addie couldn't drive. She thought I meant the car was broken, so, when she looked under the hood and saw that the only thing wrong was that the coil wire wasn't hooked up to the distributor cap, she just fixed it," he explained apologetically. "She learned to be a mechanic in the army. She was a WAC."

"Wacky," Rachel muttered darkly.

"That too."

She wheeled on him suddenly, jabbing an index finger to his sternum. "I never should have let you talk me into leaving Mother with her! She's certifiable; any sane, responsible person can see that."

Bryan winced. "Rachel, I'm sorry. I should have been more thorough about disabling the car. I'll accept responsibility—"

"Since when?" she asked angrily. All the fear and fury and frustration crested at once inside her, and she unleashed it on him without hesitation. "Since when do you accept responsibility? You're the most irresponsible person I know. You with your don't-worry-be-happy mentality. Everything will take care of itself. Everything will turn out fine," she said bitterly. "If you knew anything about accepting responsibility, this never would have happened! I would have been home to keep an eye on Mother, not off in the wild blue yonder with you!"

She paced away from him, shaking her head in self-reproach.

"Don't beat yourself up with guilt, Rachel. An accident happened. Nobody was hurt. I'll take care of the rest. It'll all work out."

He couldn't have chosen a worse phrase had he been deliberately trying to goad her. His last four words rang in her ears. She could hear Terence saying them and Bryan saying them, and she could see herself dealing with the messy reality while they blew it off because nobody had gotten hurt.

"Why can't you face reality?" she asked, her violet eyes full of pleading and pain. "Things don't just work out, Bryan. Things don't just turn out fine. We struggle to do the best we can and we still get kicked in the teeth. *That's* reality, not buried treasure and eating Brie in a hot air balloon."

She shook her head again, lifting her hands to cradle it as it hung down. "I should have known better. I should have known from the start."

I should never have gotten involved with you.

Bryan's head snapped back sharply. She didn't have to say the words; they arced between them like an electrical current that seared his nerve endings with excruciating pain. Their love meant so little to her, she was wishing it away. It was inconvenient, getting in the way of her noble self-sacrifice. His own defense mechanisms snapped into action to stem the flow of blood from his battered heart.

"Fine," he said tightly. "You shouldn't have any enjoyment in your life. God forbid! There's work to be done, sins to be atoned for, hair shirts to be worn."

Rachel grabbed his arm as he started to turn away from her. "Don't you go calling me a martyr. I'm a sensible, practical person trying to deal with a nightmare in a sensible, practical way."

"Oh, right," he said sarcastically. He smiled a rueful parody of a smile. "Maybe I should have taken my cue from you and behaved in a sensible, practical way, because I sure as hell didn't need the kind of aggravation falling in love with you has been."

It was Rachel's turn to wince. The pain wasn't entirely unexpected. She'd told herself from the start Bryan would cut his losses when the going got rough. That was what dreamers did.

"Well, don't let me stand in your way," she said softly, opening her arms wide in a gesture of resignation. "There's no time like the present. I'm certainly not going to try to stop you."

Bryan stared at her long and hard, doing everything he could to hide his own hurt while he looked for some evidence of hers. She was bitter and disillusioned and had meant every word she'd said. She hadn't believed in his love from the beginning, not really, not in the way that mattered most. It was clear she was determined to carry out her plans for her penance, and he had no part in them. Or maybe in some perverse way he did. It made her sacrifice only greater if she could look back on their relationship and think of what she had given up, of what might have been.

"Fine," he said, looking past her to the crumpled powder-blue Volvo, where Aunt Roberta was having an animated conversation with the erstwhile flower vendor. "I'll move my aunt out to Keepsake. I'll stop by tonight for our things."

He didn't look to Rachel for confirmation or approval. He didn't look at her at all. He simply walked away. She watched him go, thinking he looked like a stranger. There was an air of cold authority about him as he took his aunt by the arm, murmured a few curt words to her, and led her away.

Rachel wondered if she had ever really known him. But the point was moot. She was never going to have the chance to find out now. He was walking out of her life, taking all the light with him. As the fog bank rolled in around her, she thought of her future and ached at how empty it would be.

THIRTEEN

"Now, keep your eye on the dollar bill," Bryan said.

He sat back on his barstool, his concentration on the trick rather than on the small group of semi-interested onlookers. He folded the bill into an intricate bow shape, squeezed it between his palms, turned his hands. When he turned his palms outward again, the bill was gone.

"Great trick," Dylan Harrison said from behind the bar. He wiped his hands on a towel and leaned against the polished surface. "Now make it reappear, Houdini. I want my buck back."

Bryan sighed, took a sip of his whiskey, and performed the trick in reverse. The bill did not reappear. On three tries the best he could manage to produce was a wilted flower and a lint ball. He frowned, his broad shoulders slumping dejectedly as his audience wandered away.

Dylan reached across the bar and patted him on the shoulder. "Don't sweat it, Bry. I'll put it on your tab."

"I've lost it again," Bryan mumbled. "I've lost my magic."

"You're having an off day, that's all."

"There's an understatement."

Losing Rachel put the day in the catastrophic category. He'd seen it coming, of course. It was just that his unflagging optimism had convinced him he would be able to prevent it when the time came. He'd been wrong.

After the fight to end all fights, he had taken Aunt Roberta out to Keepsake—Faith and Shane Callan's inn—dumped her there, and made a beeline for Dylan's Bar and Bait Shop, the popular waterfront establishment owned and run by Alaina's husband. He still needed to return to Drake House for Roberta's and his belongings, but he hadn't been able to face that task without a little fortification of the distilled variety. He needed something to dull his too-sensitive senses. Time, mostly, but in lieu of that a nip or two of Dylan's Irish wouldn't hurt—especially since Dylan was liberally watering the stuff when he thought Bryan wasn't looking.

That wasn't the standard practice at Dylan's. It was a neat bar that catered to tourists and locals alike. The floors were swept, the glasses clean, and the booze uncut. He was getting special treatment because he was obviously in such rough shape. Dylan was looking out for him, like any good, conscientious friend would. It made him feel a little better to think that Alaina had ended up with such a good guy. If he had to be lonely and miserable for the rest of his life, at least his best friends had found happiness.

"My, you look like hell," Alaina said mildly, sliding onto the stool next to his.

"I know, I know." He sighed. "I need a haircut."

"That too."

She was immaculate as usual, every chestnut hair in place, not so much as a speck on her Ralph Lauren ensemble of gold slacks and a midnight-blue silk blouse. Bryan, on the other hand, knew he looked as if he'd been sleeping in an alley. His jeans were rumpled. Roberta had burned a hole in his sweatshirt, and the tail of his white T-shirt hung down beneath the hem. It might have been a style popular with the fraternity crowd, but it didn't cut the mustard with Alaina, who probably would have given up her civil rights before her Neiman-Marcus charge card.

He shot her a look, wincing at the tender sympathy and concern in her gaze. He didn't know if he was up to having Alaina feel sorry for him. She was more in the habit of giving a person a swift kick in the britches and telling them to buck up and get on with it.

"Oh, don't get nervous," she said, extracting one of her precious, rationed cigarettes from her monogrammed case. Ignoring her husband's scowl, she lit it and took a deep, appreciative drag. As she exhaled, her shrewd gaze shifted to Bryan again. "I'm not going to do the poor-Bryan routine. Faith tells me she already failed in the attempt."

"Have the three of you ever considered sharing your amazing communications skills with the intelligence community?" he asked, his brows pulling together in annoyance. "I could give you a phone number."

Alaina ignored the remark if not its implication. "And if it's spiritual analysis you want, Jayne will be more than willing to provide that. Practical advice is more my line of expertise."

He cringed at the mention of the word. "Please. I've had all the practicality I can stand for one day. I think it's giving me a rash."

"Can we see?" Dylan asked with a bright smile. His wicked sense of humor actually managed to cut through Bryan's cloak of pain and coaxed a chuckle out of him.

Alaina rolled her eyes. "Don't you have to go gut fish or something?"

Her husband leaned across the bar, grinning as he touched the tip of his nose to hers. "Yeah, but I was saving that to share with you later, sweetheart. I know how you like to get slimy."

"Beat it, Harrison," she said without batting an eyelash. The polar ice caps would melt before Alaina Montgomery-Harrison would put her manicured hand on a dead fish.

"You don't want me around?" Dylan shrugged. "I get it. I can take a hint."

"Since when?" she said dryly, tilting her cheek up for his kiss.

He waved to Bryan and let himself out from behind the bar so he could help attend to the many customers who had wandered in before heading off for dinner at one of Anastasia's several fine seafood restaurants.

"You've got a good one there," Bryan commented.

"Yes, I have. How about you?"

"Dylan? Gee, honey, I like him, but . . ."

She gave him a look that ended his nonsense in mid-sentence. "Don't pull that act on me, Bryan. I'm sure you fool the uninitiated on a regular basis, but I am hardly that, now, am I?" She paused with typical lawyerlike drama to let her point sink in, then started her line of questioning over. "Rachel?"

Bryan sipped his drink and stared across the bar at the crowded shelves that lined the wall. "It's not working out," he said shortly.

Alaina took another long pull on her cigarette. She had been afraid something like this would happen. Still, her instincts told her Rachel Lindquist really loved Bryan, and an idiot could have seen how in love Bryan was with Rachel. The man was absolutely besotted. She even knew the problems—irreconcilable differences of philosophy, and extenuating circumstances. The question was, how to reconcile the irreconcilable?

"Look," Bryan said, hoping to avoid any more painful prodding of his feelings for one night, "maybe it's best this way. I didn't come to Anastasia looking to get embroiled in another hopeless situation. I did what I could to help Rachel and Addie. . . . It didn't work out," he finished lamely.

Alaina chose her strategy with ruthless calm. Delivering the blows, however, was another matter. She didn't enjoy inflicting pain, especially when Bryan had suffered so much already, but it seemed the only way.

Taking a deep breath, she braced her shoulders and launched her attack. "Yes, maybe you're right. You're really not up to this. You gave it a shot, you failed the test," she said with an idle shrug. "Let it slide. Heaven knows a chance at everlasting love comes along as regularly as the bus to Mendocino. You might as well wait for a woman who isn't so much trouble."

Bryan sucked in a surprised breath, but Alaina retreated before he could voice his rebuttal.

"If you'll excuse me, sweetheart, I think I'll go help my husband gut fish." She slid gracefully off her stool, leaned over to kiss Bryan's cheek. "You have fun wallowing in your self-pity."

She left him sputtering, sauntering away in a cloud of Chanel and smoke.

"Dirty player," he muttered. He should have known better than to go against her. He probably had a note someplace reminding him of that, but he was too tired to look for it.

So he was feeling sorry for himself, he thought angrily. So what? He had a right to.

So does Rachel.

"Right?" He sneered. "She practically makes a living at it."

That's not fair.

"Oh, shut up," he said to his little voice, ignoring the stares he drew from several other patrons at the bar. He wrapped his hand around his chunky tumbler of liquor and took another sip.

It was a matter of circumstances conspiring

against them, he reflected. If he and Rachel had met at another time, in another place. If he had been able to prove to her Wimsey's existence. If he had found the gold.

To take his mind off his self-pity, he thought about the gold. Lorraine Clement believed Wimsey had stolen it. But if Wimsey had stolen it and Addie truly spoke to Wimsey on a regular basis, if Wimsey was indeed the force he knew was present in Drake House, then why wouldn't Wimsey have led Addie to the treasure?

No. His mind kept turning to Arthur Drake. He knew with certainty that Ducky was their man. If only the clever thief had thought to leave a clue for some worthy adversary . . .

"Adversary," he mumbled, his brows pulling together. He pushed his glasses up on his nose. Suddenly his eyes went wide. "Ad*versity*."

Realization roared through him like a flood tide, leaving him awash in goose bumps. It had been there all along, right under his stupid nose!

He swiveled around on his barstool just as the front door opened and Felix Rasmussen slipped in and slinked along one wall like the rat he so resembled. Bryan fought back a grin. Maybe his luck hadn't all run out.

Helping himself to the whiskey bottle, he splashed a little more in his glass, then on his hands, and he baptized his cheeks with it as if it were aftershave lotion. He rubbed a little through his hair, took a quick swig, and gargled before swallowing. Then, with his glass in one hand and the bottle in the other, he made his way unsteadily across the room to the small table where Rat had taken a seat.

"Mister Rasmussen!" He gave the man a lopsided grin. Rasmussen's eyes darted back and forth as he searched hastily for an escape route. He found none, and his bony shoulders drooped in resignation as Bryan straddled the chair across from his. "How ya doin'?"

"I'm—fine—Mr. Hennessy," Rasmussen said solemnly, the way a dying man might say he was fine.

Bryan slapped a big hand down on the tabletop. "Glad to hear it! Me, I've had better days." He leaned back in his chair and took a gulp of his drink, letting it dribble down his chin. "Yeah, yeah. Got tossed out of Lindquist's, you know. She gave some feeble excuse about my drinking, but . . ." He waved a hand. "Women, huh, Felix? Women! You know how it is."

"Women," Rasmussen echoed. He looked as uncomfortable as a man who had accidentally sat down in something wet. "A—yes." He nodded, but his expression clearly said he had not the slightest idea of how it was.

Bryan gave him a shrewd sideways look. "You'll never get that house away from them. You know that? You never will."

Rasmussen's thin mouth tightened to the point of disappearing entirely.

"You know what I think?" Bryan asked, breathing heavily in the man's face. Rasmussen coughed and blinked. "Do you know what I think, Felix? She said she didn't believe me, but I think she wanted it all to herself, the little—"

He paused to belch, tapping his sternum with his fist. Rasmussen was on the edge of his seat, waiting to hear the rest of the statement, but Bryan waved it away.

"Forget it. What do I care? Huh, Felix? What do I care? I don't need her with her loony mother. Rich babes are a dime a dozen." He paused to take a swig right out of the bottle and wiped his shirt-sleeve across his mouth. Leaning across the table, he pointed at Rat. "Hey, you got a dime?"

Half the bar turned to stare as he burst into loud, obnoxious laughter, reached across the table, and thumped Rat on the arm in a gesture of male camaraderie that nearly knocked the man to the floor.

"Jeez, I kill me!" Bryan laughed. "I'm a damn genius. Did you know that, Felix? Huh? Did you know you were up against a damn genius?"

"Genius," Rasmussen murmured, his furtive gaze zipping nervously around the room.

"Let 'em rot in their ugly ol' house. Ha! I can get what I want. It's in the wall behind that por-hic!-trait. I can get what I want just like that." He tried to snap his fingers and managed to overturn his drink in the process. The watered-down liquor pooled on the table and ran over the edge and onto the floor, the whole process enchanting Bryan. He smiled boyishly, leaning down close to the mess. "I made a waterfall. Look at that, Felix."

Dylan suddenly appeared beside the table, looking sad and sympathetic. He dropped a towel into the miniature lake and put a steadying hand on Bryan's shoulder, just saving him from falling off his chair. "Come on, pal. I think you've had enough."

"Says who?" Bryan demanded. His chin jutted out at an aggressive angle.

"Says me."

"Yeah? Both of you?" He dissolved into giggles and reached across the table toward Rat, who arched back out of his way. "Maybe they're right!"

"Come on," Dylan said with the tolerance of long experience. "You can sleep it off out back. There's nothing like the smell of live bait to sober a guy up."

He helped Bryan up and led him toward the door that separated the bar from the bait shop. Rasmussen bolted for the front without hesitation. The instant he was gone, Bryan straightened and stretched and grinned at his friend.

"Well, that was fun!" he said brightly. "Can I use your phone?"

Dylan shook himself out of his incredulous stare. "Yeah, sure."

Bryan was already across the room and behind the bar. He dialed the number of Keepsake from memory.

"Shane, it's getting exciting."

Rachel went into her bedroom, barely dredging up enough energy to put one foot in front of the other. She was exhausted, done in, wrung out. She couldn't imagine being more tired without actually lapsing into unconsciousness.

After straightening out the situation at the accident, she had packed Addie into the Chevette and gone to a fast-food place for dinner. That had been a disaster in its own right, with Addie accusing the help of giving her food she hadn't ordered because they wanted to poison her. Neither of them had ended up eating very much. By the time they had returned to Drake House, her mother had insisted on going straight to bed. Rachel hadn't argued.

She had spent a couple of hours sorting out the papers she had left in neat stacks on the dining room table. They hadn't been neat upon her return. They had been shuffled into one enormous multicolored mountain. The sight had brought tears to her eyes. She supposed she was lucky Addie hadn't set the pile ablaze, but lucky was the last thing she was feeling. Finally she had given up on trying to concentrate and had dragged herself upstairs.

Maybe things wouldn't look quite so bleak in the morning.

"Now I sound like Bryan," she muttered, pulling her Bach T-shirt out of the dresser drawer. "A good night's sleep won't make everything better."

But it would have been a comfort. To sleep in Bryan's arms, snuggled against his warm body, her legs tangled with his. To have him hold her and kiss her hair and sing in his sleep.

She shook her head. "Whoever heard of anyone singing in their sleep?"

She pulled her sweater off and dragged her T-shirt on in its place. She let her jeans drop to the floor and lay there, too tired even to dream

about being neat. Taking her hair down from its
messy knot, she turned toward the bed.

There was a red rose lying on it, a perfect red
rose lying on the bodice of another old dress. This
dress was pearl-pink satin encrusted with seed
pearls and trimmed in lace that had turned dark
ivory with age. It was of the same era as the
burgundy dress. It was beautiful.

Rachel let her fingertips brush across it as she
picked up the rose. Tears flooded her eyes. Bryan.
When had he put it there? She tried to sort out
the answer to that question as she brushed the
rosebud against her cheek, but her brain was too
exhausted to function. He couldn't have had time
to do it that morning, but he had to have. The only
other explanation was that he had come back after
. . . after and done it, but that made no sense at
all. Besides, she knew his things were still there—
his clothes and magic tricks and juggling balls and
all the paraphernalia associated with his odd
work.

He hadn't come back. He probably wouldn't
come back while she was in the house. She had
made it more than clear that she didn't want him
around.

Sniffing back a tear, she sank to the bed and sat
there clutching the rose and the satin dress. She'd
never felt so empty in her life, not even when she'd
left Terence in Nebraska and headed west. That
was probably because she hadn't loved Terence
anymore, had never loved him in that deep, soul-
searing way she loved Bryan. She couldn't have felt

this empty, because she hadn't lost nearly as much.

She tried to tell herself it was best they had ended it now. She'd known all along it would have to end before she and Addie left for San Francisco. But she had never wanted it to end so bitterly. She would have preferred they part as friends, that they let the passion simply fade away into sweet, gentle memories. That would have been nice, to have those memories stored away inside so she could take them out on long, lonely nights and smile at them and hold them close to her heart. Now there would always be a certain sadness attached, even to the best of them. And every time she took them out, there would be regret for the way they parted, for the things that might have been if only she had been able to believe in magic.

Closing her eyes, Rachel tried to block out the pain. It was no good having regrets for being practical. Someone had to face life's problems and deal with them in a sane, rational way. It didn't do any good wishing that someone weren't her.

Addie stood at the door to her daughter's room, peeking in, hesitant to enter. Rachel looked tired and miserable, and Addie couldn't help but wonder how much of that was her fault.

She had awakened from a deep sleep, feeling strangely calm and clearheaded, but also feeling a sense of urgency. She needed to see Rachel, to speak to her.

The accident had etched itself in her otherwise foggy memory with a clarity that made her heart clench every time she closed her eyes. She had been behind the wheel, driving toward town, when whatever knowledge she had possessed about driving went right out of her head. She had suddenly looked at the steering wheel and had no idea what to do with it. She knew the pedals on the floor served some purpose, but she hadn't been able to recall what it was. And when her brain had tried to send a message to her hands or her feet to do something, anything, the message had never arrived.

It turned her stomach to think of it. The result could have been disastrous. She might have hit someone. That strange woman who had been with her might have been injured or killed. She might have been killed herself, and then she never would have seen Rachel again.

The chill that drifted through her frail old body made her pull her robe more closely around her. She had it on inside out, but she hadn't been able to fix it, and it didn't really matter anyway. The only thing that mattered right now was Rachel.

The door drifted open a little wider, and she was suddenly stepping forward with her heart in her throat.

"Rachel?" she asked softly.

Her daughter looked up at her with luminous eyes that were brimming with tears. "Mother? What are you doing up? Is everything all right?"

"No," Addie murmured. "It's not."

She shuffled into the room and sat down on the bed, her back perfectly straight, her hands folded on her lap. They had done this before. It might have been a long, long time ago—she wasn't sure—but it seemed like yesterday. They had sat on her bed in the little house in Berkeley and made plans about Rachel's future. Now her daughter sat across from her expectantly, waiting for her to say something.

"Don't slouch, Rachel," she admonished, tapping the girl's knee. Then sadness settled over her like a veil, and she drew her hand away. "I've always pushed you too hard. Talent needs a firm hand directing it, but I pushed too hard. That's why you left with that guitar player, isn't it?"

"Yes," Rachel whispered.

Addie shook her head. "He's not good enough for you."

Rachel smiled sadly. "I know, Mother. I don't see him anymore."

"Good," she said decisively. "You've always been a sensible girl, except for that business."

"I wanted you to love me in spite of that. I wish you could have."

"Love you?" Addie asked, incredulous. She stared at her daughter, certain Rachel had taken leave of her senses. "I've always loved you. You're my life."

"But you wouldn't forgive me."

"I wouldn't forgive myself either. That doesn't mean I didn't love you, it means I wouldn't forgive you. They are two quite different things," she insisted.

"Do you forgive me now?"

"You threw away all our dreams," Addie began, but she cut herself off. What good were those dreams going to do her now? They were gone forever. Rachel had to run her own life.

She straightened her shoulders and stared at the floor, at the green rubber garden boots she wore all the time because they were easy to get on and off. The hem of her pink robe hung above them, inside out. "I'm not a well woman, Rachel. I know I do a good job of hiding it, but I forget things. All the time, more and more. I forgot how to drive that car today."

"It's all right—"

"No, it isn't," she insisted sternly. "It isn't all right at all. It's the pits. I had a perfectly nice collection of bird cages. Do you think I have any idea where they've gone?"

"We sold them," Rachel said carefully. "At the tag sale."

Addie just stared at her, drawing a blank.

"Never mind. I came back to help you, Mother. We'll manage."

Addie mustered a smile and patted her daughter's knee. "We'll manage. We always have. We have each other. And we have Hennessy."

Rachel closed her eyes against the wave of pain. "No, Mother, we don't have Hennessy."

Addie's brows pulled together in concern. "You sacked Hennessy?"

"He can't come with us to San Francisco. It wouldn't work out. He's not a butler."

"Oh. Well . . ." She guessed she'd known Hennessy wasn't a butler. He had played along so well with her, she had eventually decided to believe their little game was real. She waved her hand in a regal gesture that managed to combine resignation and regret. "He made me laugh."

"Me too," Rachel murmured. She bit her lip against the tears, but they fell nevertheless, down her cheeks and onto the bodice of the beaded dress.

"You mustn't cry on satin, Rachel," Addie said in gentle reproach. "It stains."

She took the dress from her daughter's hands and brushed it off before hanging it over the foot of the bed. She got up then and went to the dresser to fetch the hairbrush.

"We have to move, Mother," Rachel said, watching as Addie plied the brush to the squirrel's nest she'd made of her hair. "Do you understand that?"

"Yes," Addie said, staring at their reflection in the mirror above the dresser. She didn't want to talk about moving. The idea frightened her more and more. She didn't precisely understand why they had to move. Rachel would explain it to her if she asked, but what was the point? The decision was no longer hers to make. Her independence had slipped through her fingers. Fighting it only made her tired.

"One hundred strokes a night," she said, shuffling across the floor to stand behind Rachel. Slowly, gently, she drew the brush bristles through her daughter's pale gold hair. "You'll have to count, dear, I can't get past forty anymore. Or is it sixty?"

"That's all right, Mother," Rachel said, smiling through her tears. "I'll count."

"No." Addie brushed steadily, methodically, her ability to accomplish the simple task calming her.

"Sing for me. You have a voice like an angel. Sing the aria from *Zaïde*. Mozart was an idiot, but he made wonderful music."

Rachel took a deep breath, swallowing down the knot in her throat, and she sang the aria from *Zaïde*, *"Ruhe sanft"*—rest quietly. It was a sweet song, the notes all purity and light and innocence. She was out of practice, but she had been blessed with a natural talent that made practice seem redundant. Her voice held an ethereal loveliness, a purity of its own that carried the song throughout the old house though she sang softly. And when she finished, the silence was absolute, as if the house itself were holding its breath in awe.

Addie put the brush aside and rested her thin, age-spotted hands on her daughter's shoulders. "You're a good daughter, Rachel."

Rachel smiled. This was what she had prayed for, what she had pinned her hopes on, some sign from Addie that all was forgiven. There would be no emotional reconciliation scene full of hugs and kisses and tears of joy. That wasn't the way of the Lindquists. But this, in its own way, was just as touching, just as meaningful. It was certainly every bit as precious to her. She had feared this moment would never come, that Addie would slip away from her and they would never be anything but strangers with nothing between them but bitterness.

She reached up to cover her mother's hand with her own and wished fleetingly that she could have shared this moment with Bryan. But Bryan was gone. All she had now was Addie.

"Thank you, Mother."

Addie sighed and shuffled toward the door. "Go tell Wimsey dinner will be ready soon. I just have to feed the bird first."

That quickly Addie was gone. The fragile connection between reality and her mind was lost.

What a gift these last few minutes had been, Rachel thought, watching her mother shuffle away. Like magic.

Maybe there was such a thing after all.

Addie's shriek pulled Rachel from her musings and catapulted her off the bed. She pulled her jeans on and ran out in to the hall, heading in the direction of her mother's angry voice.

"I'll get you this time, you ugly thing!"

Addie stopped halfway down the hall and flung a rock at the apparition standing wreathed in smoke near the secret door. Her form would have done a major league pitcher proud. The stone sailed high and inside, catching the ghostly figure squarely on the forehead.

He grunted in pain and fell back against the partially opened door, closing it and sealing off his own escape route. His sunken eyes went wide with panic. He turned toward the two women, raising his arms and his white cape along with it.

"I am the ghost of Ebenezer Drake!" he wailed, stepping toward them, smoke rolling out from behind him accompanied by a high-pitched wheezing sound. "I come to cast you from my— ouch!"

Addie let fly another stone, bouncing this one off his chest. Rachel grabbed her by one arm and attempted to drag her away from the advancing figure, but her mother shook her off long enough to reach into her pocket. She heaved a half-finished cheeseburger that hit her target smack in the face. Ketchup trickled down his long nose.

"Mother, come on!" Rachel insisted, pulling Addie down the hall. "We have to get the police!"

"Leave!" the ghost wailed. "Leave this house!"

Miles Porchind let himself into the study through the French doors. Dressed all in black in a vain effort to hide his considerable bulk, he waddled across the room with a flashlight in his hand, going directly to the portrait of Arthur Drake III that hung on the paneled wall behind the desk. He shined his light up at the man's face.

"Thought you were so clever, didn't you?"

"As a matter of fact, yes," Bryan said, stepping out from behind the curtains. "I think I was awfully clever, don't you?"

"You!" Porchind gasped, wheeling away from the wall. He made a dash for the door to the hall, grabbing the knob, twisting and rattling it. The door didn't budge.

"Oh, that door sticks something fierce," Bryan said mildly, flipping on a light. "You know how these old houses are. Actually, I like to think the ghost is holding it shut."

"There is no ghost, you moron!" Porchind snapped, wheeling back around to face him, his florid face contorted with rage.

"No?" Bryan frowned in mock disappointment. "I guess that means Shane might get to use his gun after all." He shrugged as the fat man blanched. "Well, that'll make him happy. So, Mr. Porchind, to what do we owe this not-so-unexpected visit? Doing a little after-hours art shopping?"

"I came to claim what is rightfully mine!" he declared emphatically.

Bryan looked surprised. "Yours? Hmmm. I think the authorities might have something to say about that, seeing how you don't own this house or anything in it."

"Drake stole that gold."

"From a notorious criminal."

"I will have the gold, Mr. Hennessy," Porchind said purposefully.

Bryan raised a brow as the man produced a revolver from behind him. "Deciding to follow in the family tradition, I see."

"Shut up," Porchind ordered, his breath coming in short gasps. "Come over here and take this picture down."

Bryan shrugged. "If you say so."

He sauntered across the room and easily lifted the heavy gilt frame from its hook. The wall behind it was blank.

"Where's the safe?" Porchind demanded, his chest heaving like a bellows. Sweat beaded on his bald head and ran down the sides of his face in little rivers.

"There is no safe."

The fat man's eyes bulged as his cheeks turned crimson. "But—but—you told Rasmussen—"

Bryan grinned engagingly. "I lied."

His admission met with a murderous look. "You rotten . . ."

Porchind lifted the revolver and aimed. Bryan swung the portrait sideways, catching the man hard across the stomach with the thick frame. Porchind staggered back as his breath left him in a gust. Suddenly his feet kicked out from under him, and he fell backward with a strangled squeal. The revolver discharged as he hit the floor, the bullet exploding into the fireplace, nicking a chunk out of the brick.

The study door burst open, and Shane Callan charged into the room with a nine-millimeter Smith & Wesson in his hands. He trained the gun on Porchind and smiled a purely predatory smile, gray eyes gleaming.

"I'd drop that peashooter if I were you, sport," he said, his voice a low, rough caress.

"Where's Rasmussen?" Bryan asked.

"Out front with Deputy Screwup."

"Bryan!" Rachel exclaimed, rushing into the room, her face white, eyes wide. "Are you all right? We heard a shot!"

"I'm fine," he said coolly.

Turning away from her, he hung the portrait of Arthur Drake back in its place, brushing his fingertips across the tarnished brass plate that was affixed to the bottom molding.

"Are you all right?" he asked as they watched Shane haul Porchind to his feet and shove him out into the hall.

"I'm fine."

"And Addie?"

"Are you kidding? The police are here," Rachel joked, trying to muster up a laugh of her own and failing. "She's ecstatic."

The silence that fell between them was awkward, filled with unspoken questions. Bryan let his gaze drink in the sight of her, memorizing everything about the way she looked at that moment—young and frightened in a baggy T-shirt and jeans, her hair falling around her like a rumpled curtain of silk.

Finally, she broke the quiet, asking a question that had nothing to do with the ones in her heart. "How did you know they would be here tonight?"

"Oh, I had a hunch. I sort of sent them."

She gave him a puzzled look.

"I guess I just wanted to clear all this up for you before I left."

Rachel's heart leapt into her throat. "You're leaving? Leaving Anastasia?"

"I've been asked to go to Hungary."

"I see."

"I wanted to find the gold for you first," he explained. "After all, you and Addie deserve it more than Porky and the Rat do."

Rachel hung her head and sighed. He'd come back here and risked his life for something that didn't exist. All for her. What was she going to do? She would love him with her last breath, but she couldn't afford to go chasing rainbows with him.

She watched as Bryan went to the fireplace and selected the poker from the stand of heavy brass fire irons. Using the handle end, which was shaped like a hammerhead, he rapped it against the brick that Porchind's bullet had struck. The thin layer of brick crumbled and fell away, revealing a surface of shiny gold.

" 'Gold is tried by fire,' " he said, " 'brave men by adversity.' Seneca."

Rachel stared in stunned disbelief. She fell to her knees in front of the fireplace and lifted a trembling hand to touch the treasure that had lain hidden all these years, safe and snug behind a wall of false brick.

"Oh, my— It's real," she said on a soft breath. "Gold."

"Yes," Bryan murmured, watching her. "A considerable fortune's worth, I'd say, though I admit I don't exactly keep abreast of the market prices. You'll want to call Dylan Harrison. He does a little investment counseling on the side. He can tell you what it's worth in dollars and cents."

At the moment she didn't need to know what it was worth in dollars and cents. She knew what it was worth. It was the answer to all her financial woes. It meant they wouldn't have to sell Drake House. They wouldn't have to leave Anastasia. Practicality could take a flying leap right out of her life.

She closed her eyes and laughed as giddy joy flooded through her. Sighing, she pressed her cheek to the exposed bar of gold.

"It was really here," she whispered. "Like magic."

"Yes," Bryan said sadly. "It's a good thing one of us believed in it."

FOURTEEN

Bryan turned to quit the room, but the door had swung shut and refused to open when he tried it. He hung his head and let out a slow, measured breath, struggling to rein in his temper. Rachel had made it clear where he fit into her life—nowhere. He wanted only to make a graceful exit, but that privilege was being denied him. He had a feeling he knew why, but he was in no mood for interference from a sixth sense or anything else. Both his pride and his heart were still stinging from Rachel's rejection. He wanted only to leave.

Cursing under his breath, he stood back and gave the door a kick that clearly demonstrated an acquaintance with martial arts. Part of the jamb splintered away, and the door flew open. An odd thud sounded on the far side of the hall, and a vase teetered on its stand.

Rachel watched him go, her eyes wide, her heart pounding. He was leaving, leaving Anastasia, leaving her. The final barrier to their happiness had been eradicated, and he was leaving!

She scrambled to her feet and dashed out of the study and down the hall.

On the porch Deputy Skreawupp and another of Anastasia's finest were reading Porchind and Rasmussen their rights. The pair of erstwhile criminals stood glumly side by side with their hands cuffed behind their backs. Porchind's bowling-ball head was red with indignation. Rasmussen looked as if he would have been stark white even without his greasy makeup. The thin man rolled his shoulders uncomfortably against the straps of the contraption he and his cohort had devised to make the mystic smoke that had floated around him as he had "haunted" Drake House.

"I never should have listened to you," Porchind hissed. "You should have known it was a trap, stupid."

"A trap," Rasmussen mumbled miserably, his head lolling from side to side.

"Moron," Porchind grumbled.

"Clam up, Porky," Skreawupp ordered, shaking a stubby pencil beneath the man's nose. "I'll muzzle you like a fat circus bear, and I can do it."

Shane Callan leaned indolently back against a post, watching the scene with an almost feline smile of amused satisfaction. His hands were tucked casually into the pockets of his black jeans. The butt of his pistol peeked out from under his left arm.

Addie watched the proceedings from Skreawupp's elbow with avid interest.

"I knew they were up to no good," she said,
earning herself a scowl from the sour-faced deputy. "It took you long enough to figure it out,
Deputy Dope."

"They needed evidence, Addie," Bryan said.

She waved a hand at him. "Twaddle."

"You have the right to remain silent," the deputy
said to Porchind. He shot a dark look at Addie.
"That goes for you, too, honey bun."

She blew a loud raspberry at him and wound up
to sock him one. Rachel caught her by the arm
and swung her toward the door. "Mother, why
don't you go in and find a sweater . . . before the
deputy decides to charge you with harassment,"
she added under her breath as her mother
clomped away.

"Miss Lindquist, we'd appreciate it if you'd come
down to the station in the morning to make a
statement," the younger deputy said.

"And we'd *really* appreciate it if you left your
mother at home," Skreawupp added. Rachel's narrow look glanced off his double chins as he turned
to his captive scoundrels and herded them down
the steps. "All right, you two scum balls, it's the
slammer for you. The cooler, the can, the county
condo. I've seen your kind a hundred times. You
stalk the helpless on little cat feet and strike in the
dark of night. Makes me sick."

"He's one of a kind," Shane commented mildly
as the deputy's voice faded away and the doors
slammed on the squad car. He lit a cigarette and

sighed a stream of blue smoke into the night air. "Thank God."

"Thank you for helping, Mr. Callan," Rachel said, wrapping her arms around herself in a vain attempt to ward off the damp chill of the night as it seeped through her T-shirt and into her skin.

Shane just shrugged as he pushed himself away from the post. "That's what friends are for." His cool gray eyes slid from Rachel to Bryan. "I'll see you back at Keepsake?"

Bryan nodded. "Later. Thanks for the hand."

"You made my day," Callan said dryly, shooting his friend a handsome grin. He trotted down the front steps and disappeared into the night.

"He's an intriguing man," Rachel said, more to fill the uncomfortable silence than anything. Bryan was standing less than five feet from her, and yet he felt as distant as the moon—and as cool.

"I have to go pack." He turned stiffly toward the door.

"Would you like a cup of coffee first?" she asked, stalling for time. She felt like a coward for the first time since she'd stood up to her mother five years earlier.

"No."

The blasted man wasn't going to make this easy for her, was he? She swallowed a little more of her pride and tried again. "I'd like to hear the whole story behind the gold and Porchind and everything."

"Does it matter?" Bryan asked, giving her a

sharp look. "The gold is yours. I wouldn't think you'd care how it got there."

Rachel sucked in a breath at the blow. "That's not fair."

Bryan steeled himself against the hurt he'd caused her. She had dealt her share of it earlier. He gave a careless shrug of his broad shoulders. "Well, as I've been told time and again," he said, a sardonic smile twisting his mouth, "life isn't fair. Now, if you'll excuse me?"

"Bryan." Rachel abandoned all pretense of subtlety or pride and grabbed at the sleeve of his sweatshirt as he started through the door. She looked up at him with pleading eyes. "I don't want you to go."

"That's not what you told me this afternoon," he said, his expression carefully blank.

"Things were different this afternoon. I was upset and angry and—"

"And now you're rich?" he suggested sarcastically.

Rachel took it on the chin and plowed right ahead. "I won't have to sell the house. I won't have to worry about the kind of care I can provide for Mother. The gold changes everything."

He gave her a bleak look. "Does it?"

"Bryan, I love you," she said, the beginnings of desperation coloring her voice.

Instead of filling with joy, his earnest blue eyes only grew sad behind his glasses. "And it took something as solid, as tangible as gold to get you to trust in that love, to get you to believe it can work and last," he said quietly. "I wasn't worth taking a chance on before, but now, since you're rich, what the heck? How is that supposed to make me feel, Rachel?"

She didn't answer. She knew how it made him feel. That same horrible, hollow feeling was yawning inside her. At that moment she would have given the lion's share of the gold to be able to take back everything she'd said to him that afternoon.

"Love can't be contingent on financial security," Bryan said gently. "It can't be contingent on anything at all. Tell me what happens when the gold runs out? Will you stop believing? Will it no longer be sensible or practical to be in love with me? The vows say for richer or poorer, Rachel. For better or worse. In sickness and in health. They don't say anything about convenience. I sat by and watched someone I loved die. Do you think that was easy or convenient or fun?"

"No," she whispered, tears clinging to her thick golden lashes.

"No," he echoed softly, his eyes shadowed with remembered pain. "I won't stay here because it's suddenly become easy for you to love me, Rachel. There are lots of times when love has to subsist on nothing more than hope and a belief in magic. When you're ready to believe that . . ." His words trailed off on a tired sigh, as if he had already given up on the idea. "I'll leave you the number of a Mr. Huntingheath in London. He knows how to find me."

He turned then and went into the house. Rachel's hand fell to her side. Her fingers closed around the memory of touching him, and she raised her fist to press it to her mouth. She watched Bryan go up the grand staircase, but she made no effort to stop him. She wasn't sure if she had the strength or the right to. Instead, she went to the study and curled up in the corner of the leather love seat to think.

To her left, amid the dark bricks of the fireplace, the exposed bar of gold gleamed dully in the soft light. She stared at it dispassionately. It was the answer to all her prayers save two: It couldn't bring her mother's health back, and it couldn't keep Bryan from walking out on her.

What was it worth, then? Nothing. Less than nothing. It would pay her debts and secure her future, but her future would be empty without Bryan and the magic he brought to her life.

Bryan folded his shirts mechanically. Packing was a routine that had long ago become automatic to him. His hands knew what to do. His mind was free to wander.

He had no taste for a trip to Hungary. The work might prove to be a good diversion, but he could dredge up none of his usual enthusiasm. Maybe he would go home first and visit his parents or take a trip to Connecticut and spend some time with his brother J.J. and Genna and their kids.

But thoughts of family only sharpened the ache of loneliness inside him. He wanted a family of his own. He wanted a wife and children and a home he wouldn't be a visitor in. For the second time in his life he had had that kind of happiness within his reach, and again the rainbow had eluded his grasp.

It hurt. Maybe it hurt worse because he believed so strongly that wishes could come true. Maybe Rachel was right in expecting the worst from life. At least then you couldn't be disappointed when that was what you got.

Rachel. He loved her. She loved him. But she wasn't willing to believe in magic, and he wasn't willing to settle for less.

"Being a bit hard on the girl, aren't you, Hennessy?"

Bryan looked up at the sound of the cultured British voice. His gaze went to the cracked mirror above the dresser. In the reflection of the room he could see himself and a shadowy figure standing some distance behind him, near the armoire. The man was tall and slender, an elegant figure in formal attire; a pale, thin man with the insolent bearing of aristocratic breeding. His hair was combed straight back. His suit was immaculate, his bow tie just slightly imperfect—the mark of a true gentleman of his day.

"Archibald Wimsey, I presume," Bryan said, not exhibiting the least sign of surprise. "I was wondering when you were going to come out of hiding."

"Hiding?" Wimsey frowned but chose not to challenge the remark. "Work to be done, don't you know, dear fellow. Couldn't be the life of the party what with all these good deeds to do, now, could I?"

"Good deeds?"

Wimsey leaned against the armoire as if the thing could actually support his translucent form. He tucked his hands into the pockets of his trousers and scowled up at the ceiling. "I've been stuck in this wretched house for fifty-nine years, waiting for some great humanitarian act to perform so I could go on to a more appropriate afterlife. Fifty-nine years! Rather the ultimate story of a house guest overstaying his welcome, eh?"

He dropped his gaze back to Bryan and shrugged. "I wasn't inclined to muck up my chances by showing myself to one and all just so you could get your name into some bloody obscure pseudoscientific journal."

"In fifty-nine years you haven't had a single opportunity to redeem yourself?" Bryan asked dubiously.

"The closest I came was setting fire to Cornelia Thayer's collection of miniskirts in 1969," Wimsey reflected with a fond smile of remembrance that faded into a look of disgust. "The woman possessed thighs to rival the trunks of the great redwoods, don't you know. Unfortunately, eradicating an affront to refined sartorial tastes was not deemed sufficient to get me out of my spiritual exile. To make matters worse, Cornelia took to wearing hot pants." He shuddered in revulsion at the memory. "Confined myself to the attic over that ghastly turn of events. Finally drove the Thayers to sell by pouring buckets of ooze down the walls of their bedroom. Don't reckon that garnered me any brownie points in the great beyond," he added thoughtfully, rubbing his long chin.

"I don't imagine," Bryan agreed, rolling his eyes. "What landed you here in the first place?"

Wimsey gave him a shrewd look. "I think you've figured that one out, chum. You tell me."

"All right. While your pal Ducky was quietly robbing everyone blind, you let people think you were the gentleman bandit because the ladies thought it was romantic. Unfortunately, the ladies weren't the only ones who believed it. Pig Porchind believed you stole his gold and he—"

Wimsey made a face and held up an insubstantial hand to cut him off. "Don't let's relive the truly unpleasant past."

"You didn't know where the gold was, did you?"

"You think I'd be here now if I had?" he asked incredulously, straightening away from the armoire and hovering near the bed. Frowning darkly, he shook out one of Bryan's dress shirts and refolded it to his own satisfaction. "I'd have bloody well told old Pig where it was and what he could do with it. Ducky had it hidden someplace until it was already too late for me, then he apparently brought the stuff in already disguised as bricks. I hadn't the vaguest idea where it was."

He directed his frown at Bryan again. "If I'd figured it out ahead of you and revealed the stuff to Addie or the girl, perhaps I wouldn't still be here."

"Sorry."

"Sorry?" Wimsey snorted. "After fifty-nine years of dead boredom I finally get a shot at redeeming myself. You pinch it, and the best you can do is tell me you're sorry? I say, that's really frightfully inadequate."

Bryan shrugged helplessly. "Well, what would you have me do?"

Wimsey smiled brightly and patted Bryan's shoulder. "Do kiss and make up with the girl. There's a good chap."

"Rachel?"

"Of course Rachel," he said irritably. "Who do you think I mean? I've been playing cupid for you all along, you ungrateful swine. The least you can do is marry her."

Bryan sighed. "I'm afraid that's up to her."

"Bloody hell," the ghost murmured, crossing his arms over his chest. He shook his head. "I'm not cut out for this humanitarian work. Never been comfortable with charitable behavior." He waved a hand as if to ward off a denial that wasn't forthcoming. "Oh, yes, I gave the odd quid to Oxfam in my day, but all this—this—*personal* stuff." He shuddered again, his distaste for his task more than apparent. "All that selflessness goes quite against my grain, I don't mind saying."

"Probably has something to do with why you're here," Bryan suggested dryly.

"Don't be glib, Hennessy. It's really quite irritating."

"Sorry."

"Don't tell me, tell Rachel," he insisted. "Getting the two of you together is my last hope of getting out of here. I did what I could to help her reconcile with Addie, and that didn't solve my dilemma. You've got to be the key. So stop slacking off and do your duty. I'm fed up with being subtle, holding the doors shut and shoving the two of you together. By the way, I was not amused by your little jujitsu demonstration downstairs."

"Tae kwon do," Bryan corrected him with a bland smile.

"Don't split hairs," Wimsey snapped. "This facetious manner of yours is damned annoying. 'Pon my soul, if I were alive, you'd be giving me a roaring headache. Do make up with the girl and get on with it."

Bryan arched a brow. "Does coercion count in the good-deeds category these days?"

Wimsey screwed up his mouth in annoyance. "You really are too flip by half. Just wait until you get stuck in an alternate plane of existence. We'll see how amusing you are then."

Bryan sighed and put on his most contrite look. He wasn't in the mood for jocularity. Encountering Wimsey had lifted his spirits, but the fact remained, he was losing Rachel. Their difference of philosophy was a wedge between them, and he could see no way over, under, or around it. The next move had to be hers.

"I'm truly sorry, Wimsey. I've done all I can. The rest is up to no one but Rachel."

"That's what you think," the ghost muttered darkly.

A knock sounded at the door. Rachel's voice floated through. "Bryan? Can I come in?"

"Yes." At least he would get the satisfaction of seeing her face when he introduced her to Wimsey, he thought with a wry smile. He went on folding clothes as she swung the door open and stepped inside the room.

"Who were you talking to?"

He opened his mouth to tell her as he straightened. His gaze went to Rachel's reflection in the mirror, then his own, then—Wimsey was gone. A black scowl pulled his brows together. He pushed his glasses up on his nose and grumbled, "Myself."

"Oh." Rachel looked confused. "That's funny. I thought I heard another voice."

"I do that when I'm talking to myself," he said irritably. "I make up another voice. It makes the conversation seem so much more realistic."

"That's kind of odd."

"I'm an odd person," he said curtly, snapping his suitcase shut and reaching for another. "What do you expect?"

"I expect you to give me a straight answer," Rachel said, more than a little irritated by his nasty mood. She'd come there in contrition, after all. The least he could be was polite.

"Fine," Bryan said, abandoning his packing. "You want a straight answer? I was talking to a ghost. I was talking to a man who was killed in this house fifty-nine years ago. Archibald Wimsey. He was here, but now you can't see him, so, as we all know, he must not really exist. He's just a figment of my overactive, irresponsible imagination."

Rachel winced. "I'm sorry I called you irresponsible. We have different ways of looking at things, you and I. We have different ways of dealing with problems."

"But I *do* deal with them, Rachel. I don't just brush them off and expect you to clean up the mess."

"I know," she mumbled, head down.

"Do you?" he asked sharply.

She looked up at him, nibbling the corner of her lip. "I'm willing to learn," she said sincerely. "Are you willing to show me?"

Bryan sighed wearily, his wide shoulders sagging in defeat. "I've been trying to show you all along."

Rachel thought back across the memories she had stored up in the past weeks, memories of Bryan intervening when things had been going badly between herself and Addie, of his silly diversionary tactics that had kept her from dwelling on her problems. She thought of the way he had come back to find the gold for her and to trap Porchind and Rasmussen. If it hadn't been for him, she probably would have sold Drake House to the pair and been glad to get what little she could for the place.

Bryan had looked out for her all along. He was simply so unorthodox in his methods, she hadn't realized what he was up to. Still, she had fallen in love with him in spite of his eccentricities, in spite of thinking he was just another hopeless dreamer. Now she loved him even more.

She put her hands on his solid forearms and looked up at him with her heart in her eyes. "I love you, Bryan. You said you needed me to believe in magic. I believe I love you. I believed that even when I was sure you were the last thing I needed in my life. Isn't that a kind of magic—believing in something even when you think you shouldn't?"

"I guess so," he whispered, lifting a hand to brush at the soft, wild tendrils of spun gold that curled around her face. She was so lovely, and he loved her so much, the thought of leaving her was like cutting out his own heart.

"I do need you in my life, Bryan," she said, leaning closer. "I need you more than all the gold in California. Please don't leave me."

As he stared down at her, his blue eyes misty, there was a strange scraping noise in the hall. It sounded suspiciously like heavy furniture being pushed across the floor. Rachel's eyes rounded as something bumped against the closed door. She snuggled closer to Bryan, her arms sneaking around his lean waist.

"What was that?" she asked weakly.

Bryan smiled and shook his head. "Just someone trying to make sure I don't leave you."

She gave him a puzzled look.

"Don't worry about it," he said, giving in to the powerful longing. "I don't have any intention of leaving you for the next hundred years or so."

Rachel's spirits soared. "You mean that?"

"I do."

"What about Hungary and Mr. Huntinglodge?"

"Neither one of them is as important to me as you are. Will you marry me, Rachel?" he asked softly.

"I will," she whispered, tilting her face up to meet his kiss.

His lips were warm and solid against hers, mas-

culine and welcoming, and trembling just enough
to bring a lump to her throat. She melted into his
arms, never questioning the sensation of coming
home. This was where she belonged. This was
where she was safe and warm. This was where she
wanted to spend the rest of her days—in the arms
of a man who brought magic to her life, who
lightened every darkness and put a rainbow in her
heart.

"I say, good show."

Rachel bolted in Bryan's arms, but he held her
fast. He raised his head to shoot the intruder a
meaningful look. "No show. Beat it, Wimsey."

"Wimsey?" Rachel asked, goose bumps pebbling
her flesh to the texture of sandpaper.

Bryan nodded, tilting his head in the direction
of the mirror that hung above the old dresser.
Rachel turned and looked. Her mouth dropped
open so hard, it was a wonder it didn't put a dent
in her chest.

There he stood—the figment of her mother's
imagination, the whimsy Bryan had refused to
give up on, the ghost she didn't believe in. His
image was slightly translucent. He was handsome
and smiling, decked out in formal attire. And he
was holding a rose.

Her heart skipped a beat as her gaze fastened on
the perfect white bud of the flower. Then her eyes
went to the eyes of the man who held it. Wimsey
nodded in answer to the questions she couldn't
quite force into words. It had been Wimsey all
along.

Now he held the rose out toward her. Rachel

turned away from the mirror, twisting in Bryan's arms to face the apparition that stood by the armoire.

"Thank you," she whispered, taking the flower by the stem.

"Thank *you*, my dear," he murmured in return, his pale eyes shining as he handed her the rose.

Then, in a flash of brilliant white light, he was gone.

"Where did he go?" Rachel asked, never once questioning that he had been there.

"Where he belongs," Bryan said with a soft smile. "Where he belongs."

"Then we're alone?"

He nodded.

With a beguiling smile, she wound her arms around his neck. "It seems like now might be a good time for you to start teaching me all about magic."

"Hmm, yes," Bryan agreed, his eyes twinkling as he pulled her with him to the bed. They tumbled across the coverlet, laughing and breathless, Rachel's hair spilling around them like moonlight.

Bryan kissed her cheeks and her eyelids and the corners of her mouth.

"Why don't we start with making the earth move?" he suggested. "That's a trick you seem to have a natural aptitude for."

Rachel grinned and hugged him, loving him with every fiber of her being. He might have been slightly crazy, and he might have been something of a puzzle, but he was all hers, and he would fill her heart with magic every day of her life.

She threaded her fingers through his tawny hair
and pulled him down for a long, slow kiss that left
him with only one reverent word to say.

"Abracadabra."

Some killers are born. Some killers are made. And sometimes the origin of desire for homicide is lost in the tangle of roots that make an ugly childhood and a dangerous youth, so that no one may ever know if the urge was inbred or induced.

He lifts the body from the back of the Blazer like a roll of old carpet to be discarded. The soles of his boots scuff against the blacktop of the parking area, then fall nearly silent on the dead grass and hard ground. The night is balmy for November in Minneapolis. A swirling wind tosses fallen leaves. The bare branches of the trees rattle together like bags of bones.

He knows he falls into the last category of killers. He has spent many hours, days, months, years studying his compulsion and its point of origin. He knows what he is, and he embraces that truth. He has never known guilt or remorse. He believes conscience, rules, laws serve the individual no practical purpose, and only limit human possibilities.

'Man enters into the ethical world through fear and not through love.' – Paul Ricoeur, *Symbolism of Evil.*

His True Self adheres only to his own code: domination, manipulation, control.

A broken shard of moon glares down on the scene, its light faint beneath the web of limbs. He arranges the body to his satisfaction and traces two intersecting Xs over the left upper chest. With a sense of ceremony, he pours the accelerant. Anointing the dead. Symbolism of evil. His

True Self embraces the concept of evil as power. Fuel for the internal fire.

'Ashes to ashes.'

The sounds are ordered and specific, magnified by his excitement. The scrape of the match against the friction strip, the pop as it bursts with flame, the whoosh of the fire as it comes alive and consumes. As the fire burns, his memory replays the earlier sounds of pain and fear. He recalls the tremor in her voice as she pleaded for her life, the unique pitch and quality of each cry as he tortured her. The exquisite music of life and death.

For one fine moment he allows himself to admire the drama of the tableau. He allows himself to feel the heat of the flames caress his face like tongues of desire. He closes his eyes and listens to the sizzle and hiss, breathes deep the smell of roasting flesh.

Elated, excited, aroused, he takes his erection out of his pants and strokes himself hard. He brings himself nearly to climax, but is careful not to ejaculate. Save it for later, when he can celebrate fully.

His goal is in sight. He has a plan, meticulously thought out, to be executed with perfection. His name will live in infamy with all the great ones – Bundy, Kemper, the Boston Strangler, the Green River Killer. The press here has already given him a name: the Cremator.

It makes him smile. It makes him proud. He lights another match and holds it just in front of him, studying the flame, loving the sinuous, sensuous undulation of it. He brings it closer to his face, opens his mouth, and eats it.

Then he turns and walks away. Already thinking of next time.

Murder.

The sight burned its impression into the depths of her

memory, into the backs of her eyeballs so that she could see it when she blinked against the tears. The body twisting in slow agony against its horrible fate. Orange flame a backdrop for the nightmare image.

Burning.

She ran, her lungs burning, her legs burning, her eyes burning, her throat burning. In one abstract corner of her mind, she was the corpse. Maybe this was what death was like. Maybe it *was* her body roasting, and this consciousness was her soul trying to escape the fires of hell. She had been told repeatedly that was where she would end up.

In the near distance she could hear a siren and see the weird flash of blue and red lights against the night. She ran for the street, sobbing, stumbling. Her right knee hit the frozen ground, but she forced her feet to keep moving.

Run run run run run run –

'Freeze! Police!'

The cruiser still rocked at the curb. The door was open. The cop was on the boulevard, gun drawn and pointed straight at her.

'Help me!' the words rasped in her throat.

'Help me!' she gasped, tears blurring her vision.

Her legs buckled beneath the weight of her body and the weight of her fear and the weight of her heart that was pounding like some huge swollen thing in her chest.

The cop was beside her in an instant, holstering his weapon and dropping to his knees to help. Must be a rookie, she thought dimly. She knew fourteen-year-old kids with better street instincts. She could have gotten his weapon. If she'd had a knife, she could have raised herself up and stabbed him.

He pulled her up into a sitting position with a hand on either shoulder. Sirens wailed in the distance.

'What happened! Are you all right?' he demanded. He had a face like an angel.

'I saw him,' she said, breathless, shaking, bile pushing up the back of her throat. 'I was there. Oh – Jesus. Oh – shit. I saw him!'

'Saw who?'

'The Cremator.'

All Orion/Phoenix titles are available at your local bookshop or from the following address:

Littlehampton Book Services
Cash Sales Department L
14 Eldon Way, Lineside Industrial Estate
Littlehampton
West Sussex BN17 7HE

telephone 01903 721596, *facsimile* 01903 730914

Payment can either be made by credit card (Visa and Mastercard accepted) or by sending a cheque or postal order made payable to *Littlehampton Book Services*.
DO NOT SEND CASH OR CURRENCY.

Please add the following to cover postage and packing

UK and BFPO:
£1.50 for the first book, and 50p for each additional book to a maximum of £3.50

Overseas and Eire:
£2.50 for the first book plus £1.00 for the second book and 50p for each additional book ordered

----

BLOCK CAPITALS PLEASE

name of cardholder ....

address of cardholder ....

*delivery address
(if different from cardholder)*
....
....
....
....

postcode ....   *postcode* ....

☐ I enclose my remittance for £............................

☐ please debit my Mastercard/Visa (delete as appropriate)

card number ☐☐☐☐☐☐☐☐☐☐☐☐☐☐☐☐☐☐☐

expiry date ☐☐☐☐

signature ....

prices and availability are subject to change without notice